The Return

The Return

Rachel Harrison

HODDER &
STOUGHTON

First published in Great Britain in 2020 by Hodder & Stoughton
An Hachette UK company

This paperback edition published in 2020

I

A CIP catalogue record for this title is
available from the British Library

Hardback ISBN 978 1 529 35195 8
Trade Paperback ISBN 978 1 529 35196 5
eBook ISBN 978 1 529 35197 2

Printed and bound in Great Britain by Clays Ltd, Elcograf S.p.A.

Hodder & Stoughton policy is to use papers that are natural, renewable
and recyclable products and made from wood grown in sustainable
forests. The logging and manufacturing processes are expected to
conform to the environmental regulations of the country of origin.

Hodder & Stoughton Ltd
Carmelite House
50 Victoria Embankment
London EC4Y 0DZ

www.hodder.co.uk

For Grandpa, Babi, Nanny, and Pop Pop.
Sorry about the bad words!

I

"What do you mean she's missing?"

I watched frantic ants descend upon a nearby apple core and a facedown slice of pizza. A renegade splinter faction marched across the parking lot with tiny bits of food on their backs. The raccoons must have been in the garbage behind my office again, and I made a mental note to report it when I got back inside, but of course I would forget.

"She's missing," Molly said, her exasperation creeping through the receiver. "I don't know how else to explain it to you."

"She's not missing."

Above all else, I knew two truths about Julie. The first was that she was the most stubborn, most determined person I'd ever met. And the second was that she loved attention. Julie would never be missing. She might go dark, intentionally disappear for a few days here or there just to make sure someone noticed. A pop quiz: "Do you love me?" That, she was capable of. That, I believed. But missing, as in milk cartons and posters and hounds in fields—no way.

I told Molly as much.

"What year do you think this is? Milk cartons?"

"That's my point. People don't go missing anymore."

"What? What world are you living in?"

I'd been asking myself that question for a long time. I didn't have an answer for her.

"She left her house last Friday morning to go hiking, and she never came back. Tristan filed a missing person report. They have a team out looking for her."

"Looking where?"

"Acadia National Park."

"How'd you find out?"

"He called me."

"He called you?"

"I don't know why me, Elise, so don't start."

Tristan was Julie's husband. None of us had ever met him. They had gone to the same high school and reconnected when Julie returned to her gloomy Massachusetts hometown to take care of her sick mother. They got married before her mom died so she could be there. The ceremony and reception were held in someone's backyard. We were sent two pictures from that day. One was of Julie and Tristan cutting a two-tiered pale yellow cake topped with sugared daisies. The other was of Julie standing in a patch of generous sunlight, smiling with her head back, as if she was midlaugh, or the weight of her happiness was too much for her neck. She wore a birdcage veil.

It was a shock to all of us. It might have been the shock of our lives, had she not gone missing.

"What do we do?" I asked Molly.

"I don't think there's anything to do. Just gotta wait. And prepare ourselves."

I dug into my back pocket for my lighter. It was a white one. Julie once told me white lighters were bad luck. I cleared my throat. "It's been how many days? Four? Five?"

"I thought you'd be freaking out."

"Have you told Mae?"

"Are you smoking?" she asked me.

"No."

"Yes, I called Mae first, because I thought she'd be the calm, logical one. She was very upset. I know because she said she was very upset."

Mae was hardwired to think showing emotion was bad manners. She had a sensitive nature, but she tried her best to suppress it. She never wanted to put anyone out by acknowledging she had feelings of her own.

An airplane groaned somewhere above the clumpy gray clouds. The rush of nicotine distracted me, and I missed something Molly said.

"Sorry?"

She scoffed. Molly was the funny one, so it was easy to forget that when she wasn't being funny, she was being mean. She was capable of empathy, but on a case-by-case basis. Childhood bone cancer had taken her left leg below the knee, and sometimes she joked that was where all her patience had been.

"This is serious."

"I know," I said, the lie leaving a chalky residue in my mouth. She wasn't missing.

This was classic Jules. She could fool Molly and Mae, but not me.

She and I were made of the same stuff. It was the special sauce of our friendship, and the curse that made it turn ugly sometimes. Molly described our passive-aggressive fights as "tangos." Mae would frown and say, "There's only tension because you two are so similar." When things were good between us, we would brag about our similarities, say we were soul sisters. When they weren't, we both knew it was like spitting at a mirror.

There were times when I fantasized about vanishing. Chucking my phone through a sewer grate and taking the train to God knows where with nothing but a stack of cash. Cutting my hair with dull scissors in a shitty motel room. And if I had thought about it, Julie had thought about it, too.

During one of our late-night dorm room confessionals, we had bonded over obsessively imagining our own funerals. Which exes would show? Would they cry? Who else would cry? Who would give the eulogy? What would they say about us? Would our parents ever move on?

"We're so fucked-up," she said, giggling into her beloved puffer-fish pillow.

"If I die first, will you give the eulogy?" I asked.

"You know I will," she said. "And I'll make it all about me."

The end of my cigarette was pure ash. I flicked the butt into a nearby puddle.

I didn't know what else to say to Molly. In a few days, Julie would resurface and exonerate me and my lack of reaction.

"What do you think happened?" I asked.

"You really want to know?"

"Yeah."

"Honestly, Lise, I think she's gone. I feel like she's dead. I looked up the park, and it's all woods and cliffs and ocean, and she was

4

there by herself. Alone! I don't want to be negative, but I have to say it out loud or I'll explode. Don't tell anyone. Especially not Mae."

"I won't," I said. "And Julie's not dead. Don't worry."

I told her I had to get back to work, said I loved her and would call her later. After we hung up, I walked around back to check the garbage bins. Raccoon ravaged. Trash everywhere. Possessed by some dormant Girl Scout goodness, I went to turn the bins upright. I leaned over with my hands outstretched, and beyond the tips of my fingers, I noticed movement. A wriggling. White spots. The spots swam in and out of the banana peels and half-eaten sand-wiches, the fuzzy avocados and open containers of yogurt.

Maggots.

I thought I should scream, but I couldn't muster one. Instead, I backed up slowly, as if from a crime scene, until I was far enough away to safely turn my back. Still, I felt like they were on me. Like maybe one had burrowed in through the bottom of my shoe, crawled up my leg, my spine, and was now perched on my shoulder, waiting to climb into my ear and, eventually, eat my brain.

What I remember most about that day is I was more disturbed by the maggots than I was by the news about Julie. I didn't think for a second that she could be gone.

I went back to my desk and let the day pass.

When the day bled into a week, I looked up Acadia National Park. I scrolled through images of sprawling nature, a lighthouse nestled atop a rocky bluff. A mountain called Cadillac, its slope etched with trails. It seemed awfully mild. Blue sea, blue sky. Pine trees. Piles of stones worn smooth by the ocean. I refined my search.

"Acadia National Park—death."

It was possible to die there. But people die everywhere. People die at Disneyland.

"Acadia National Park—missing."

There it was.

Julie's face.

I closed my laptop and stuffed it under my bed, kingdom of dust bunnies and lone socks, among other things I didn't want to deal with.

I woke up every morning forgetting. I would remember with my toothbrush molar deep, or while beating an egg, or on my third attempt to start the damn car. If I hadn't already, I would remember on my way to work, when I passed the roadkill, what was maybe once a deer? A large fox? An unfortunate dog? It was on the shoulder now, a pink mound of guts that refused decomposition.

One day the roadkill was gone, and when I got to work, I shut myself in a bathroom stall and tried to make myself cry. I told myself Julie was gone. Dead. Had died alone in nature.

"Ninety-nine percent of the time, it's good," she had told me during one of our last conversations, a few weeks before she had gone missing.

"Then what's the problem?"

"The one percent."

After years of practice, I had finally figured out how to deal with Julie's relationship drama. Instead of voicing my concern, huffing and puffing, disapproving, giving advice that would go untaken, offering ultimatums, I was now relentlessly supportive. It disoriented her. She'd spin around in circles until the truth spilled out.

"I mean, you guys are so in love. And you're starting this bed-and-breakfast. It's really exciting! Not all couples can go into business together," I said. "You're super compatible."

"We're not, though. He's simple."

"That's bad?"

"He doesn't understand me," she said. "He's my husband, and he doesn't get it."

"Did you end up making it legal?"

When she had sent us the pictures from the wedding—her way of telling us she'd had one—they were captioned "Don't worry, not legal. For mom." I figured it was a lie, an attempt to rationalize why we weren't invited and diminish the gossip the three of us would inevitably engage in behind her back. She knew we would be talking about it, about her. She wanted to protect herself. But we knew the truth.

The wedding hadn't been for her mom. The wedding was because she really did love him. That was how she loved. Hard and fast. Until whoever she loved loved her back, or until she got bored.

"He's my husband," she repeated, which could have been confirmation but maybe not.

"It's not like with Dan. You're not fighting all the time."

"He doesn't react to anything. Sometimes I want to push him into a wall just to see what he'll do."

"Healthy."

"Lise."

"Maybe you miss your mom. Maybe you need time to clear your head. To allow yourself to grieve."

There had been no funeral. Julie's mom, Beth, was a character. A chain-smoker, silk nightgowns with feather slippers at the supermarket, fake eyelashes and red lipstick. She'd been married three times. The first when she was seventeen, after legally emancipating herself from abusive parents. The second to Julie's father at twenty-two. She'd had Julie's sister, Jade, then Julie. Then, after something happened that Julie never talked about, Beth married her third husband, a guy who did something with boats and had a lot of money. She got half of it in the divorce.

Beth's illness had been long and drawn out. She got to say all her good-byes. At the end, she told Julie, "Burn me and scatter my ashes someplace pretty, would you?"

"I was there every day," Julie said. "I grieved."

"Okay," I said. "I just think it's a lot all at once. You went from being a caretaker to being a wife, and now you're opening a business in a new state and doing a whole renovation. When did you have time to process any of this? Have you had any time for yourself?"

"No. I haven't. You're right."

"Take a few days. Get back to yourself."

"Right. I know you're right."

"I go crazy without my alone time," I said. That had been true at some point in the past, but then I was alone all the time, and that was bad, too.

"I miss you."

"I miss you, too."

"I want to get this place up and running so you guys can come. But I want you to come first so we get some one-on-one QT. I miss you most. Don't tell them, though."

"Secret's safe with me."

"We've got the great big porch that wraps all the way around. I keep picturing us out there, drinking whiskey under blankets and stargazing. I love Maine. The sky is so beautiful here, Lise. I don't understand how some patches of sky are more beautiful than others. How does that work?"

"Nature! Science!"

She laughed. "That stuff."

"All right, I should get going," I said, surrendering to sleepiness. "G'night. Love you."

"Love you. Talk soon."

I pressed down on the memory like a bruise and felt nothing.

At six months, Mae suggested we write Julie letters and bury them someplace special to us.

"My therapist thinks it's a good idea," she said.

"Since when are you in therapy?"

"Does it matter?"

"No. I'm sorry."

"What are we doing?" she asked me.

"What do you mean?"

"We're not doing anything. We have no control over the situation. It's not constructive. It's not good for us. Mentally, emotionally."

Yeah, duh. Of course our best friend's going missing wasn't good for us emotionally. But I couldn't say that to Mae. Besides, she had a point.

"Did you write her something?" I asked.

"Not yet."

I thought about what it would be like to give Julie the letters when she came back. How she would hold them in her hands, then up to the light like diamonds, then tight to her chest, as if they might absorb through her clothes and into her skin. The precious evidence of how much we missed her.

This vision was uniquely mine. By then, I was the only one who believed she was still alive. I was the only one who believed her disappearance was a sham. I was convinced Julie was somewhere reveling in solitude and not willing to give it up just yet. She'd come back for us, though.

I'd committed myself to this belief. It was the only way I could function.

"I bought paper," Mae said. "This beautiful, expensive stationery from a shop in Soho. And a wax seal kit I'll never use again."

"I'm going to get a letter from you in a few weeks with a wax seal. Written with a calligraphy pen."

"I bought one of those, too."

I laughed.

"It made perfect sense at the time."

"I'm sure it did."

"Elise," she said, "you should probably see someone."

"A therapist?"

"Yes."

"I don't do therapy," I said. "Julie doesn't, either."

Mae made a clicking noise with her tongue, signaling to me her displeasure. It was a habit she had picked up from her mother. I thought maybe it was a Southern thing. Mae had been raised in a suburb of Atlanta by two born-and-bred sweet tea come-to-Jesus Georgians. She had an accent she tried her best to subdue because it only provoked more of the "Where are you from?" and "What are you?" questions she was inundated with daily.

"I'm from China," she would answer. "I'm Chinese."

But it was never enough, because then they wouldn't understand the Southern accent, or because they were still wondering about her skin and her hair.

So, for a while, she ended up giving away her life story to satisfy obnoxious strangers.

"I was adopted from China. I grew up in Atlanta. I have albinism."

"It's exhausting," she told me once.

"Then don't do it anymore," I said. "Just don't say anything."

"Doesn't work that way."

She and Molly would talk, but with Molly it was different. Not many people asked about her prosthetic. They assumed cancer or combat. They tried to be polite. Not with Mae, though.

To think about it was a quick way to hate the world.

"I love you, Maebs. I'll think about the letter."

"It's an idea. You don't have to," she said. "But it's something."

A week passed, and I considered it. But then I thought, *Why write a letter? I'll just tell her when she gets back. Whatever I have to say, I'll tell her in person.*

At a year, their hope expired. They weren't looking for a body; they were looking for bones. Julie's husband decided to hold what he called a "memorial service."

"Funeral. It's a funeral," Molly ranted while we coordinated travel. "Why not call it a fucking funeral?"

"I don't know. He only talks to you. Why don't you ask him?"

"He doesn't talk to me. He only has my number."

"How?"

"No idea."

"Is he nice?"

"He's fine," she said. "I'm getting in at two p.m. I hate flying east. I'm going to be wrecked."

"That's what you get for living in Los Angeles."

"Don't city-shame me right now. We're going to our best friend's funeral."

"Don't use our best friend's funeral as an excuse to get out of being city-shamed."

"Fair. But you live in Buffalo, so get off my ass."

I wanted to remind her it wasn't quite by choice, but that was a whole thing, so I decided it was better to change the subject.

"What are you wearing?"

"We're dysfunctional. You know that?" she asked me.

"I'm aware."

"Just checking."

"When does Mae get in?" I asked.

"Three, I think. Let me see," she said. "Oh, Tristan offered for us to stay there. At their house slash bed-and-breakfast or whatever."

"Really?"

"I don't think it's, like, a functioning bed-and-breakfast. I think he still lives there, though."

"Interesting," I said.

"Do you think we should? Or would it be too weird?"

"I'm poor, so yes, let's."

"All right, all right."

I spent the long drive with my hands clasped tight around the steering wheel, my knuckles ten pale hills. I looked down at my black dress, my black shoes, my black jacket crumpled in the passenger seat, the black road ahead going on and on like a cruel fate. She wouldn't be there. She wouldn't be stiff in a box, fenced in by flower arrangements and sniffling aunts. But I knew that didn't matter to anyone except me. They would all mourn her anyway.

Even if her body was there, lying in an open casket with her hands folded, in a modest dress she undoubtedly wouldn't have been happy about; even if I walked up and saw her, touched her cold cheek; even then, would I believe it? What was the proof I needed, and was I crazy for needing it in the first place? Not neurotic crazy, or crazy with grief, but clinically insane?

When I got to the house, I found Molly and Mae sitting on the great big porch Julie had told me about. The house didn't disappoint. A mammoth Victorian she had bought with her mother's money. A giant dollhouse. It was really something to see it in person.

"This house is just like her. A little too much," I said to them as we hugged. They both hung on too long, limp with grief.

I saw a man hovering nearby. I recognized him from the wedding picture. He recognized me, too.

"Hi," he said. "You must be Elise."

"Must be," I said. I shook his hand because he offered it. I could feel his calluses.

"Tristan. Thank you for coming."

He got called away by someone delivering food. As soon as his back was turned to us, we huddled.

"He's not her type," I said. He was too generic. All-American. Probably knew all the words to "Sweet Caroline." Drank a lot of milk.

"He seems nice," Mae said. "Genuine."

"He keeps messing with his tie," Molly said.

We had our suspicions back then. He had been the last person to see her. They had gotten married pretty quickly, and people always blame the husband.

When she had first gone missing, he sat through long police interviews, underwent questioning. They searched the house, his truck. They did an extensive background check. They called up his ex-girlfriends to ask about him. "Was he ever aggressive toward you?" Stuff like that.

The cops never officially announced him as a suspect, but that wasn't enough to silence the speculation. There were people who thought, *Yeah, well, maybe he was just after her inheritance.*

Of course we wondered.

But as the day went on, he was so clearly distraught, all it took was one look among the three of us, and he was acquitted.

"I think part of me wanted to believe it was him, just to have an answer," Molly said later that night when we were on the porch sharing a thick wool blanket and a bottle of whiskey.

"He's just so sad," Mae said. "It's so sad."

We stayed up all night, not wanting to leave one another's company. They swapped stories about Jules or cried or passed the bottle back and forth in time-bending silence. I stared at the sky, a dizzying display of stars that seemed to multiply in the blur of their own brightness, melting the darkness out of the night for shades of purple and evergreen, swarming up toward what might have been heaven.

A year and five months. I took a painfully long bus ride from Buffalo to Manhattan to visit Mae. She gave me the grand tour of her luxe new Tribeca apartment. Money had never been an object for Mae. Her dad was a successful lawyer and her mom a sought-after interior designer. An only child, she had wanted for nothing. Horseback riding and ballet lessons, multiple trips to Disney World, a miniature castle of her own custom-built in the backyard. She had been given creative freedom and a credit card, a combination that birthed a love of fashion. She worked as a stylist and, apparently, did well for herself.

I wasn't jealous. I skipped straight to shame. I thought of my sad studio apartment with disgusting old carpet, kitchen cabinets loose on rusty hinges, a bum landlord who would never forgive me for that one time I paid my rent late. I thought of my dumb office job, the credits I had squandered abandoning my master's degree, the behemoth of student loan debt that haunted my life. I made all the wrong choices. Mae made the right ones.

There was a framed picture of the four of us on her nightstand. We stood on some street corner with water bottles full of vodka, on our way to a party that wouldn't be worth it. We smiled, our teeth white from the drugstore strips we used religiously, our cheeks fat and rosy with youth. Molly and Mae were in the middle, Julie and I the bookends.

Julie wore her favorite jeans with rips at the knees, a T-shirt too tight and too low, her bottle blond hair down and curly, and her ridiculous black heels. She always wore heels to parties. She was her mother's daughter.

"It's a good one of us," I told Mae.

She ignored me, shifted the conversation to our dinner plans.

She took me to a Mexican restaurant where we ordered prickly pear margaritas and overpriced tacos. After, we went barhopping in the West Village with her fancy fashion friends. They asked me minimal questions before veering the conversation to industry gossip. I had nothing to contribute so I drank excessively and excused myself for cigarettes.

"If Molly knew, she'd kill you," Mae warned me.

"But she doesn't know," I said.

Standing on the city sidewalk, with drunk college kids stumbling past, good-looking couples holding hands and eating ice-cream cones, I wanted nothing more than to call Julie. She was the only one who would understand. She knew what it was like to feel so lonely you could die. I wouldn't have to explain it to her, or how being in this city of millions of people was worse than being alone in my apartment. I could say all of that, and she would relate. Then I wouldn't be lonely anymore, because she was out there. She existed.

Looking back, I realize it was the first time I allowed her absence to panic me. Too much time had passed. How come she hadn't surfaced? I knew she wasn't in the park anymore. I supposed she had left, gone to Canada, sublet a room. But how long could she keep it up?

Mae came out to check on me.

"You okay?"

"Yeah," I lied. "Tired from the bus."

"You want to go?"

I nodded. "Sorry."

"That's okay," she said. "I have to close my tab. We can get a car."

When we got back to her apartment, she pulled out the couch for me and made it up with clean sheets that smelled like the beach in a good way.

"We'll brunch in the morning," she said. "Thank you for coming. I like having you here."

"I like being here."

"We need to see each other more. The three of us."

"I know."

"Molly's a lost cause. But I keep faith I can convince you to move back to New York."

"I'd have to sell a kidney," I said.

"I'd find you a buyer."

"I hope you're kidding."

She raised an eyebrow. "Good night."

. . .

A year and ten months, six days. A snowstorm on the first of April. Ha-ha.

It was apocalyptic snow. White as marshmallows but dense as cement. Cars swallowed. Roofs collapsed.

Work was canceled. Everything closed. Fair warning and a backup generator were my saviors. I moved my bed away from the window, piled on every blanket I owned, ate peanut butter sandwiches and drank hot chocolate I made with half-and-half. I tucked a jug of water in bed next to me. A tip I got when I first moved to Buffalo was to stay hydrated in winter, because the weather's so harsh it'll dry out your skin. It was advice I had ignored at first, only to watch my extremities turn to ash.

I witnessed the accumulation of snow through my window until it covered the glass, and on the third day I couldn't remember what sunlight was like.

"Jules," I said. Talking to her out loud when I was alone was a habit I had developed after coming back from Manhattan. "Look, Jules."

Julie liked the snow. In college, she would drag me to the common room and make us "hot toddies" (microwaved water, contraband bourbon, honey, a splash of ginger ale), and we would watch the flurries shimmy their way down.

In the absence of light, time became something fun and elusive. I would guess. Midnight? Three p.m.? Had I slept past noon, or was it five o'clock in the morning? Did it matter?

I stalked the far reaches of my apartment. I cleaned out my closet, manufacturing a mountain of doleful clothes to donate to

Goodwill. I threw out two boxes of long-expired Pop-Tarts, stale English muffins, unsalted peanuts I had bought by mistake. I scrubbed my oven. I opened the record player Julie got me for my twenty-fifth birthday so I could play the only record I owned, *Back to Black*, Julie's gift for my twenty-fourth birthday.

I danced around in my socks.

"Julie, you're the best dancer," I said. "In general, but definitely out of the four of us. Mae would just find a wall to lean on and do that sort of swaying thing. She didn't need to do much. Her in her, like, satin bomber jacket and Ray-Bans. Molly doesn't really dance, either. She goes and plays beer pong or darts or whatever to get out of it. I figured it's pretty much impossible for me to look cool, so why not dance with you? You liked to dance. I acted like I hated it, but I always had fun dancing with you."

I paused for a response, and when I didn't get one, I said, "Yeah, yeah. You knew it, too."

I said, "You'd think after being stuck in the same room for days, the room would seem smaller, but it doesn't.

"You forget what it's like to leave. To be somewhere else.

"We're adaptable," I said with a definitive nod. Outside, the wind howled like somebody dying.

"Stay somewhere long enough, it becomes your world.

"Actually," I told Julie, "I hate this place."

And I could see her beside me, rolling her eyes, chewing on a straw.

It was around then that it really started to eat at me, in a way I could no longer control. What if something had gone wrong? An unsettling amount of time had passed. What if she was chained up in some cult leader's basement, carving notches into the wall to mark the passing days, subsisting on pastelike oatmeal and brownish water and the occasional kindness from Mr. Discount Koresh, who was crazy but conflicted?

Children are taken from sidewalks. Plucked from bus stops by strangers in old, unassuming station wagons. You read stories. Ones that turn your eyes into magnets. It's almost like it's against your will, or that's what you want to believe. You don't want to admit that you're interested. That you want to know about the duct tape or the DNA evidence found in the trunk of the car when it turns up months later, even though the kid never does.

Women are kidnapped in parking garages, at Laundromats, from their beds, while out for their morning runs. It happens all the time. Taken by men who feel a sense of entitlement, a right to female bodies. Men who were dropped on their heads as babies or raised by mommie dearest.

Julie wouldn't have gone quietly. Julie would have screamed, thrashed around, bitten, scratched, gouged. Julie would have made things bloody. She wouldn't have vanished without a trace.

But she had. They never found anything. Not a scrap of clothing. Not a scent. Not a single witness.

Had she been abducted by aliens? Would I turn into one of those conspiracy theorists who put newspapers over the windows and hissed at the mailman?

Would I take the case into my own hands? Buy a corkboard and a bunch of red yarn from a craft store, stand in line at checkout among the disgruntled parents helping with science projects or costumes for the school play? Would I print out a map of Acadia State Park at a FedEx Office? Pay the extra few bucks for color? Tack it to my wall and stare at it, waiting for clarity?

My friends thought I was in denial. They discussed it together and confronted me separately.

"I don't know if you're dealing with it well or not dealing with it at all," Mae said.

"You have to accept the reality of the situation," Molly said.

"I hear you," I said, an acknowledgment to get them off my back. I lied and told them I would look into therapy.

I didn't need therapy. I explored it on my own, this idea of denial. It didn't feel like denial. It felt like I knew the truth and everyone around me was a skeptic. I wasn't bothered by it at first because the truth was enough, but it wasn't anymore. It was isolating.

It would have been easier to trade my truth for the ordinary Kübler-Ross, weekly sessions on a somewhat comfortable couch with a box of cheap sandpapery tissues. But I couldn't. I clung to it.

Two years to the day after she went missing, Tristan found her sitting on the porch swing. She was wearing the same clothes she'd had on when she disappeared. She did not seem confused or disoriented, but she had no memory of where she'd been for the past twenty-four months.

Her return was national news.

She was taken to the hospital. The doctors invaded her with needles and cotton swabs, attached her to sinister-looking machines that made unpleasant sounds. She was analyzed by psychologists and questioned by police.

Aside from the gap in her memory, she seemed to be perfectly stable.

"She's doing great," Tristan said. "She's been very calm."

Calm? Julie? I'd never known Julie to be calm. She had caught the flu sophomore year, and I'd had no choice but to carry her to the school nurse for Tamiflu. She had cried like I was taking her to the gallows. She hated, hated, *hated* doctors. All doctors. She refused to get a physical. She had a severe phobia of needles. She was panic-stricken whenever there was a blood drive nearby. Seeing the Band-Aid on someone else's arm was enough to make her shriek. I didn't buy that she was "calm" about being confined to a hospital, at the mercy of doctors.

"Are you sure it's her?" I asked. A joke, kind of.

"That's not funny," he said. But then he added, "It's her."

"Can I talk to her?"

"Not yet."

"Who decides that?"

"The doctors. Not me."

I relented.

I expected more relief. Relief that she was back safe. Relief that I wasn't crazy. That, actually, I was very intuitive and should maybe consider an alternate career as an oracle. I thought relief would fill the vacancy of anticipation. The wonderings and what-ifs that had occupied my mind for so long.

But there was no relief, not really. Only more questions.

Her return disturbed my rituals. It created new ones. After work, I would run five miles, take a hot shower, a cold shower, drink an indeterminate amount of whiskey, put myself to bed and wait for sleep. When it eluded me, I would check the news to make sure I hadn't dreamed up her return. I would reread the articles about her coming back.

Sometime after I stopped reading but before morning, I would notice a numbness in my fingers and toes. It spread slowly, and I would lie there helpless as I lost parts of myself to it, until I became completely paralyzed.

I couldn't move my head to see, but I felt like there was something there, at the foot of my bed, or maybe standing beside it. I imagined its breath, hot and rancid. And when I was so sure of its presence I thought I might scream, I would fall asleep.

I would wake up in the morning to a new truth. Dread.

"Elise?"

"Julie?"

"Hey, it's me."

"Yeah?"

"Yeah."

The sound of her voice did it. Two years' worth of tears burst out.

"Don't cry," she said.

"Don't tell me what to do."

She laughed, and I was certain. It was her.

"I missed you, Jules."

"I miss you always," she said. "Before you ask, I have no memory. None."

"I wasn't going to ask."

"But you're thinking about it."

"I promise you I'm not."

"Good."

"Am I allowed to ask if you're okay?"

"Yeah. Yes, I'm okay. I've essentially woken up a lab rat, but overall, I'm fine. I feel fine. I feel good."

"Good?"

"I mean, a little freaked out. But good. I always knew I would be famous. I thought it would be for winning an Oscar or whatever. Not for this."

"Marrying famous."

"Yeah, meeting an A-list actor in rehab and walking the red carpet. Who's so-and-so's new mystery girl?"

"Five facts about Hottie McHandsome's new girlfriend."

"Right?" she said. "But, yeah, I don't know about this."

"Mm."

"I don't want to be known for this."

"You won't be," I said.

"I lost two years, Lise."

"I'm sorry." What else could I say? A mass of sadness lodged itself in my throat.

"The last thing I remember is waking up that morning, sitting on the porch, drinking coffee out of my favorite mug and thinking about the hike. Then nothing. Not until I was back on the porch."

I wasn't sure I believed her, but I was sure I didn't care.

"I knew you'd come back," I said. "M and M thought I was crazy. They tried to get me to see a shrink."

"Did you?"

"Come on."

"I wouldn't have, either."

"I know, Jules."

"I love you."

"I love you, too. So, so much." And because I can't resist ruining a moment, I asked, "You sure it wasn't aliens?"

"Don't even."

"I'm kidding. Kind of. When can I see you?"

She erupted into a coughing fit so brutal, I pulled the phone away from my ear. It lasted a solid minute.

"Julie?"

"Yeah," she said between coughs. "Sorry."

"You okay?"

"I'm fine."

"You sure?"

"Don't keep asking me."

"Okay."

"Can I call you right back? I need water."

"Yep."

She hung up. I took the opportunity to pee. Living alone, I had developed a habit of leaving the bathroom door open. I don't know why I did it. Because I could. Because I'm horribly lazy. Ever since I had moved into my studio, I peed with the door open.

I kept my phone faceup at my feet in case she called back right away, and I was looking at the screen when I heard the creak of hinges. I turned just in time to watch as the bathroom door crept forward, shutting itself almost completely.

I knew it was a draft. My building was old, decrepit. Still, what if it wasn't? What if there was someone in my apartment? My best friend had just reappeared after vanishing for two years. Anything was possible.

I wiped myself, flushed the toilet, locked the door and washed my hands. I checked behind the shower curtain, which I had failed to notice was pulled across even though I usually left it open to save myself the trouble of wondering what was behind it.

I couldn't tell what was worse—feeling alone in my apartment or not alone.

I don't know what I would have done if Julie hadn't called back right then. Hid in the bathroom forever, maybe.

"Hey," she said. "Sorry about that."

"It's okay," I said. "I missed you."

"Just now?" she asked.

"Yeah, just now."

"Me, too," she said. "I want to see you, too. I need a few weeks."

"Oh," I said, pushing the bathroom door open and sticking my head out, scanning for something unusual. Coast was clear.

"Don't be mad."

"I'm not mad."

"You sound mad."

"I'm not. Cross my heart," I said. "Take all the time you need. Only not too much."

"I think I just need a good mope, you know? I'll get back to feeling like myself again. I'm not there yet, but I will be. Soon."

"I'll mope with you. If you want to mope, I'm happy to mope."

"That's sweet. But we'll see each other soon, I promise," she said. "We'll go somewhere. Do something fun."

It wasn't unlike her. Julie was never good at sitting still, but under the circumstances, it caught me off guard.

"Are you sure? I'll come to you, Jules. Just say the word."

"Tristan's been hovering nonstop since I got back. Not that I blame him, but it'd be good to get out of the house. Be back in the world again. But sorry. I've actually got to go. I love you."

"I love you. I can't tell you how good it is to hear your voice again."

"Oh, darlin'. I'll call you tomorrow."

I couldn't stop myself from opening my laptop and searching for her name. Reading the articles for the thousandth time. A form of pinching myself.

. . .

Her coming back didn't surprise me. Not on any level. What did surprise me was her genuine lack of interest in media attention. I expected her to lean in, do interviews, pose for the cover of *People* magazine, fish for a book deal. The interest was there—she was headline news, but she wasn't keen on the spotlight. I found that highly unusual.

Julie had grown up wanting to be an actress. She had taken the bus to New York by herself at fourteen and been told by a casting director she was too fat. It devastated her. She remembered crying on a bench in Washington Square Park, callous strangers walking past. The more they ignored her, the louder she cried, until she realized she wasn't crying because she was sad anymore; she just wanted someone to notice.

She marched back uptown to the casting director and insisted on seeing him again. She made such a scene that the receptionist caved. The guy said she was pretty and had potential, and to come back and see him after she lost fifteen, no, better make that twenty pounds.

She returned to Massachusetts with an eating disorder. It outlasted her acting dream. Acting shifted to singing, which somehow evolved into a marketing major. After graduating, she had moved out to California with Molly and gotten a job as an assistant at a record label. She was there for about a year before working her way up the West Coast, doing a short stint in San Francisco, then in Seattle.

"I want to focus on travel," she had said when she called to tell me she quit her job.

"What about health insurance?" I asked.

"What about it?"

After a bad breakup in Seattle, she had moved to Tokyo for six months. She taught English to cute, enthusiastic students she got too attached to. But she couldn't stay in Tokyo—some visa issue, I think—so she took herself on a wild European adventure: Croatia, Greece, Italy, Switzerland, Germany, France, the Netherlands. She spent all her money and called me from a café in Amsterdam, laughing. "I don't know how I'm going to get home."

"Put on the red light," I told her.

"Don't joke."

I think Mae ended up transferring her the money for a return flight. She slept on Mae's couch for a few weeks when she got back to the States. She contemplated putting down roots in New York City, but then her mom got sick.

Then she met Tristan. He had the idea to start the bed-and-breakfast in Maine. They found an old place with good bones. They were going to live off the summer tourist income and travel during the winter. It was a romantic plan, but all of Julie's plans were romantic. Mine were, too. The only difference was hers always seemed to work out. Mine crashed and burned.

Mae and Molly were both, in general, considerably more realistic. But something in Julie's return sparked a temporary lapse in their practicality.

"Girls' trip," Molly said.

It was so obvious to me that it was a bad idea. I started shaking my head, the way a baby does to avoid a spoonful of mashed peas. "I don't think Julie is ready."

"It was her idea. She said she talked to you about it."

"Kind of."

"Wouldn't be until the fall. We give her the summer to recuperate and then the four of us go away together."

"Go away where?"

"Mae has a place. This hotel in upstate New York. You wouldn't even have to fly."

"Good, because I can't afford to fly. Is the hotel expensive?"

"I don't think so," she said. "I thought you would be excited."

I was, but I'd envisioned some time for just me and Julie. I had no doubt Julie was struggling more than she let on. If I had her one-on-one, I could probably get her to open up. Plus, the group dynamic overwhelmed me sometimes. It could be the most fun I ever had. It could also unearth insecurities. Who was in on what inside jokes? Who was present for what? Who remembered what? Who knew the secrets the others didn't? Were Molly and Mae closer than Julie and I? Were Mae and I actually the closest? Who talked the most, saw each other the most? Was I everyone's least favorite? Would they even notice if I wasn't there?

We were out of practice being together. The four of us hadn't been in the same room in more than three years, not since Mae's twenty-fourth birthday party. She'd held it at some überchic rooftop club. Molly and I had wedged ourselves in a corner and avoided mingling. We'd taken turns sipping tequila out of her flask because the bar was overpriced. I couldn't afford it, and Molly held out on principle. She didn't like places like that, where you got side-eye for wearing sneakers. When the tequila was gone, we acted like we were on a desert island and had just drunk the last of our water supply.

"I just want you to know," she said, clutching my hands and fake crying, "you're my best friend."

"I wouldn't want to dehydrate to death with anyone else!"

Mae scowled at us. Julie was busy flirting with a male model wearing an outfit I assumed to be couture but could have just as easily been from Walmart. Camo cargo pants and a matching camo button up.

"Elise," Molly said, tapping on the receiver to get my attention.

"Yeah?"

"What's in your head?"

"I am excited. I just don't know if it's a good idea for Julie."

"Well, Julie brought it up and Mae went into full Mae mode."

Mae was the default organizer for all events. It satiated her type A personality. Knowing Mae, I assumed she was desperate to orchestrate pretty new memories to eclipse the trauma of the past two years. It was her coping mechanism—tying ribbons over open wounds.

"And you're on board?" I asked.

"I don't know, man. I said I'd go to Maine, but Jules wasn't having it. We need to see her. If it's on her terms, whatever. I mean, she seems fine. But if she's not fine, we need the chance to be with her and see what's up."

"Yeah."

"Sounds like this is what she wants. What's the alternative? We just show up at her house? I don't know what else to do here, Lise."

"How are you feeling about all this?" I asked her.

She did a sigh-laugh combo. "How are you supposed to feel when your friend comes back from the dead?"

"What's your therapist say?"

"Don't be a bitch."

"I'm not! I'm genuinely curious."

"She says I need to practice acceptance. Accept every thought I have about her coming back, even the bad ones. Acknowledge them, accept them, but not to hold on to them. Not to get stuck on the questions."

"Sounds smart. Solid advice."

"Only problem is, I have a lot of fucking questions." She delivered it like a punch line, but I could hear in her voice she was having a hard time with Julie's return.

"Molls."

"I can't wrap my mind around it. It's too much. Too big a thing. We buried her, essentially. I buried her. We had a funeral."

I remembered Molly's long, wide-legged black pants. Her flowy blouse. She had looked like a seventies icon in mourning. I'd never seen her dressed up like that. I remembered her quiet pearlescent tears, the used tissues packed inside her fists like snowballs.

"I don't want it to come across like I'm not happy. You know I am. This is miracle shit. But I don't know what to do with that."

"You don't have to explain to me, Molly."

"I do, though. You never grieved."

"I did," I said. A lie. "In my own way."

"If you say so."

"It was different. I held on to hope. I don't think you guys did."

"No," she said, "we didn't. You know. I told you from the minute I heard she was missing, I felt in my gut she was gone."

"You just don't like being wrong."

"I'm going to reach through this phone and slap your beautiful face."

"I'm glad that's not possible. You're freakishly strong."

"Live strong," she said. Molly was queen of the sarcastic cancer comment. "All right. So are you good with this?"

"I guess."

"You guess?"

"It's not just the Julie of it all. I'm poor."

"I don't think it's expensive," she said. She didn't sound convinced. She knew as well as I did that money wasn't an issue for Mae and that she was incapable of understanding it was for other people.

"How did Mae find the place?"

"She was there for a photo shoot a few months ago."

"We talking *Vogue* or . . . ?"

"Lise."

"Never mind," I said. "I don't want to ruin everyone's hopes and dreams."

"We'll work it out," she said.

"Do we have a date in mind?"

"Columbus Day weekend, I think."

"All right."

"I've got to go. Mae will iron out the details, and we'll take it from there," she said. She didn't sound excited, either.

"Okay, talk to you soon."

"Laters, baby."

It wasn't that I didn't want to see them. I did. It was the dread. It moved under my skin like a sickness. It spread. I could feel it, always, as it manifested as a pinch in my throat when I swallowed or a slight ache in my neck, a migraine, a random sneezing fit, buckling knees. A range of symptoms that came and went, that had no intelligible connection, that persisted despite medication and heating pads and stretching and herbal tea. Something was wrong with me, physically, every day. It could be a different thing or the same. It could last for a few days or a week or two before switching to something else.

It was psychosomatic. I wasn't beyond admitting that. It was my mind's way of reminding me of my dread, of locking me inside it. I couldn't be happy or free or excited about anything. I was in constant discomfort.

I went to see a doctor who took my blood and chastised me for smoking and for my erratic eating habits.

"It'll catch up with you," he warned.

"I know," I snapped back. I didn't like his condescending tone. "I know smoking is bad, and I need to eat more green things."

"You should think about quitting."

"I have thought about it."

He didn't care for my tone, either.

"I haven't been sleeping," I said, hoping for a prescription. I got one. He wanted to get rid of me.

"Thank you," I said.

He said, "I need you to quit smoking."

I left cranky. I chain-smoked on the way to the pharmacy. It gave me a headache and made me dizzy. I took one of the pills, went to bed too early, woke up too late. I considered the extra sleep a victory.

I made myself chocolate chip pancakes and ate them standing at the counter. I had dried chocolate on my cuticles. I remember noticing it when I picked up Mae's call.

"How are you?"

"Good. You?"

"I'm crazed for Fashion Week," she said. "But I want to book our rooms as soon as possible."

She was out of breath and there were sirens wailing in the background, horns squawking, people yelling.

"Rooms?"

"This hotel is amazing, Lise. When I went for the shoot, I was thinking about how perfect it would be for a girls' trip, but I thought it could never happen because of Julie. Now she's back and it's just . . . I don't know. It's like fate."

"Fate?"

"Yes," she said, resolute.

"When are we going?"

"Over Columbus Day weekend. We'll get there that Thursday before and stay through Tuesday. Five nights. But we'll only have to take off three days because of the holiday."

"I don't get Columbus Day."

"What?"

"I don't get it. I'll have to take four days."

"Is that a problem?"

"Don't think so."

"I'll e-mail you and Molly the info."

"What about Jules?"

"She has the dates. I'll book her room."

"What do you mean, 'book her room'? We're not sharing?"

"The whole point of this place is to get different rooms. The rooms are themed."

"Oh."

"It's reasonable, Lise. Don't worry. If you need, I can help."

"I don't need charity."

She huffed. "That's not what I said. This hotel was my pick. If it's too much for you, I can help. It's not a big deal, okay?"

"I can pay for my own room."

"All right. I'll send you the link. Or should I book them and then you can get me back?"

"Whatever works for you."

"Okay, I'll book them."

I figured it was better to commit before I saw how much it would cost me. If I saw the number first, I would back out. Or cave and take the help. It was best to get the bill and deal with it once it was already set. Mae was going to do what she wanted, Julie and Molly would go along with it, and if I was the only one with a problem, I would be the only one to blame. Solidify my status as the least favorite, the most problematic. Killjoy extraordinaire.

Later, Mae sent me the link to the hotel and a number that made me clutch my chest like I'd been delivered bad news in an old movie. I cried myself to sleep over that number and the realization that the gap between my friends and me had grown so wide that soon I wouldn't be able to jump the distance. It hurt. It was bad enough to be poor and unsuccessful, to make half of what they did, but to know they knew it and weren't sensitive to it? That made it all so much worse.

Resentment began to take shape.

This trip would be the last time I would tolerate it. In the years I'd been in Buffalo, no one had come to see me. Not once. They had the means. They found other excuses. I understood that where I'd ended up was far less glamorous than where they had, but it shouldn't have mattered. The fact that it did told me something about them I didn't want to hear.

I sent Mae half the money right then to get it over with, get it off me. Flick it away like a bug on a picnic blanket. I would need to live on peanut butter sandwiches for the next month to pay the rest.

I was too mad and too sick over it to click the link and check out the hotel.

The trip was jeopardized in late August when Julie's estranged sister, Jade, decided to resurface.

"My sister is a problem" was a phrase I was familiar with. Julie never went into detail, but what I pieced together was a story of a turbulent childhood that Jade remembered much better than Julie did. Jade had taken an early interest in boys, and she'd had a rebellious streak, a penchant for opiates. She dropped out of high school her senior year. She lived with a string of deadbeat boyfriends who had long hair or bad tattoos or missing teeth or arrest warrants or, usually, all of the above. One left her to die after she overdosed. A friend called the ambulance. One beat her up so badly she decided she'd had enough and wanted to get clean. That didn't last.

When their mother got sick, Jade couldn't be bothered. She was curious about the will, but her curiosity condemned her. She was written out of it. Julie got everything.

"I don't feel bad," Julie told me back when it happened. "She would spend it on drugs."

"Have you thought about trying to get her back into treatment?"

"You think I'm heartless," she said.

"I don't." I did. A little.

"You've never dealt with an addict. They lie. My sister is a compulsive liar. She's terrible at it, too."

"You could tell her she'll get the money if she goes to rehab. As motivation."

"Elise, would you just believe me?"

"All right. I do."

"I know she's my sister, my blood. But she's not my family. Not like you and Molls and Maeby baby. You're my family."

"You're closer to the situation. I trust your judgment."

Watching Jade pop her gum during her big TV interview, I realized Julie had a point. Jade looked twice her age, but young, too, somehow. It was her eyes, wide and desperate. Her eyebrows were overplucked, or they'd fallen out. She'd drawn them back on with what appeared to be black Sharpie. Her teeth were brown. Her jaw squarish, her face long. She didn't look anything like Julie.

"She went away because she took all my mom's money after she died," Jade said. "When my mom was sick, she was hanging around, waiting to get that money. She took it all, turned our mom against me. She knew I was coming for her, 'cause it was my money, too. I had a right to that money. So she went away."

"Where do you think she was?"

"Don't know, don't care. But she's lying if she says she can't remember. She knows. She did it on purpose. She's the world's biggest manipulator. You can't believe a word she says."

"Do you think her husband knew?"

Jade shrugged. "Never met him. But Julie can get people to do things. She shows them this sweet side, but it's not the real Julie."

"Do you think you'll see your sister?"

"Nah. But people should know about her. What a liar she is. It's a fake story."

It was obvious Jade had done the interview for money, to get on TV, whatever, but it didn't matter. It poisoned the public with suspicion. Julie was no longer a miracle case. No longer a sweet, beautiful young wife who had vanished on a hike. She was a schemer. A manipulator. Someone who would cheat her ailing sister out of her inheritance. Someone who would invent an elaborate two-year-disappearance plot.

"Have you seen?" Julie asked. It was one a.m., but I was up anyway, pacing around my apartment, trying to exhaust myself to sleep without any pharmaceutical assistance.

I decided my best course of action was to lie and say, "Seen what?"

"It's Jade."

"What happened?"

"She called me a liar on TV."

She said it with the moderate annoyance of someone who got a flat tire or who was taking out the trash and the bag ripped. She wasn't hysterical like I expected, which was strange, considering I'd known her to be obsessed with her public image.

"No one will believe her," I said. "How does she look?"

"Not good."

"Do you feel like you need to give a statement or something?"

"I don't know," she said. "What do you think?"

"Maybe. So people's minds don't run away." I settled on my bed, lying back with my legs up the wall.

My studio was a narrow rectangle, the kitchen on one side, designated bedroom area on the other. My bed was positioned in the back corner, below the only window in the apartment. I lived on the ground floor and kept the curtains drawn 95 percent of the time. I hated the idea of someone looking in on me. Hated it more than I valued the natural light.

I set my gaze up to the window and noticed there was a gap between the curtains. Almost wide enough for a face. A set of eyes. A nose, a mouth. I tried not to let it bother me. It was late; no one would be passing by. But I couldn't shake the feeling that, at any second, a strange face would appear in that space on the other side of the glass.

I sat up and closed the gap.

"Elise?"

"I'm here."

"You sound different."

"I'm fine," I said. "A little anxious. I've been having trouble sleeping."

"We must have traded," she said. "I used to be an insomniac, but lately I sleep like a baby."

"That's good," I said, nibbling on an already stubby nail. "Good you're getting sleep."

"You get pills?"

"Yeah, but I don't want to have to take them every night."

"Are you not supposed to?"

"Dunno."

"I should let you go. I'll call you in the morning. You seem distracted."

"I'm not. Talk to me. Talk, talk, talk."

"Okay, so, if I give a statement, it makes me look guilty. I don't want to be defensive."

"I don't think it'll come across that way. You have the right to protect your reputation."

"My reputation?" she said. "My reputation as the missing newlywed?"

"That's not your reputation."

"Level with me, Lise."

"I told you before. This is temporary. You'll get back to your life."

"What life?"

I sat on the edge of my tub and lit a cigarette. I tried not to make a habit of smoking inside but kept a loose definition of what constituted a habit.

"What's going on?" I asked her, tapping ashes into an empty soap dish.

"Nothing," she said. "Readjusting. I don't know if I'm ready for a girls' weekend at some kitschy hotel."

"No?" My ribs clenched. I missed her. I wanted to see her. I also didn't want to pay all this money for a contrived experience. All I really wanted was Jules and me on the couch eating Nutella with spoons and waxing poetic about reality TV.

But there were Molly and Mae. And the money I had already spent.

"I want to go. I really do," she said. "But I'm afraid to leave. Not only because of the media stuff, but because what if I lose my memory again? It's stupid, but sometimes I'm afraid to leave a room because what if I'm never seen again? Poor Tristan—he follows me around the house. I know he's worried about the same thing. If I don't know what happened, how do I know it won't happen again?"

I didn't know what to say. I watched the ember burn steadily toward the filter, my fingers.

"Don't listen to me," Julie said, breaking the long silence. "I'm just in a mood because of this whole Jade thing."

"It'll blow over," I said.

"I want to see you," she said, "and Molly and Mae."

"It's going to be good for you. For all of us," I said, sounding more confident than I felt.

"The hotel does look cool, doesn't it? It'll be fun to take pictures."

My curiosity won out. I abandoned the bathroom for my kitchen, stood at the counter, opened my laptop and searched.

As I scrolled through the photos, I convinced myself that everything would be fine, that we would have a good time, that the trip was exactly what we needed. And it worked, because I had spent the past two years becoming very convincing.

II

The Red Honey Inn hovers somewhere between the soft peaks of the Catskill Mountains, miles from the nearest nameless town. The purpose of its seclusion is unclear. It's not a place trying to hide from the world. It's not quiet. It stands among the trees, screaming.

It's a sprawling storybook estate. Aggressively whimsical. Cloying. A pastel Frankenstein's monster.

The original, central structure was an early-twentieth-century ski resort. Swiss chalet–style. All balconies and gables. Distinctly European. The expansion was an identity crisis. The place seems to grow off itself, multiplying in unnatural ways. There's a part that's Gothic, with tall, ornamented arches and stained glass. Part is made up of a series of conjoined cottages with thatched roofs.

I watch it from the parking lot, anticipating that if I take my eyes off it for a second, when I look back, it will have proliferated, adding a sweeping porch or a French château.

I made the drive in good time and need to reward myself with this cigarette, my last for the weekend. I can't smoke around Molly. Mae doesn't approve, either, though after a drink, she'll be pulling on my hands, asking sweetly to bum one. Julie doesn't mind but doesn't partake.

"I refuse to turn into my mother," she says.

Trees guard the parking lot. These trees have been around for a while, been around the block before. Seen some things.

It's been a warm fall, and the leaves are confused. Some are fiercely green, ignorant of the fact it's October, or perhaps aware and defiant. Others got the memo and have dutifully turned themselves yellow, orange, red. The surrounding wood is dense. It gives me the feeling the hotel shouldn't be here, shouldn't have intruded. It gives me the feeling that *I* shouldn't be here.

There are cars in the parking lot, but I see no other evidence of humans. It's dead quiet. I should check in, get to my room, take a nap, change. That would be the normal, natural thing to do. I should want to. I shouldn't want to wait in my car. But I'm afraid if I walk into the hotel, no one will be there. It'll be empty.

Or it won't be empty, and I'll have stumbled into that old trap. A witch will greet me in the lobby, lock me up and, in a few days, cook and eat me.

It would be a ridiculous thought if the place didn't look so otherworldly, like it had dropped straight out of some warped fairy tale.

Molly landed in New York two hours ago. She and Mae rented a car and are driving up together. They shouldn't be much longer. Jules will be at least an hour late, as a rule. She said two p.m. It's one now.

I take a good, long, final drag of my cigarette. I get my duffel out of the trunk, gather my purse and its spilled contents from the passenger seat. Dig around the crease for rogue lip balm. When I lock the car, the screechy beep echoes, scattering dark birds across the cloudless powder blue sky.

The stone walkway is lined with browning flowers, retiring for the season. Moss has begun to crawl up the side of the building, initiating its inevitable takeover. There's a hint of manure smell in the air. Maybe someone was trying to give the flowers a few more weeks to live. Some make-my-own-granola Hudson Valley resident who couldn't be happier with a groundskeeper job. Or maybe it was the garden gnomes, with their painted smiles, with their can-do attitudes, with their shovels and rakes, with their ulterior motives.

The front doors are nearly twice as tall as me, iridescent teal with gold trim, gold handles and two giant gold lion's head knockers. I push the handle. Pull the handle. Nothing.

"Hello?" I ask the lions, with immediate regret. What if they answer me?

There's a humming, and the doors begin to open on their own. Outward, toward me. I have to jump back out of their way.

My eyes adjust to the influx of color. They struggle to accept the sheer absurdity of the lobby. It's vast. Far above me, exposed beams drip with Edison bulbs. The ceiling is clean silver. Hundreds of framed mirrors and paintings, each a different style, cover the walls. They're interspersed with sculptures: spiral things, a big shoe, Venus's head, an angel's wing. It's like a five-year-old's idea of an art museum. Light bounces between the mirrors and makes the space seem bigger and brighter and more fantastical.

"Good afternoon. Welcome to the Red Honey Inn. How may I help you?" asks the bouncy blonde behind the reception desk. I open my mouth to answer her but am distracted by a trio of spiral staircases beyond the lobby and the way the place seems to go on and on without any visible end.

"Miss?"

"Yes, sorry. Checking in. My name is Elise Webster, but the reservation is probably under Blake. Mae Blake."

"Let me see here," she says, vanishing behind a huge, shiny white Mac. "Yes, I have a reservation for Mae Blake. Four rooms. May I please see an ID and a card to keep on file for your room?"

"Yep."

"Thanks so much."

I feel bad for my credit card. It's sad and tired.

"Okay! I have you in our Cassandra suite. Here is your room key." She hands me a silver key attached to a large turquoise tassel. "Here are your card and ID, and here is a map of the hotel with a list of our amenities. If you give me just a moment, I'll have someone see you to your room."

She reappears from behind the monitor. She's young and sunny. She wears vintage cat-eye glasses with thick lenses that magnify her eyes. She looks like she belongs in a Keane painting. She has on a green-and-white-striped housedress. I wonder if it's a uniform or something she dug up in her grandmother's attic.

"I can help!" Another woman appears. She's also wearing a housedress, but hers is brown, and she has on moccasins. She's got untamed gray hair that falls down to her waist. She's sturdy-looking. Broad shouldered.

"Hello! Welcome! Please let me take that bag for you, and I'll lead the way!"

"She's in Cassandra," the receptionist says. "If you need anything, Ms. Webster, please don't hesitate to ask! We're so happy to have you. We do hope you enjoy your stay!"

This girl was definitely in her high school drama club. Sings along to show tunes in her car. "Practices" yoga. Knits.

"Right this way."

I follow brown-dress lady down the main hallway, past the three spiral staircases. To the left there's a cave of a room with stone walls and a fireplace like an enormous mouth. There's a series of hallways that veer off at odd angles, a disorienting side effect of the additions built off the original structure. We come to a grand staircase with an elaborate gold banister carved with flowers and grapes and whatnot. The spindles are each painted a different color. Deep blue, sage green, burgundy. Mustard, rust, purple. The attention to detail in this place is impressive. You can't escape the theme. The theme being pure cuckoo-bananas quirkiness. But tasteful, kind of? None of it looks cheap.

"Right up here," she says.

"Do the spiral staircases lead up here, too?"

"Those go to our private suites, popular with honeymooners. Or anyone in need of some relaxation and self-care. Those suites feature private balconies with outdoor Jacuzzi tubs and gorgeous views. Gorgeous."

"How long have you worked here?" I ask her. What I really want to know is what her job is, but I think it would be rude to ask outright.

"Since we opened two years ago," she says. "The inn has such a rich history. It was built by Oskar Berlinger, a wealthy art dealer. He contracted tuberculosis in 1898 and came up to the Catskills for the mountain air. Once he recovered, he loved the area so much, he didn't want to return to the city. He had a vision of creating a luxury resort for elite New Yorkers."

"Mm," I say.

"The original building, inspired by Swiss chalets, was completed in 1907. After Berlinger's death in 1931, it remained vacant until the forties, when it was purchased by Richard Abraham as a family summer home."

I didn't ask for a history lesson. I'm also certain this is all on the website. We're standing outside the door to my room, and she's still talking. I appreciate her enthusiasm, her tea green eyes wide as disks, her smile revealing porcelain teeth and receding gums. I appreciate the huskiness of her voice, like she might sing me a folk song. But if I don't interrupt her now, I'll be here all goddamn day.

"Are you the manager here?"

"Oh, yes," she says. "Apologies. My name is Patsy."

She shakes my hand. Her grip is firm. Too firm. From the intensity of her eye contact, I can tell she's the kind of lady who appreciates a good, firm handshake. She's burly. I bet she eats a lot of stew.

And children, maybe. Who knows? Might not be out of the woods yet.

I'm being a bitch today. Judgmental. The four of us bring it out in one another. They aren't here yet, but they're close enough. When we're all together, we can be downright evil.

"Here we are," Patsy says, gesturing to the door.

It's difficult to unlock it with a giant tassel in the way. The strings keep getting twisted around the key. Patsy clears her throat, and I decide I don't like her.

The lock clicks, and Patsy pushes the door open from behind me, ushering me in.

It's an assault of turquoise. Everything is turquoise. The theme might be baroque? There are two regal high-backed chairs, a fainting couch, a dainty love seat. The upholstery perfectly matches the shade of the walls. There's crown molding painted cotton candy pink, same as the ceiling medallion that anchors the crystal chandelier. There's a mirror with a dramatic gold frame that takes up most of the wall above the love seat. On the wall across from the love seat, there's a turquoise fireplace mantel, but no fireplace. There's a conspicuous mini fridge, which would be guilty of shattering the illusion if it wasn't already broken by the massive flatscreen TV that sits on top of the mantel.

The bed is past the sitting area, separated by a step and a duo of floor-to-ceiling columns, painted to look like marble. There's a queen bed with a formidable tufted headboard. It's flanked by two nightstands, each a round of glass held up by a wrought iron flower stem, complete with leaves and thorns. There is an abundance of pink satin pillows on top of a turquoise duvet. Beyond the bed, velvety turquoise curtains run the whole length and width of the wall. I pull them to the side and find a large window and a short, narrow glass door.

"Oh!"

"The shared balcony is through there," she says.

"Huh," I say, replacing the curtains over the door. I don't like the idea of a shared balcony. Of people walking back and forth past my window. You would think a second-floor room would buy you some privacy. It's like I'm back at home.

"The bathroom is just through there," Patsy says, pointing to a door next to the mantel.

I peek inside. It's spacious, tiled pink. Pink tub, pink toilet, pink sink. There's no shower curtain, only a pane of frosted glass that folds in and out of the wall.

I oscillate between delight and indifference. I can't tell if I like the room or if I find it obnoxious.

"Thanks, Patsy."

"You're very welcome. I'll leave your bag right here, and if you need anything else, please let us know."

"Thank you."

She lingers a little too long, looking around the room as if she's never seen it before. I smile and wait for her to go. Eventually she nods and says something I miss. She gives a final wave as she closes the door.

I take my phone out of my back pocket. A message from Mae. She and Molly will be here in thirty. Nothing from Jules.

Something catches on the fringes of my vision. My body tenses, startled, but it's just my reflection in the mirror above the couch. I lean toward myself. My nose looks extra big, my hair extra flat. The persistent patch of eczema on my left temple is pink in contrast with the rest of my face, my cheeks and lips ashen.

"I'm not too happy with you," I tell my reflection.

I reach up to touch my face, pinch some life into it. My fingers are freezing cold. I spy a thermostat near the door. It's at sixty-seven, but it doesn't feel like it. I turn it up to seventy. I remember I'm in a hotel and don't have to worry about the heating bill. Seventy-five. Seventy-seven.

I dig a book out of my bag and spread myself across the fainting couch. I like the book but can barely get through a sentence. I'm too antsy to read. Restless.

I put the TV on for some company. It's set to a classic channel, some old Hollywood movie. Black-and-white. A beautiful, distressed actress in the arms of a slick, barrel-chested actor too handsome for his own good. The volume is all the way down. I turn it up.

I expect words. I expect her voice to be high and melodic, his deep and smooth. I expect her to ask something like "Don't you love me, darling?" Him to answer, "Well, of course, I do."

It takes a second to register that they aren't saying anything. As I turn the volume up louder, it's clear they aren't speaking words. What's coming from the TV is a low moaning noise. I look down at the remote as if there'll be an obvious solution, a button that reads WORDS or ENGLISH or something. I smack the remote against the side of my hand as if that'll fix the problem.

The noise gets louder. There's another noise growing inside it. A hissing, scratching tone. Angry static. The sound reverberates.

I press MUTE, but nothing happens. I start to panic. It's too loud.

I search for a button on the TV itself. I feel like the actors are looking at me. Like there's no fourth wall; they see me. Their mouths move like they're trying to tell me something, like what goddamn button to press to make this sound stop.

The hissing static has taken over. It's the loudest now. It's quick. It's like it's speaking, like it's saying something. But it's on some other frequency. It's away, it's above me or below or it's in my ear but I'm rejecting it like a body rejects a transplant.

I feel around the side of the TV and start pressing buttons at random. In come the romantic violins, the actors' voices. It's too late now. I've got zero interest in watching TV. I find the power button and turn it off.

Flustered, I go into the bathroom and splash cold water on my face. I change into a cuter outfit. Dark-wash high-waisted jeans, black tank, comfy cardigan. White Converse, spotless, brand-new. All outlet finds. I'm an outlet shopper now. If Mae only knew.

I check my phone again. No word. I cautiously pull back the curtains, anticipating that someone will be there: a patient voyeur ready to see who's on the other side of the glass.

There's no one there. Just the balcony, shadowed by the roof above it, and beyond the ledge a grassy lawn pale with the change of season. And the woods, still lush enough to be mysterious.

The sun feels good. I relax into it, fall back on the bed. Something smells sweet and lavender-y. There's a hidden air freshener somewhere, or some crazy-potent laundry detergent was used on these sheets. I turn my face to the pillows and inhale. That's it. I wriggle under the covers.

I didn't notice before. The patch of ceiling above the bed is painted to look like the night sky. It's dark blue, and there are tiny specks of stars that sparkle. They fade in and out. It's a little cheesy, but I can't be mad at it.

I sigh and check my phone again. It's my own fault for getting here so early, for subconsciously needing to get here first, because if I didn't they would have the opportunity to hang out without me. Realize they didn't miss me. Decide I wasn't integral to the friend group. I know it's crazy. I'm allowed.

And Jules. What if Jules got here first? I wouldn't want her to be alone in a new place. It's the first time she's going away from home since she got back.

I close my eyes, imagine my phone chiming over and over again until it actually does.

From Molly: **We're here! Just pulled into the parking lot. Come meet us up front!**

Running, I reply.

I grab my room key. It's heavy and awkward to carry, and I'm gaining a whole new appreciation for key cards.

I go to lock the door behind me. As the gap between the door and the frame shrinks, I think I see someone standing in the middle of my room, right in front of the mirror, turning toward me.

I push the door back open. The room is empty. I shake off what I thought I saw, lock the door, check the handle and hurry down the hall. I think I'm going the right way. Maybe?

Yes.

I see the stairs and have to slow myself down. What if I fall on my way to see them? Tumble down this swanky staircase, end up in a cast or limping around the rest of the trip. What if I break my neck?

Dark. Why does my brain always do that? Consider the worst, most ridiculous scenario?

I hang on to the bannister, tight, not willing to risk a self-fulfilling prophecy.

This place is a maze. It's bigger than I remember, even though my memory is from less than an hour ago. I walk what seems like forever until I hear Molly's voice.

"I'm getting low-key brothel vibes," she says.

She's walking around the lobby with her hands on her hips, her head tilted up toward the ceiling. She cut her jet-black hair short, and it's tucked behind her ears. Her Bettie Page bangs have recently been trimmed. She's chewing on her aviators.

"Molls!"

"There she is," she says, reaching out for me. She's significantly taller than me. She rests her chin on my head when she hugs me. "Always early."

"I want some," Mae says, inserting herself into our hug. She smells amazing. Bergamot and fig, her signature scent. She has it specially made by a friend of a friend who works for a perfumery in Paris. Underneath a wide-brimmed hat, her silvery white hair falls pin straight down past her shoulders. She rocks longer, fringy bangs.

When we release the hug, I get to take in her full look. Purple crushed velvet overalls with flared legs, a white T-shirt underneath. Her jacket is tucked under her arm. It's white and fluffy like a baby polar bear. She's wearing a new pair of glasses, like she is every time I see her. These ones are roundish with thick gold frames.

Molly is wearing her typical sweatpants-and-T-shirt combo, an old jean jacket, sneakers. "I had chemo," she says whenever Mae tries to get her to dress up. "I earned the right to be comfortable for the rest of my life."

"Did you guys get your rooms?"

"I'm in the Jane, and our little ingenue over here is in the Juliet," Molly says, yawning. "Fucking time zones."

"How do you like your room?" Mae asks.

"It's intense," I say, and immediately add, "in a good way."

"I picked it for you because it's very dramatic."

"What are you trying to say?" I ask dramatically.

"You like all that stuff. *Jane Eyre*. It said Gothic romance."

"What?"

"Your room?"

"I don't think my room is Gothic romance," I say.

"What room are you in?"

"Cassandra."

Mae's glossy pink mouth inverts into a frown.

"What is it?" I ask, looking to Molly to see if she knows. She shrugs.

"It's okay," Mae says, waving her hands in front of her face like she's clearing smoke.

"What?"

"I booked that room for Jules. I meant for you to be in the other one. But it's fine. Julie likes all that stuff, too."

51

"I can switch," I tell her, feeling guilty for something that isn't my fault but feels a whole lot like my fault. "That's the room they put me in. I don't care."

"No, no. It's okay."

"I'll switch. Really. Don't care at all."

"Doesn't matter," Molly says. "Let's leave it up to Jules."

"Do you know when she's getting here?" Mae asks me.

"I was about to ask you the same question."

"No one knows where she is?"

"She said she was on her way around eight thirty this morning," I say. "Shouldn't be too much longer."

"Hello!" Patsy's back. She introduces herself to Molly and Mae. Mae smiles politely. Molly gives me a sideways look. When Patsy starts to lead Mae down the hall, Molly hangs back and whispers to me, "What's almond butter's deal?"

"Right? She gives off a vibe."

"It's the intensity of her eye contact. It says, like, 'I'm going to bring you homemade gluten-free pastries but also watch you while you're sleeping.'"

"I envy people who enjoy their jobs, but I also think it's weird when someone is too into their job, you know?"

"She fucking loves her job."

"*Loves* it!"

We walk past the spiral staircases. Mae looks back at us and points excitedly. We pass the grand staircase and make a right into a small corridor with a series of rooms.

"Here we are," Patsy says. "This is the Jane. Which one of you is staying in the Jane?"

"That would be me," Molly says.

"Okay, this is your key." Patsy lifts the key. It's attached to a bunch of feathers.

"Is that a bird?" Molly asks. "Oh, fuck. I thought that was a bird for a second."

Mae looks back at her, shooting daggers through her glasses. We're embarrassing her already.

Patsy opens the door for us. Molly heads in first. When she steps inside, she makes a loud gurgling sound, like something went down the wrong pipe.

I peek around.

This room, apparently, is jungle themed. The walls are covered in vines, and there's a whole lot of animal print. The biggest bed I've ever seen takes up most of the room. It's made to look like a tree growing around the mattress in the form of a four-poster frame. Hanging vines and flowers and leaves make up the canopy. What might be a hundred pillows in the shapes of different exotic flowers cover the bed, the floor, everywhere. There's a dark wood dresser that doubles as a TV stand, but that's the only other piece of furniture. There's a window covered in tiger-and-cheetah-print curtains on the other side of the bed.

"I love the walls," Mae says, running her hand against what I presume to be fake stone. I reach out and touch it, and it feels real to me.

"Oh, shit! A waterfall!" Molly points. There's water running down the back wall, caught in a narrow basin.

"The bathroom is just through here." Patsy pushes open a door next to the dresser. I wouldn't have noticed it if she didn't point it out; it's made of the same stone as the wall. The knob is a miniature ship wheel.

There's a short hallway with racks for clothes. It leads to a decent-sized bathroom, tiled green with a waterfall shower, a stall for the toilet behind a door (a piece of driftwood) and a sink that's essentially a big glass bowl sitting on top of a tree stump.

"Isn't this crazy?" Mae asks, her pearly cheeks glowing.

"I'm into it," Molly says. When Mae leaves the bathroom, Molly turns to me and whispers, "How many cheetahs had to die for this hotel room?"

"At least twenty."

She laughs. "All of them. They're extinct."

"Do you like it?"

"Yeah," she says. "I think? I don't know. Like, I do, but I hate myself for it."

"Same."

She puts her arm around me. "It's so good to see you."

"Mollsy."

"Let's go see what room Mae picked for herself. If we dare."

Patsy hands Molly her key. Molly looks down at it, brow furrowing. Her mouth twitches. She bites her bottom lip. When Patsy turns her back, Molly looks at me, lifts the key and mouths, "What the fuck?"

When Mae and Patsy are out of earshot, I say, "Made from *real* birds! Can you believe it?"

"I'm calling PETA."

Ahead of us, Patsy gives Mae the same history lesson she gave me earlier. Mae is nodding graciously, asking the occasional question. We walk back to the main staircase.

"Very Scarlett O'Hara," Molly says as we go up. "I look forward to falling down these drunk."

"I thought the same thing. But better these than those," I say, pointing to the spiral staircases. "Totally impractical."

"I don't think they're going for practical here," she says, taking her key out of her pocket and dangling it in front of me. "I'm curious about the other rooms. I wish we could go in all of them."

"How many do you think there are?"

Patsy turns around. "We have thirty-seven rooms here. Fourteen in the wings on the ground floor, four guest cottages accessible from the ground floor, sixteen rooms on the second floor and our three guest suites. Okay, we're right over here."

The room is directly across from the top of the stairs. Patsy takes out the key, which is attached to a hot pink poof.

"This is the room we used for the shoot," Mae says, punctuating her words with a single clap.

"Yes, this is our Juliet," Patsy says like a proud mother.

It's obscenely pink. Hot pink carpet, metallic pink floral wallpaper, crystal chandeliers dripping from the ceiling like stalactites. The room is pretty spacious, even with the large boatlike bed. A silky magenta bedspread makes sporadic appearances beneath an excess of fuzzy pink pillows. There's a heart-shaped mirror hung above a vintage French dresser. There's a small mirror-topped writing desk in the corner. A matching mirrored nightstand showcases a flowery, retro-style rotary phone.

The whole room has an overpowering smell of rose. I spy a few fancy reed diffusers.

The bathroom door is hidden behind a bead curtain. It's completely princess pink. It's got an impressive claw-foot tub that Mae is especially giddy over.

The heart-spotted tiles are a nice reminder of what hotel we're in, so we don't forget for a second and think we're somewhere else: somewhere with claw-foot tubs and rose-scented reed diffusers and subtlety. I pick some fuzz off my tongue. No idea how it got there.

We shuffle back into the bedroom, where Patsy points out a closet with a mini fridge.

"Hey, do I get a mini fridge?" Molly asks.

"Yes. You'll find a small handle to the left of the dresser. It's embedded in the wall."

"Cool," she says, falling backward onto the bed. She settles herself in, hugging a pillow. She looks at Mae. "You're going to masturbate tonight, aren't you?"

"Molls!" Mae hides her face.

"What? This is the masturbation room."

Patsy clears her throat. "May I get you anything else? Any questions for me?"

"No, we're good," Molly says. "Thank you."

"Actually, Patsy, could you please let us know when our friend arrives? She's the fourth on the reservation. Julie." Mae pauses, taps my shoulder. "I forget if I used her maiden or married name."

"Does she have a married name? Like, legally?" I ask. In the articles they used the name I knew her by. Julie Ryan. If she took Tristan's name, she would be Julie Harbour.

"No idea," Molly says.

"Ryan," I say.

"I will ring you here when Julie Ryan arrives," Patsy says.

"I want to see your room, Lise," Molly says.

"Could you please call us there, Patsy?" Mae asks.

"Surely." Patsy hands Mae her key, nods and excuses herself.

"You don't think Julie will tell us when she gets here?" Molly asks.

"Not necessarily. I don't want her to be alone, even if it's for five minutes in her own room. We have to keep in mind we haven't seen her in over two years. And with what she's been through, she could be different. We have to prepare ourselves for that."

"We know," Molly says. But if she's speaking for me, she's wrong. My heart is set on seeing the same old Julie. I've been counting on it.

"It's still Julie," I say.

"Oh, no. I'm not saying it's not our Julie," Mae says. "I'm saying that she might be a little different. Just not what we're used to. I mean, we've all changed in the last two years. But we've been around to witness it, so there's been a natural progression. With her we were cut off from that time."

"So was she," Molly says, and adds under her breath, "Supposedly."

"You don't believe her?" Mae asks.

"Don't gimme that. I believe her. But I can't say I don't have doubts. Don't you?"

Mae shakes her head and looks down, hiding under the brim of her hat.

"Did you watch Jade's interview?" Molly asks.

"No," Mae says. "I didn't."

"I was just asking."

"Julie would never do what Jade said."

"So you did watch it?"

"Should we go to my room?" I ask, interrupting before it escalates any further. It's rare for them to bicker. "We told Patsy to call us there."

"Yep," Molly says, rolling off the bed. "Good ol' Pat."

"One more thing," Mae says, stepping onto the bed and waving us up. We get on, hold hands instinctively. Jump, jump, jump. Squeal like hot teapots.

"Okay, okay," Molly says. "Enough."

Mae wheels her suitcase over to the closet. She sets it down on its back.

"Ready," she says, shepherding us out of the room. She locks the door and puts the oversized key in her oversized pocket.

"This way," I say, leading them down the hall.

"I thought our rooms would be next to each other," Molly says.

"There weren't four adjacent rooms available," Mae says. "Besides, I picked the cutest ones."

"I wasn't complaining."

"Here we go." I take the key and wriggle it inside the lock.

Again, same as when I left, I get the sense that something or someone is standing in the middle of my room, dodging out of view just as the door opens. It's like its shadow is too slow, and that's what I'm seeing. Its residue.

I check behind the door.

"What?" Molly asks.

"Nothing," I say. "What do you think?"

"Classy," she says, putting her pinkie up.

"I love, love this one," Mae says. I remember that she didn't intend it for me. "The color."

"You get two rooms," Molly says, stepping into the area with the bed. "Is that a balcony?"

"Yep."

"Dope."

"I can't wait for you to see the rest of the hotel," Mae says. "The pictures don't do it justice. The dining room is vintage gorgeous. There's a lounge with a huge fireplace. You can make s'mores. There's an indoor pool. A spa. A cute little movie theater in the basement."

"Bar?"

"Yes, there's a bar next to the dining room."

"Nice."

"I also brought liquor," she says, "because you two are lushes."

"I'm offended," Molly says dryly. "It's cold in here. Are you cold?"

"I just raised the thermostat," I say, checking it again. It's at seventy-seven. "I guess it takes a while to heat up? Do you think it's broken? Should I call?"

"Yeah, get that Pat in here. Say, 'Pats, we got a problem.'"

"Oh, God," Mae says, pulling her hat down over her face.

Molly opens the door to the balcony, and we file outside.

"Oh, this shit is shared?"

"Yup."

"I'm not jealous anymore," she says.

"Thanks."

"Welcome."

We air-kiss like Europeans.

Mae gives a huff of disapproval.

"What? Isn't that what you do for a living, Ms. High Fashion?" Molly asks her. "Kiss, kiss."

"You two are crazy," she says, pushing past us. "Pretty view."

"It's cold out here, too," Molly says. "Is it always this cold in October? I've been in LA too long."

"This is like summer to me, coming from Buffalo, so I can't say."

"It's cold," Mae says. "I wanted it to be warmer."

"You can't control the temperature."

"Can't I?" she asks, with a hint of a smile.

"Let's go back inside. I'm freezing my tits off," Molly says, opening the door for us. It's just as cold in my room as it is outside. I'm going to have to call the front desk. *Uggghhhhh.*

"I'm getting nervous Julie isn't here yet," Mae says, tapping a superbly manicured nail on her bottom lip. "I hope she's all right."

"You're only worried because of what happened. This is Julie. Julie is always late. It's not unusual, Maebs," I say, taking off her hat and trying it on. I check the mirror. It looks stupid on me.

"You're right."

"I know," I say with a wink. She does her tongue-clicking thing.

"What's on the agenda, Maebs?" Molly asks. "What do you have planned for us?"

"Happy hour and dinner tonight. Tomorrow I thought we could explore the grounds, maybe go for a walk if anyone's interested. If not, there's a trip to a local distillery I signed us up for. Come back. Watch a movie downstairs in the theater. Saturday there's a crafts class in the afternoon. Or it's wine and painting. I forget. I reserved us spots for that, too. We don't have to go if you guys don't want to."

"No, that all sounds good," I say. I put her hat back on her like it's her coronation. She plays along. "Your hair is so soft."

"I started using this coconut-oil-and-aloe shampoo from René Alexi. He's a hairstylist who strictly does runway and print, but he's developing his own product line for release."

I steal a look at Molly, who flicks her hair back and sticks her nose up in the air.

"Don't make fun! She asked!"

There's a knock at the door. A single loud knock. The three of us freeze. Did we imagine it?

Another knock, too long after the first.

I take a step toward the door. I wait.

A third knock.

A chill nips at the back of my neck.

It's probably Patsy. Back to check in, ask how we're doing. Offer us complimentary honey-roasted chickpeas or a bottle of cheap rosé. It is that kind of place. They want to keep the guests happy. They want the experience to be personal.

My imagination trolls me. It's a clown, it says. A clown holding a single red balloon. No, it's an ordinary suburban dad, with a dark secret and a soundproof shed. It's the guy in the room next door. He just wants to say hello—"I can see you through the little hole I drilled" or the camera he installed just before I got here.

I attempt to swat the fear away, not knowing where it's coming from or why it's here, but it circles back. It won't leave. It insists.

Another knock comes when I'm about a foot from the door. It's loud, more of a pounding than a knock. Who knocks like that? Taking so long in between?

I get up on my tiptoes to look through the peephole.

It's Jules.

Of course. I'm dumb.

I pull back the door.

I lean in to hug her but am stopped by her appearance.

She's emaciated. She smiles and her skin pools like melted wax. Her teeth are chipped and discolored. Her eyes are bloodshot, and the green of her irises skews yellow. Her hair is stringy, simultaneously greasy and dry.

I'm horrified, but I don't want her to see my shock. I hide it by bringing her in close, holding her.

This is why she didn't want to go on TV. Why she was hesitant to see us. Makes sense.

Doesn't matter. It's Julie. Here she is. Breathing in my arms, against my chest. She's alive. She's back.

"I love you," I tell her, surprising myself by crying.

"I love you, too," she says. Her breath is awful. So awful I gag. I play it off like a sob but have to turn my head away.

"Come in, come in," I say.

Molly and Mae rush forward. I watch them hug her. I can't get over how small she is. Skeletal. She wears black leggings that hang loose and an oversized gray sweater. Her shoulders jut out underneath the sweater, and the way the fabric moves over her bones is upsetting.

Julie has never been this thin before. Her weight always fluctuated depending on the tenacity of her eating disorder, but never to this extreme. She was a Marilyn. She had the biggest boobs out of the four of us, and we weren't shy about expressing our envy. She would say, "It's because I'm the fattest." We would say, "You're beautiful. You're a total smokeshow." Or I would say, "I'm the ugliest. I'm ugly." Then Molly would threaten to beat us with her prosthetic leg, and Mae would purse her lips, shake her head.

"Together again," Julie says, waving me in for a group hug.

Mae is full-on weeping. Silently, of course. Tastefully. Julie wipes away Mae's tears with her bony fingers.

Molly, the tallest (a fact), looks over the tops of Mae's and Julie's heads to me, and in her eyes I read shock and concern. I nod slightly, so only she can see, and join in the hug.

It doesn't feel right. It's an awkward assembly of bodies. There's a reluctance in the way our torsos angle out, in our rigid arms and suspended hands. No one wants to touch one another. Or no one wants to touch Julie.

"Okay, okay," Julie says, breaking out. "I don't want it to be weird. Let's pretend nothing happened, okay?"

"You mean pretend you weren't missing for two years and we didn't think you were dead and have a funeral for you?" Molly asks.

Mae gasps and smacks Molly's arm.

"Exactly," Julie says.

"Cool, no prob," Molly says.

"Did you check in yet? You were supposed to call us. I was worried," Mae says.

"I wanted to surprise you. I got your room number from the lady downstairs."

"I think we've had enough surprises from you," Molly says. "And that's the last I'll talk about it."

Julie rolls her eyes. "It's going to be the hardest for you, and I like it."

"Fine, fine." Molly puts her hands up, surrendering.

"Do you want to see my room?" Julie asks. "This place is really cool, Mae. A good escape from the world." She looks back at Molly, who mimes zipping her lips.

"You like it?" Mae asks. "You like your room?"

"This was supposed to be your room," I tell Julie. "I took it by mistake."

"It's okay. I like my room. It's different. You want to see?"

"Yes! Give us the tour!"

I grab my key off the mantel. I leave everything else in the room—my wallet, my phone—I realize as I'm locking up. I could go back for them but don't bother.

When I turn around, Julie is there.

"You okay?" she asks me.

"Yeah," I say, my voice too high.

"Are you sure? You can tell me."

"I'm trying not to get emotional," I say. Mostly true.

"We should get drunk later," she says. She turns to Molly and Mae. "Drunk later? Like, absolutely hammered?"

"Freshman-year drunk?" I ask.

"Yes."

"I don't think I can get that drunk anymore," Molly says.

"Sure, you can," I say.

"I believe in you!" Julie says. "It's this way. First floor."

I let her walk ahead. She links arms with Mae. Molly slows her pace to get in line with me. She takes out her phone and types, **I wasn't expecting that.**

I nod and mouth, "Me, either."

She puts her phone back in her pocket. "Are we there yet?" she asks.

Mae points out her own room, and we make a pit stop to show Julie. I sit on the bed and cuddle a pillow. Squeeze it as a form of stress relief. My thoughts are slow and sticky, like they stepped in gum. Everything is so surreal. Julie. This place. Seeing all my friends together after so long.

I realize my toes are numb. Cold. My fingers, too. I blow into my hands.

"Are you cold?" I ask Molly.

"Not anymore. Your room is cold, though."

"We'll talk to Patsy," Mae says, the hint of a break in her voice. Anything we say against the hotel she'll take personally because she suggested it. It's hers.

"My turn!" Julie says, wiping her mouth with her sleeve. "Ready? It's intense."

We step out into the hall. I notice the carpet for the first time. Gold fleurs-de-lis over dark green. I trace the pattern, but it dizzies me. I'm hit with a sudden splitting headache. I rub my temples.

"What's up?" Molly asks.

"Headache," I tell her. "I think I'm dehydrated."

"I have water in my room," Julie says. "There's a little fridge."

We walk downstairs, past the hall with Molly's room, to a longer, narrower hallway.

Julie takes the key out of her small, beat-up leather bag. She bought it in Florence, along with matching wallets for the four of us. The guy who sold them to her took her out on a date. They drank Limoncello and ate gelato and made out on the Ponte Vecchio. He was a terrible kisser.

It's good to know someone's stories. I'm glad to be here with them, the ones who know mine, and I'm grateful to know theirs.

But I guess I don't know all of them. There are gaps in our knowledge. I used to feel like I kept the biggest secrets. Now Julie takes the cake.

Her key is attached to a tiny book.

"Is that a real book?" I ask her.

"No, it's plastic covered in cloth."

She puts some effort into pushing the door open. She's fragile. I wonder if she's been eating.

Julie's room is very, very red. Crimson walls and matching carpet. An epic Gothic canopy bed reigns from the corner. On the walls there are sconces that hold electric candles made to look partially melted and flicker like real ones. There's a set of red velvet chairs next to a clunky wooden desk topped with a vintage typewriter. Above the typewriter is a round stained-glass window. The right wall is a series of bookshelves, interrupted in the center by a grandfather clock. Red string lights wrap around the exposed ceiling beams, and the ceiling itself is cream with black ink scripted across. I can't make out the words.

"What's this room called?" I ask her.

"The Lenore," she says. I notice she keeps messing with her lips.

She was wiping them on her sleeve; now she's licking them. They're pink, on the verge of breaking. I want to offer her ChapStick, but I don't want to be rude. Like, hey, you look like you need this.

"I have to show you the best part," she says with what might be a spark of excitement in her eyes, or it could be a trick of the light. She walks over to one of the bookshelves and runs her fingers along the spines with a bit of dramatic flair. That's my Julie. She tugs on a copy of *Frankenstein*. The bookshelf jerks back, revealing an opening. Beyond it is a short hall with a closet on one side, a mini fridge on the other and a bathroom at the end.

We ooh and aah.

"Cool, right?" Julie says. "Patsy had to show it to me. Don't think I would have found it on my own. You might have, Lise."

This is the room Mae picked out for me. I'm mildly offended. I like Gothic fiction, but I've never shopped at Hot Topic. This isn't Brontë. This is Edgar Allan Poe.

I know Mae saw the room and thought, *Books!* and automatically associated it with me. I'm the reader of the group. Julie will read poetry when she gets angsty, and Mae reads, but she isn't a lover of classic literature like I am. She reads magazines, biographies, history. But only glamorous history. The life of Audrey Hepburn, fashion in the Jazz Age. Things like that.

There's not enough room for all of us to step inside the hall, so we rubberneck from the doorway, where the bookshelf was and will return, thank God, to conceal the atrocity of a bathroom. It's blood red, floor to ceiling. Red tub, red toilet, red sink, red tiles, red towels. The only exception is a black soap dispenser shaped like a crow. No. A raven. The soap must come out of its beak.

"I thought my room was bad," Molly whispers to me.

"This was supposed to be mine," I tell her.

Mae catches us conferring and gives us the eye.

"They thought of every detail," Julie says. "I can't believe I've never heard of this place."

"It's relatively new. It's only been open two years," Mae says. "They didn't do a lot of advertising. They sent postcards to people in the fashion and entertainment industries. Influencers. They built word of mouth from there. I'd never heard of it before the shoot."

"It must've been expensive to do all this," I say. I'm always thinking about money. I guess it's because I don't have any. It bewilders me.

"Oh, definitely," Julie says. "Getting the B and B up and running was expensive. I can't imagine this."

"It's open?" Molly asks.

Julie shakes her head. "Not yet. Almost there. Tristan's been working on it. Keeping busy."

"How is Tristan?" Mae asks.

"He's good. It took some"—she swallows—"readjusting."

"You'll have to tell him we say hello," Mae says. "He was very hospitable when we were there."

"I will," Julie says, noncommittal. She won't. Julie doesn't pass along messages. She'll forget, or she'll remember but a small, rebellious voice inside her will say, "Why don't you tell them yourself?" I know because I'm the same, and we've talked about it. The ways our unfounded passive-aggressiveness manifests.

"Okay, it's three thirty. I was going to change and freshen up. Then did you want to meet at the bar for happy hour?" Mae asks.

"Sounds good," Molly says. "Have to see if I can find my room again."

"What's your room like?" Julie asks.

"It's like if a fur trapper moved into a Rainforest Cafe," Molly says. Noting the expression on Mae's face, she adds, "But refined."

"Got it," Julie says. "All right, darlings. I'll see you at five, then?"

Mae hugs her. "Oh! I don't want to leave you!"

"I'll be right here. Down the hall."

"Promise?"

"Cross my heart."

"Okay."

We file out of the room. Julie blows us a kiss before shutting the door. The three of us walk in silence until we're at a safe distance. Upstairs.

"I'm worried," Molly says.

"Me, too," I say.

"Don't," Mae says, stern. "She needs us."

"Yeah, she does. She needs our *help*," Molly says. "Why didn't Tristan warn us?"

"She's lost weight. Why would he tell us that?" Mae asks.

"She's lost, like, thirty pounds!"

"Molly, I mean it. We have to let it go. She asked us."

"I wonder why. Are we really going to let her get off that easy? Ask no questions? Pretend it never happened?"

"Yes," Mae says. "I am. Elise?"

I guess I'm the middleman. "Let's see how she is. If by the end of the weekend we're still concerned, we should say something."

"Good," Mae says. She thinks I'm agreeing with her because she hears what she wants to hear. She takes out her key. "Five. Downstairs. There are signs for the bar. You can't miss it."

"Sir, yes, sir." Molly salutes her.

When Mae's inside her room, Molly puts her hands on my shoulders, shakes her head at me. "You know I'm right."

"I know," I say. "But I don't want to jump the gun, overwhelm her right away. We need to give her time to warm up to us again."

"Okay. I'll try to keep my mouth shut. But this is really weird. This whole situation is fucked. And if I feel like something isn't right, I'm going to say something."

"That's fair. You do you."

"I'm going downstairs to my room, my lowly downstairs room," she says. "Why did I come up here?"

"To put in your argument," I say. "And to make sure I'm on your side."

"Are you?"

"I don't take sides."

"Bullshit. Yes, you do," she says.

I raise my hands.

"Okay. Back to the jungle."

"Don't hurt yourself. Watch out for wildcats."

"Don't sass me. You lucked out of the Goth room. I didn't get so lucky."

"Later, gator."

"Deuces." She gives the peace sign over her head as she turns toward the stairs.

Back in my room, I'm hyperaware of their absence. Of how much space there is to occupy and how I don't fill it. They're just down the hall, but I miss them.

I'm hesitant to turn on the TV after what happened earlier. I play music on my phone instead.

The room is steeped in gentle afternoon light. I consider leaving the curtains open, but the anticipation of someone walking by turns my stomach. I notice the trees bending, trunks yielding like rubber. I don't remember it being that windy outside. The wind must have kicked up suddenly, because now I hear its distinct howl, and it's so loud, I can't imagine having missed it before.

The weather won't be good for the weekend. I worry how Mae will take it.

I'm fine staying inside. I close the curtains.

I put on a heavier sweater, check the thermostat again. It's at sixty. Maybe it's set to default back to that? I turn it up. I'm too much of a coward to call down and complain. I'll wait until I'm spitting mad to do anything about it, and even then, I'll work myself up to be firm and end up polite.

"Is there any way you could, please?"

That's how I operate.

I'll make Molly do it. Molly doesn't care. Julie, either. When we were roommates, Julie was the one who took care of things. Who got lightbulbs changed and carpets cleaned. I showed my gratitude with chocolate and coffee and by doing all our laundry.

I wonder if she does her own laundry now. When she was in Europe, she told me she would throw away her dirty clothes and buy new ones at thrift stores or cheap fast-fashion chains.

"Isn't that a waste of money?" I asked her.

"Better than wasting my time. I'm not doing *laundry* in *Italy*."

The room is dark, even with the chandelier, so I turn on the bathroom light and leave the door open. I turn on all the lamps.

I put on a second pair of socks to warm myself up, and it works. The extra layers, the extra light. The thermostat kicks in. Finally, I hear it clomping awake, and I feel the warm air generously spilling out of the vents. I can almost see it, carrying clouds of little nothing dust.

With time to kill, I fish out my makeup pouch and take it into the bathroom, rest it inside the sink. I study my face in this new light. I inch closer to the mirror to examine the size of my pores, play a game of freckle or zit. Pluck rogue eyebrow hairs.

I'm almost nose to nose with myself when there's a loud thump. I startle, tweezers coming alarmingly close to deflating my left eyeball.

I poke my head out into the room. My bag is on the floor, its guts spattered around. Gravity must have nudged it off the edge of the bed. But I remember thinking it was in danger of falling when I got my makeup, and I remember pushing it toward the middle of the bed, but maybe I just thought about pushing it and didn't actually do it.

I'm disturbed by how the bag fell and by the way it sits now, slumped against the side of the bed like a teen rebelling against good posture. It's unzipped, and I can see it's completely empty. My clothes, my plastic bag of toothpaste and floss and small travel face wash, my knots of socks, have all been ejected halfway across the room, between the columns, and are practically at my feet.

The way my clothes are, it's like there's a body there. Like there's some flat, invisible person wearing them, lying down on the floor. My oversized sleeping T-shirt is splayed out, and below are my black pajama pants, each leg perfectly straight, pointing out in a different direction.

I can't stand to look any longer, afraid if I do the clothes will stand up or crawl toward me.

I hurry over and gather everything up, shove it all back into my bag, zip it, leave it on the floor at the foot of the bed.

I grunt at it.

My phone sings on, some silly pop song about forbidden love. I turn it up a few notches and go back into the bathroom.

There was a time when I never got ready alone. When the bathroom was crowded with bodies, when eyelash curlers and warnings of hot flat irons flew back and forth. When there was always someone to turn to and ask, "Is my eyeliner even?" Or "What do you think of this shade?" Or "Can I borrow your red lipstick?" Julie had a makeup arsenal. She ditched it when she went to Europe, to prove to herself she could learn to live without it and still feel beautiful, and not have to lug it around.

Mae believed in good skin care. She was always spritzing us with something, offering us green tea masks.

Molly believed in Vaseline. She used it as lip gloss, mascara, highlighter. She had big vats of it and little mini ones she kept on her at all times. She would take it out of her back pocket and offer it to us, and we would always take it.

III

I count the fat flowers, follow the winding vines patterned on the carpet downstairs in the bar. I'm waiting for my friends to arrive. I waste a lot of time being early.

To get to the bar, I had to walk through the lounge, which projects a different atmosphere from the rest of the hotel, with its weathered leather couches, stone fireplace, taxidermy—all rustic appeal. The lounge is a remnant of the building's original form and intention. Not much has been done to it. No pastel paint or eccentric art. Absolutely no flowers. It's got a masculinity to it, which, honestly, is refreshing after the tour of rooms earlier.

The bar, alternatively, is a return to what's typical of this place. Too much. The walls are painted black. The ceiling is low, enforcing intimacy. The long mahogany bar snakes around the corner. It's fenced in by bronze-legged barstools with red leather upholstery on the seats and seat backs, tufted with small bronze buttons. Above the bar, thick blue fabric drapes from the ceiling. I suspect to cover the generic track lighting that illuminates the liquor-lined shelves. The room isn't particularly large; there's maybe three feet between the stools and the sets of round glass tables with mismatched armchairs against the wall. I'm sandwiched in.

I read and reread the cocktail menu, resist the bowl of mixed nuts. Who knows who stuck their fingers in that bowl before I got here?

"Where's everyone else?" Mae asks. She's wearing a lace maxi dress and a suede moto jacket. Her hair is elaborately braided.

"What am I, not good enough?"

She sighs. "That's not what I meant."

"Frankly, my feelings are hurt."

"I'm ten minutes late, that's all."

"Have you met our friends?"

She purses her lips.

"Sit down," I tell her, patting the stool next to mine.

She climbs up, and I offer her the drink menu. She pushes up her glasses. They're different from the ones she had on earlier. Black, squarish. She had to have eye surgery when she was young. She doesn't talk much about it; it's one of the things she pretends she's come to terms with. It came up during one of my recent visits to Manhattan.

"I know it could be worse," she told me, ever brave and graceful, sipping a pink cocktail out of a speakeasy champagne coupe.

"You can be upset," I told her. "You can feel bad for yourself every once in a while."

She shook her head. "No, I can't."

Later that night, when I was out of cigarettes, she agreed to go with me to the corner bodega to get another pack. I bought Marlboro Golds and a couple of scratch-offs for the hell of it.

"What should we buy when we win?" I asked her, scanning the sidewalk for a coin to use. Neither of us had one.

"Hmm," she said, pulling the cigarette from my mouth and taking a drag. "A magic lamp. So we can get a genie. For wishes."

"Are you making fun of me?"

"No. Some wishes would be nice." She tossed the cigarette. "You should really quit smoking."

"Lavender," she says, snapping me back to the present. "I like drinks with lavender. My grandma used to make this lemon-lavender punch. She said it was her special recipe, passed down through generations, but she definitely used tea bags and Country Time lemonade, the powder mix that comes in those plastic barrels. You know what I'm talking about?"

"Yeah. Tastes like summer."

"What are you going to have?"

"Starting without me?" Molly asks, sitting on the opposite side of me. I like being in the middle.

"You're late," Mae says.

"I took a power nap. I'm ready to start drinking. What we got?" Molly reaches for the menu. "Oh wow. Egg whites and shit. Pinkie up. Cool glasses, Mae."

"Thank you."

"What are you getting, Lise?"

I shrug. "The signature one?"

"Which one is that?"

"The red honey. Only one with whiskey."

"Honey whiskey, orange bitters, cherry. Into it. I'll have that, too."

Molly signals the bartender, a guy with a beard that acts as his only defining characteristic.

"Should we wait for Julie?" Mae asks.

Molly pauses. I can tell she forgot about Julie. Her eyes widen and her right brow twitches upward. It's an embarrassment she's about to play off. Her lips flatten.

"Nah," she says. "She won't care."

The three of us know that to be untrue. Julie and I are equally sensitive about inclusion. We always need to be invited, even if it's to a sushi restaurant, and we both hate sushi; even if it's to go see a movie we've explicitly said we don't want to see. If we're not invited, we get mopey. If we're meeting at a bar or a restaurant, we expect to be greeted outside, not at the bar or the table, even if we're late. (This is more a Julie thing, because I'm never late.)

But none of us objects. We order our drinks and gossip about the famous people Molly has run into in Hollywood. We pretend we aren't distracted by Julie's absence. When we get our drinks, we take tiny sips.

"Should I call her?" Mae asks, interrupting a story of a washed-up sitcom star jerking off in a parking garage.

"Yeah," Molly says immediately. She's running out of stories, or she's sick of telling them.

Mae raises her phone to her ear.

There's a ringing behind us.

"I'm here. I'm here," Julie says, rushing up. She kisses Mae on the cheek and sits on the stool next to her. She waves over the bartender and orders a vodka soda. "Sorry I'm late."

We wait for an explanation. We don't get one.

Worse, vodka sodas are Julie's drink of choice when she's trying to lose weight, and right now her sweater hangs so I can see the pronounced V of her collarbone.

I watch her hand tremble as she reaches for her drink. I catch the shine of her engagement ring, a princess-cut diamond with tapered ruby baguettes, an heirloom from Tristan's great-grandmother. I've never seen it in person before. I almost ask for a closer look, almost stretch my hand across the bar for her hand, but something stops me. Whiskey swirls in my stomach.

Julie holds her glass up too high. She's chugging her drink. A teardrop of vodka falls down her chin. Molly squeezes my thigh under the bar, trying to tell me something I already know.

"I need to catch up," Julie says, and orders another drink.

"We're still on our first," I say, but she doesn't seem to hear me.

There are a few moments of silence Mae can't stand. She taps her nails on the bar, examines the sprig of lavender in her drink.

"We did part of the shoot in here," she says. "November issue. I'll send you copies."

"What are the winter trends?" Molly asks, elbows on the bar.

Mae sticks her tongue out at her.

"Hey, just because I don't dress up doesn't mean I'm not interested in fashion."

"Interested in it as comedy material?" Mae asks.

"No," Molly says. "I won't make fun. I like when you give us your trend forecast. Jewel tones! That was one!"

"If you really want to know, winter colors are bold. Teal is the color of the season. Rose gold is out. Yellow gold. We're going to see a return to yellow gold. But really, we're already looking at spring. A lot of geometric patterns, more playful but modern silhouettes. Asymmetric hems. Shoulder pads."

"Shoulder pads?" Molly asks. "Really?"

Mae nods.

"Huh," Molly says. "Is it time? Is the world ready?"

Mae leans in. "Is it ever?"

Julie has already finished her second drink. She keeps raising the glass to her lips and tilting her head back, as if there's a last sip eluding her.

The whiskey isn't sitting right in my stomach. All by itself.

"I'm hungry," I say. "It's kind of early, but I didn't have lunch."

"Me, either," Julie says, slapping a hand down on the bar.

"We had McDonald's, but that won't stop me," Molly says. "Mae?"

"I could eat," she says.

We settle our tabs, and Mae leads us out of the bar and into the dining room. It's savagely lavish. Circular booths twirl around the room, each covered in a clean white cloth and set neatly with mismatched vintage china, closely supervised by napkin swans. The seats are upholstered with magenta vinyl, cute but borderline tacky. The wallpaper is blush damask. Eclectic chandeliers swarm the ceiling: gold, silver, bronze, crystal. String lights occupy every spare inch in between: some the classic white, others shaped like stars or flowers. Despite the efforts of the bulbs, the windowless room remains dim, with a milky pink quality to the light.

The bartender told us to sit anywhere, so we pick a booth near the back. A cluster of tea light candles burn on the table. Without them reading the menu would be hopeless.

"There are three choices every night. They rotate," Mae says. I hope one day she settles down, gets a finance wife and a Hamptons house. She's destined to host dinner parties. Shoes off at the door, no wine outside the dining room, sliced-cucumber-based hors d'oeuvres, the tiniest salad forks that make you feel like a giant. Carefully planned courses finished off with coffee she'll grind herself. She wants to be bohemian, but at her core, she feeds on order.

I love that about her. "They each come with soup or salad and a side."

She reaches over and touches my hand, points to the menu. She's asking me without asking to read it for her. She's having trouble seeing. It's too dark. I take a sip of water. It's lukewarm, been on the table for a while.

I use the flashlight on my phone to read, "Vegetable Wellington, pork chop, strip steak."

"What are you getting?" she asks me.

"Vegetable Wellington sounds interesting. I kind of want fries ever since you mentioned McDonald's. Sides are baked potato, fries, sautéed spinach, sautéed kale with garlic or mashed cauliflower. Soup today is pumpkin."

"Pumpkin?" Molly asks. "Can you eat pumpkin?"

"You've never had pumpkin?"

"Fuck no," Molly says.

"No pumpkin pie?" I ask. "Never even seen it?"

She shakes her head. "Yuck."

"You're ridiculous."

Molly doesn't like "weird food." She likes meat and potatoes and rice and pasta and eggs and toast and turkey sandwiches and anything that comes in a plastic wrapper. It's the food she was raised on, and she doesn't stray from the path. No room for adventure on her plate.

"It's a fixed price?" I try to mask my embarrassment for having to ask. I unfold a napkin on my lap like I belong, like I'm the First Lady.

"Yes," Mae says. "It's twenty-five for dinner, thirty including bottomless house wine or one signature cocktail. Lunch is fifteen, breakfast ten. Settle at checkout."

"If it's all the same, I'll get the steak," I say.

"Hear, hear," Molly says, fanning me with her menu.

"Same!" Julie says from behind hers, allowing the three of us to trade quick expressions of confusion, asking one another with wide eyes instead of words, "Do you think this is weird?"

The answer is "Yes, we all think it's weird."

Julie is a vegetarian. She found a piece of gristle in a chicken nugget when she was nine, and she was so traumatized, she refused to eat meat from then on out. She climbed further on board after watching a few radical food documentaries sophomore year. Even the not-so-radical ones radicalized her. She tolerated us eating meat but did not approve. She forced upon us bites of her beloved veggie burgers, of her tofu scramble, which she claimed was "so good" but made Molly barf for twenty minutes straight.

Under any other circumstance, Julie ordering a steak would have caused the three of us to flip the table. But what can we do? What can we say? "Hey, Jules, did you develop a taste for meat while you were out doing whatever it was you were doing wherever you were doing it the past couple of years that you don't remember?"

A guy in a kitchen apron comes to take our order. I'm on the end, so I'm first. I open my mouth to speak. Over the muffled vanilla jazz struggling out of an old speaker system somewhere above us, I can hear Julie's breathing. Not breathing. Panting. Like she's just run sprints. No. It's more primal. A hungry dog.

I stutter out my order. I've lost my appetite for meat and get the vegetable Wellington instead of steak. With a side of fries, because I need them.

Mae orders the same, only with a side of kale. Because that's who she is.

When it comes to Julie, she's practically shouting.

"I'll have the steak, rare, and two baked potatoes with extra butter."

She hands over her menu and relaxes into the booth.

Molly's so thrown, it takes her a moment to remember what she wanted.

"I'll have the . . . uhh . . . Sorry. I'll have the . . . I'll have the pork chop. Um . . . no, sorry. Yeah. Yes. Pork chop. Side of fries. Thanks. Oh, and I'll have a bourbon, straight. Whatever you got."

"Sorry. Me, too!" I don't care what it costs.

"I'll have the lavender gin drink. From the bar menu, please," Mae says. "Thank you."

"Vodka martini," Julie says, smiling. There's something about her teeth. Aside from being chipped, not white anymore, they've shifted. Her canines have come forward. And her lips. They're so chapped, shriveled thin, even in this dark room from across the table I can see the flakes of dead skin. And one of her dimples is missing. Did it fall off?

I'm being an asshole. What's wrong with me? I shouldn't be picking apart her appearance. I should be grateful that she's here, that I get to be with her again. I'm lucky to be looking at her.

And despite the differences, she's still beautiful. Maybe that's what's scaring me.

"So," Mae says, unfolding and refolding her napkin, "I met someone."

"Ooh, what's her name?" Julie asks.

"Her name is Taylor."

"Please don't tell me she's a model," Molly says.

"She's a model."

"You have a problem."

"As I was saying. Her name is Taylor. She has her bachelor's in psychology from Columbia. She started modeling to pay for school but got a few runway shows and campaigns so she decided to keep going. She's very sweet and mellow."

"How old is she?" I ask. Mae dates beautiful, confused girls. Usually younger, usually models. These girls like to attach themselves to Mae because she's special. Hitch their wagon to her star to see what happens, see how far she'll take them. They end up stealing her clothes or her weed, mooch, cheat, decide they're straight. But Mae won't end things. She waits to be left. She doubts herself. She thinks she'll end up alone. Molly, too, but she got ahead of it. She decided she wants to be alone.

I like to pretend I'm like Molly, but deep down I know I'm like Mae. Hopeful and afraid.

"She's twenty-four."

"Younger," Molly says.

"She's the oldest of six siblings. She's from Connecticut. Her parents are teachers. She's very well-read. You could talk books with her, Lise."

"I like her already."

"All I care about is how she treats you," Molly says. "Is she good to you?"

"She is. I asked *her* out, believe it or not."

"How long have you been dating?" Julie asks, and licks her lips. I think they've split. I think I see blood. I try not to stare.

"About three months."

"And we're just hearing about it now?" I ask.

"I didn't want to speak too soon. I wanted to wait until we were official."

"Wow," Julie says. "Exciting."

Our drinks arrive. We gather our glasses.

"To Taylor," Molly says. "One lucky girl."

"Oh." Mae blushes. "No, no. To Julie."

"To being together again," Julie says, lifting her glass. There's an olive lolling in it like a dead eye. "Cheers!"

I drink too much too fast. I follow up with water, but it's too late. A headache blossoms behind my forehead. A meticulous twinge right in the middle. I dig two Advil out of my purse.

"What's wrong?" Julie asks.

"Nothing. Little headache."

"Finish your medicine," Molly says, tapping her glass against mine.

"Don't listen to her," Mae says. "Water. And here."

She picks the sprig of lavender out of her glass and holds it up.

"Smell this," she says.

"It smells like gin."

"Oh," she says. "Hold on."

She digs into her purse and takes out a small vial of something.

"This is peppermint oil. I'm going to put a dab on your wrists. Big inhale. Your headache will disappear. Promise."

I hold out my wrists.

Molly groans. "Essential oils, Mae? Really?"

"Yes, really. How you survive in LA is beyond me."

"I drink a lot," Molly says, and gulps her bourbon.

"Smell," Mae says.

I inhale the aroma of the oil. It's a nice smell but doesn't instantly fix my headache.

"Thanks, Maebs," I tell her. "It helped."

Mae shoots Molly a smug look.

Julie lurches forward, her neck slack, head rolling down. She hits the table and our glasses dance.

"Jules?" I reach out for her hand. One is on the table, the other underneath.

"Yeah?" she asks, looking up like nothing happened.

"You okay?"

"Yeah, of course," she says, and takes a sip of her martini.

Molly kicks me.

"Okay," I say. "You need anything? More water?"

"No," she says. "I'm good. So. Are you seeing anyone?"

The question feels mean. She knows I'm not. Or she doesn't. But I tell her everything. I've always told her everything. If I were dating someone, she would be the first to know.

"No," I say, and snort as if the idea is ridiculous.

"Huh," she says. Her eyes linger on me. I return to my drink.

Please, God, let the food come. I crane my neck to see the door to the kitchen. Open, open, open. Please.

"Aren't you going to ask me if I'm seeing someone?" Molly asks.

"Are you?"

"No," she says, laughing.

The kitchen door swings open. The waiter is coming with our food. A true hero.

Mae starts rearranging the glasses on the table, the salt and pepper shakers. She can't help herself.

I forgot what I ordered, but I don't even care what it is. I see fries and shove three in my mouth.

"Actually, I should wash my hands," I say, "now that I've already touched my fries with my germ hands."

"You've been spending too much time with this one." Molly points to Mae, who is already squirting hand sanitizer into her palm. It makes an obscene noise, and we giggle like a bunch of first graders.

"You want some?" Mae asks.

I open my palm to her. Molly does, too. Julie is already eating.

She holds her steak knife in a closed fist, sawing at the meat. Pink juice floods her plate. She forks a chunk into her mouth, and her eyes flutter as she chews. I can hear it from here, the click of her jaw, her back molars grinding. She gulps, and I can see the food travel down her throat, the expansion of her skin as it goes.

Molly kicks me under the table again, but she's not looking at Julie. She's looking at me. I don't know what she's trying to tell me. I ignore her.

Silverware scrapes, glasses clink. The conversation died, and we're each waiting for someone else to resuscitate it. What can I say? What do I have to talk about? There's nothing new to report. My life is in the same sorry state it's been in for the past five years.

The quiet between us starts to mean something. I steal a look at Julie, and she's almost done with her steak already. There are drippings on her chin, and she's barely chewing before swallowing. Her head bobs. No. It's jerking. There's a physicality to the way she's eating. An aggression. I've seen her binge a few times, but it was never like this. It was quick but methodical. There was a pleasure to it, interspersed with brief moments of shame, which became more and more frequent until they took over.

There's not the slightest inkling of shame here.

Mae doesn't seem to notice. She focuses on cutting up her food into teeny-tiny little pieces. She eats slowly, precisely, her perfect posture exaggerated. When she was young she went to etiquette school at the insistence of her racist grandmother. All her grandparents were racist, but according to Mae, this one was the most open about it.

"She thought I couldn't help but be uncivilized because I wasn't from here," I remember Mae telling me. "I was seven. What seven-year-old is civilized?"

"How are your parents, Maebs?" I ask. Bottom of the barrel.

"They're good," she says. "My dad is planning on retiring. Again. Every year he says he's going to retire."

"He's young to retire, no?" Molly asks.

"He's sixty-three," Mae says.

"My parents will never retire," Molly says. "It's not really in their nature. They've got that immigrant mind-set. Work, work, work."

"Have you talked to your dad?" Julie asks me.

Mae gives a mini gasp. Molly clears her throat and begins to chug water.

My family situation is in the trunk of topics we keep hidden under the floorboards, along with my fumbles after college, Julie's eating disorder, Mae's not being out to her conservative parents and Molly's cancer-consumed childhood. We dance on top of these floorboards, and though sometimes they squeak, we don't acknowledge it. We pretend we've forgotten about the trunk and what's inside it, even though we all know it's there, beating against our denial like the telltale heart.

Okay, okay. Maybe I should have been in Julie's morbid Poe room.

"Haven't spoken to him," I say.

"Did something happen?"

"Do you not remember?" I ask, more bitter than curious.

Molly and Mae look terribly uncomfortable. They're communicating now, nonverbally, in their own secret friendship language. I get a pang of jealousy. They're the closest, aren't they? Julie and I used to be on that level, but this girl sitting across the table inhaling a rare steak isn't my best friend.

She's a stranger.

"I meant since then," Julie says. She adds a single shoulder shrug.

"No," I say. "Not since then."

"And Lu?"

"She's good. Still in Florida. Rick's good."

"Good," Julie says.

She's on to potato one now, peeling off the skin and eating it with her fingers.

It's profoundly awkward for everyone at the table. For close friends, the closest friends any of us have, we don't often talk about our life struggles or our emotions. We don't share our feelings, at least not in depth. Only when we're hammered or desperate. We're all repressed, and that's how we like it. That's part of *why* we're close. We have a mutual understanding.

My mom was a teenager when she had me. Then she and my dad bailed, and I was raised by my aunt Lucia. Lu. My dad went on to have another family in Ohio, with a woman he liked better than my mom, and kids he liked better than me. My mom was killed in a car accident. She was drunk and got in a car with someone drunk, and they crashed into a tree. The tree, by all accounts, was sober. It was a few weeks shy of my third birthday. I don't remember her.

There was no void left by my biological parents. Lu is my mom. She met Rick when I was eight, and he's my dad. He's fifteen years her senior and convinced her to move from Maryland to Florida when I went to college. They're happy there. Have a nice house. Sweet neighbors they play cards with. They go dancing on Fridays. They don't mind the humidity or the lizards.

I reached out to my DNA dad when I was sixteen. Couldn't leave it alone. He was not particularly enthused to hear from me, but regardless he (reluctantly) invited me to meet his wife and my half siblings. I declined. I asked him for financial help. He had never paid a dime of child support. It could go to court, I told him. He gave me ten thousand dollars. It went toward my college tuition.

We started e-mailing back and forth, and at one point it seemed like there might be the promise of a relationship. He gave me money for grad school. I didn't even ask. He offered. What I thought was progress turned out to be a nail in the coffin. He was pissed when I dropped out. The communication stopped after that.

Why Julie would bring up my dad over dinner is beyond me.

I finish my drink.

"We should get another round," Julie says. "If we see the guy, let's flag him down."

There's a noise across the dining room. We all turn. A chair is on its side, on the floor. Back from the table. Like someone bumped it and it fell, but no one walked by there. I think about my room, about the split second before the door closed when I thought I saw someone standing inside, about my bag falling onto the floor un-prompted.

"This place is haunted," I say.

"Haunted hotel—real original," Molly says, rolling her eyes.

"No, no," Mae says. "It's not haunted. Don't say that."

"I was joking," I say, even though I kind of wasn't.

"Relax," Molly says. "None of us believes in that bullshit."

"Except you, Maebs," I say, giving her spooky fingers.

"I'm from the South!"

"Elise believes in ghosts," Julie says. "I do, too."

"I don't believe in ghosts," I say. "I like ghost stories. I like any good story."

"If anyone's room is haunted, it's definitely mine," Julie says.

"It's some *Scooby-Doo* shit. I'm not gonna lie," Molly says. "Moving bookcase? It looks like one of the mansions in an episode of *Scooby-Doo.*"

"Oh my God," Mae says, face in hands.

"What?" Molly asks. "I'm serious. You know I'm right."

Julie laughs, and she's more familiar to me now. I'm laughing, too.

"So good news is if there is a ghost, you can just pull the mask off, and it'll be Patsy," Molly says.

"Poor Patsy." Mae sighs.

"Actually," Julie says after finishing her second potato and washing it down with whatever's left of her drink, "I think I'm good on another round. Do you guys want one?"

"I'm fine," Mae says.

"Same," I say.

Molly shakes her head.

"I just got really tired," Julie says, and yawns. "Really tired." She looks tired. Her eyes are sunken, orbited by dark shadows.

"You want to go to bed?" Molly asks.

"Yeah, actually. Is that okay? I can meet up for breakfast tomorrow."

"Sure," Mae says. "I was thinking we could meet down here at nine. Does that work?"

Nods all around.

"Okay," Julie says. Molly gets up to let her out. "Good night. Love you."

"Night," we say. "Love you."

We're quiet as we watch her walk out. On her way she stops to pick up the fallen chair.

We wait a long time to say anything to one another.

"Does anyone want dessert?" Mae asks. "Last time I got this really amazing bread pudding."

"Dessert?" Molly asks. "Yeah, I could go for some dessert."

"Always," I say. I do want dessert, but even if I didn't, I would welcome the confectionary distraction. Anything to put off the inevitable conversation about Jules.

I look around for the waiter. There's no waiter. There's nobody. That hasn't dawned on me until now. We're alone.

"It's weird there's no one else in the dining room."

"There's a couple," Mae says. "I saw them. They're on the other side."

"Where is everyone else? I'm surprised it's not packed."

"It's new. They're in the process of building their brand."

"I thought you said it was booked up?"

"That's what they told me, yes. I'm sure more people will come tomorrow. Friday."

The quiet comes again. I keep looking for the waiter, but I see only empty tables, tea light candles burning feebly, chairs pushed in.

As if he can hear us or read our thoughts, the waiter comes over with dessert menus. We make him wait while we debate the options. We decide to share the peanut butter bread pudding and the apple-blueberry crumble. We all get coffee, and it appears seconds later, like magic.

We sip the coffee in silence.

"All right," Mae says, folding her hands in her lap. "I want to say that I don't think we should talk about Julie when she isn't here. After what she's been through, I don't think it's fair."

"Were we talking about Julie?" Molly asks.

"No, but it's coming," Mae says.

"Well, what the fuck?" Molly says. "Rare steak? Rare? Like, what?"

"Maybe the doctors told her she has to eat red meat," Mae says. "She could be anemic."

"Then why wouldn't she just say that?" Molly asks.

"We don't know what happened to her in the past two years," Mae says.

"Apparently, she doesn't, either," I say.

"Even if she does," Mae says, "it obviously wasn't good. She'll talk to us about it when she's ready. But she won't if we come out guns blazing with the questions and judgments."

"I'm not judging," Molly says. "But why am I not allowed to ask questions? It's shady as fuck."

"Patience. That's all I'm asking, that we be patient. Make her feel comfortable."

"I'm not comfortable," I say. "It's not just the way she looks. It's not just the steak. It's how she's acting. Asking me about my dad? She's not herself."

"And she probably knows it. We don't want to make her feel any worse than she already does," Mae says. She's playing with her hair now because she's annoyed. Or overwhelmed. Both.

"It's going to get to a point where it's obvious," I say. "She'll pick up on it."

"It'll be worse if she thinks we're lying to her," Molly says.

"We're not lying," Mae says, offended by the implication. "We're being patient. Observing. Maybe she had an off night. Maybe her issues with food have resurfaced. We need to be supportive. As her friends."

"I'm fine with being supportive," Molly says, then pauses for the waiter to drop off the desserts and get out of range. "I'm not cool with having to bullshit. I'm not going to censor myself. I'm just going to say it. She looks fucking terrible. She looks sick. And Elise is right. She's not acting like herself. Something's going on. Can we agree on that?"

"Yes, but . . . ," Mae starts.

"I won't come hot out of the gate," Molly says. "But I'm not leaving here without getting some honest answers out of her. We can't help her if we're gonna handle her with kid gloves or whatever. I'm not going to bullshit to spare her feelings. That's not being a friend. Yeah?"

"Yeah," Mae says, conquered. She eats a big spoonful of whipped cream.

"I don't know if I care so much about getting answers," I say. As I hear my words out loud, they sound true. "I just want her to go back to being Julie."

"We all want that," Mae says. "But maybe it's a selfish expectation."

"I want to enjoy this bread pudding without thinking about it anymore," Molly says.

"All right," I say. "Tabling for tonight."

"It is good bread pudding, isn't it?" Mae asks.

"I want to eat this every day for the rest of my life," Molly says, grinning.

And then everything is fine and easy. None of us mentions Julie.

We say good night to Molly at the foot of the stairs.

"Off to spend the night in the jungle," she says with sarcastic enthusiasm.

Mae sighs. "I thought she would like it."

"She's joking," I tell her. "It's Molly. She can't admit to liking anything."

"I know," she says. "I worry you guys don't like it here or you don't like your rooms. I really want this weekend to be fun and special. We don't get to see each other like we used to. And it's only going to get harder."

"Maebs."

"What if we get married and have babies?"

"Okay, well, Molly and I are degenerates. I doubt we'll go the wife-and-mother route. And I would hope Julie isn't anywhere close to considering kids. If you and your beautiful model girlfriend decide to have a chic *Vogue* wedding, I'll be there. And if you decide to have babies, I'll be your live-in nanny, and you'll see me every day."

"I thought you didn't want to move back to the city?"

"Maybe by then," I say.

"Don't get my hopes up."

"Okay. Forget I said anything."

"I think my room is this way. Yeah. Right here."

"G'night." I open my arms for a hug. I don't want to let her go. I don't want to be alone in this hotel.

The thought surprises me. I'm used to being alone. To sleeping alone. Walking alone. Everything alone. But as I look down the hall, the way back to my room, something about it is foreboding. It's dark. The lighting isn't normal hotel lighting, the standard bland but sufficient. Here lanterns dangle from the walls, inside them alternating blue and purple bulbs. The result is hazy, bruised light.

"Sweet dreams," Mae says. She's closing the door.

I want to shout for her to wait. Ask if it's okay if I stay with her. The idea of walking back to my room has set like concrete. Standing around is worse. It's dead silent. The stairs are behind me, doors all around. I'm on display. Unseen guests are waiting on the other side of the closed doors, watching me through the peepholes, or they're creeping up the stairs. Soon their heads will come up above the top step, and by then it'll be too late.

"Jesus," I say out loud, breaking the silence. I'm being insane. It's getting to the point where I'm worrying myself, always being afraid like this. I'm going to end up one of those paranoiacs who live in booby-trapped bunkers, eating canned peaches with rusty spoons.

Roll the shoulders back. Chin up. Walk it off. I'm an adult. This is an empty hallway. There's nothing to be scared of.

I start to walk. I take cool, calculated steps like a bridesmaid. My arms sway at my sides. They swish against my clothes. My footsteps sound heavier than they should. The floorboards hidden underneath the carpet creak. I count.

One. Two. One, two. One, two. One, two.

Three, four.

I pivot so fast, I trip over my own foot.

There was another set of footsteps. Someone walking behind me.

Right behind me, hiding in my shadow, out of my line of—

God. I untangle my feet and take a deep breath. What if I fell? My cheeks expand with heat. I touch my face. I'm flush.

The hall is empty. No one was following me. The only footsteps were my own, and the echo of them allowed by this quiet space.

It's behind you now.

I turn back.

Nothing.

When you look away, it skitters behind you. You'll never see it.

I quicken my pace. My hands tremble holding the stupid, heavy key.

The lock clicks, and I push open the door, reaching inside for the light switch. I feel around for it. Find it. When the lights come on, I slip inside and close the door behind me. Lock it. Exhale.

The feeling of safety I expected to greet me isn't here. Instead, I'm met with uncertainty. I'm *sure* the room isn't how I left it. The chairs and the couch have switched positions. The mirror is farther along on the wall, not across from the TV anymore. There are different pillows on the couch. The headboard is taller. I don't remember the pattern on the carpet, but I don't know how I missed it. Flowers, of course. Turquoise with little pink flowers.

I didn't put the DO NOT DISTURB sign on the knob. It's possible Patsy or the cleaning staff came in. But why would they move the furniture? And they couldn't have changed the carpet.

I'm sure, though. This I'm sure about. This isn't me being crazy or having drunk too much whiskey. Something's changed, moved, is out of place.

A few steps inside, and I doubt myself. The chairs were there. The mirror is across from the TV. It *is* the liquor. It *is* me.

I rummage through my duffel for my pajamas, change, get out my plastic bag full of toiletries and go into the bathroom. I check the corners for spiders.

I wash my face and brush my teeth. Skip flossing. I leave the bathroom light on and the door cracked. I turn off the rest of the lights and climb into bed. The duvet is heavy and warm, thankfully, because it's still cold in here. I kick my feet around to settle inside it. I'm glad I left the bathroom light on. Falling asleep somewhere new has always been hard for me. I would take an Ambien but I've been drinking. Too bad. I took one last night, and it helped.

I close my eyes.

Count backward from a hundred. Imagine an hourglass tipping

over. The sand trickling through. I transport myself to a beach, sunshine nuzzling my face as I search for sea glass.

An unknowable amount of time passes. I turn onto my side. My eyes pop open. I stare at the curtains. They sway as my eyes adjust, almost like something moves behind them.

The door.

The door *outside.* To the balcony.

I shoot up, push the curtains aside and test the knob.

It's locked.

"What's wrong with me?"

I tuck myself in, turn my back against the wall to face the room.

I hear a wheezing noise, and I know it's the air coming in through the vents. I know that, but still I imagine there's someone standing next to my bed, watching me, breathing heavily.

My mind projects the image of a witch. Dirty, matted hair, gray skin, black eyes and a cold, evil mouth. Hands mottled with open sores, long green fingernails about to touch me.

I flip onto my other side, face the windows.

No witch. No one.

But what if someone's behind one of the columns, thin enough to be concealed? What if they're waiting? What if they're slipping around now?

I make a split-second decision. I push the covers back and bolt over to the main light switch, the fear rising in me like carbonation. I slam my palm against the switch, and the lights come on. The room is empty.

"Guess I'll sleep with the lights on," I mumble out loud, hoping the sound of a voice, even if it's my own, will trick me out of my fear.

The light is a comfort, but it won't make it any easier for me to sleep. Whenever I get insomnia like this, I think about Julie. Sharing a room with her for four years spoiled me. We would talk each other to sleep, trade stories across the narrow chasm between our extra-long twin beds.

If our conversation was dying, or if she sensed I was drifting off while she was still wide-awake, she would ask me the most random question she could think of.

"Do you think God created dinosaurs?

"Do you think elves are real?

"How come people don't have other-color eyes? Like, rainbow eyes?"

I'd react by sitting up and asking, "What?"

She'd laugh and laugh.

Then I would be awake, too. She was always good at getting what she wanted. I admired that, but it also stirred envy in me.

There were times when her questions didn't work. When I didn't answer because I ceded to sleep before I could cede to her. Whenever that happened, she would climb into bed with me. Not in a male-fantasy kind of way. It wasn't like that. It was innocent.

The first time she did it, I thought it was a joke. I thought that she was trying to prove a point or to keep me up. That she really, *really* needed the attention. I laughed. I figured she would go back to her own bed in a few minutes. I patted her on the head.

I waited for her to leave but she never did. She stayed. Those dorm room beds are so narrow, the two of us barely fit. She rested her head on my shoulder. Our limbs were piled up. Her hair smelled like fruity shampoo. Like mango.

I was uncomfortable, but eventually I slept, and when we woke up the next morning, it wasn't awkward. I didn't think anything of it. It didn't compute. We brushed our teeth and went on with our day.

It hit me later, as I sat in some yellowy lecture hall. I had this swell of memory. Julie slept in my bed last night. Does it mean something? How do I feel about it? Is it normal? Should I bring it up? Will she try again?

She didn't that night. She stayed in her own bed.

But a few weeks later, she was back. This time it was because she was sad. She was after this guy, Paul, who was the epitome of nothing special, but that was irrelevant to Julie. She would chase him until he relented. It was a pride thing.

Paul was famous on campus for being the son of the Liquor King. His dad owned a chain of liquor stores and did those cheesy come-on-down TV commercials, wearing a fur cape and a plastic crown. Paul put his liquor-prince status to good use, ferrying alcohol onto campus for a hefty fee. It gave him more clout than he deserved. Paul got a lot of girls. A lot. That enticed Julie, in the way that Mount Everest entices some people when they read that others have died climbing it.

She was telling me how she was upset over something Paul said to her, something I remember she was reading too far into, and she came into my bed again. She smooshed me against the wall, and I let her because she was sad, because I felt sorry for her and because I didn't know how to extricate myself from the situation. I put my arm around her so it wouldn't go stiff beneath me, and she took my hand. I thought she might be crying, but I couldn't tell.

There were other times, too. It happened enough for it not to be special but not enough for it to be creepy. After a while, I got used to it. Liked it, even. I told myself it was because it made me feel good to comfort her, but really it was because I needed the comfort, too.

I could use it now. Even with the lights on, there's something off about this room.

I must fall asleep, because I dream. I'm dreaming.

In this dream, I reach over for my phone and text Julie. **Are you up?**

Yep, she says.

Can't sleep?

No. You, either?

Nope.

Come by!

I put on my shoes and ask for her room number, but she doesn't respond. I scroll up, and we haven't been texting at all. There are no messages in our history. None.

I think I can find her room. I think I remember from earlier.

I take my key, my phone. I wrap myself up in my favorite oversized sweatshirt. I walk. Past Mae's room. Down the stairs. Nothing makes any sound. Not the vents, not my breath, not my feet on the floor. I float.

I know it's her room because the door is open. Just a crack. From a distance, I can see a faint light. Maybe from a lamp or the bathroom. She, like me, needs a little light. The pitch-darkness makes us uneasy.

I can't tell where the light is coming from. It's green.

I open my mouth to call out for her, but my throat is dry. Her name dissolves on my tongue and leaves a bitter taste.

I try again, but this time it hurts like a sickness, like strep or a virus. Like little white spots you can see in the mirror with a flashlight if you say, *Ahhhhhh*.

I'm afraid. Not with the sensation that there's something behind me, out of view, though something is behind me, pushing me forward. It's like there are two wet palms on my shoulder blades. I can feel them, but I don't fear them. I fear what's ahead of me. But I can't stop myself from moving forward. I can't turn around. It's out of my control.

There's a shape in the shadows. Not the bed. Over the bed. On the other side of the bed, crouching in the corner. Knees and elbows up, sharp, at strange angles, like a tortured crab, head down, over something. Something dark and limp and dripping.

And there are noises. Bad noises.

Eating. Sloppy eating. Not eating. *Feeding.*

The thing looks up at me, and it's Julie, but it's not Julie. Hideous mouth open, red, red, red, red. Even in the dim light, I can see the red. Pointed teeth. Rows of them, like a shark's, things hanging between. I've never seen a mouth so wide. Only it's not the mouth; it's the jaw. It's come undone. It's disconnected from the rest of the face. The only thing holding its skull together is skin.

It sees me, but it doesn't acknowledge me. It looks at me with empty eyes and, after a moment, returns to the limp thing. Whatever the limp thing is, it's big enough to be a person.

Another noise. A guttural one, a grotesque, hard swallow.

I back away through the door. There's nothing pushing me forward now, so I go back, back to my room. Lock the door. Back to bed. Close my eyes. Fall asleep.

Wait to wake up from the dream.

IV

It's a colorless day. The kind of fall day not advertised. The trees shiver in the wind.

I take a long, hot shower. There's a tyrannical pounding inside my head. I take three aspirin and wash them down with a glass of murky tap water, because I refuse to take the bottles from the mini fridge and get charged some ridiculous amount by the hotel. I don't know how long I slept last night, but any sleep I got was marred by the dream. I need a coffee IV.

There's also this nagging voice telling me I should go home. Return to my own bed for some decent rest. Spare myself any potential unpleasantness. Hibernate. Become the hermit eternal I'm meant to be.

I know this voice will shut up as soon as I see them.

I get dressed and go down to the dining room early. It's eight thirty, but I need coffee. I find the booth we sat in last night and slide in. I don't even have to ask for coffee, just turn my mug the right side up, and they bring a whole thermos for the table, along with cream and sugar. Hallelujah.

I'm not functioning until my third cup, when my brain fizzes awake. I get flashes of the dream whenever I blink. Split-second reminders of what I saw. It makes me queasy.

I text Mae, who I know is already awake.

Hey good morning! I'm downstairs, I write. I add a sad face. **Didn't get much sleep.**

Oh no! I'm sorry! Coming down.

I'm at our table from last night.

Be right there.

And she is. With a puff of fairy dust, she appears a minute later, her skin dewy, her hair perfect. She's wearing a Prada T-shirt, red trousers and slip-on sneakers that could be from Target but are probably designer and cost more than my rent. Her pink army jacket, I know, is a thrift store find. I was with her when she got it. She was so happy, she danced around with it all afternoon. I've never seen her so happy since. Lovestruck.

"I'm sorry you didn't sleep," she says, frowning. "Was the bed not comfortable?"

"No, that wasn't it," I say, pouring her some coffee. "I've just been having trouble lately."

"Hmm," she says. "I think Molly has melatonin. She usually takes it. She's not a great sleeper, either."

"I have Ambien."

"You shouldn't take that," she says.

"I don't like chamomile," I say. She gives me the click.

"What's on the agenda for today?" I ask, redirecting.

"Well," she says, sighing, "I thought we would go for a walk, see the grounds, but it's dreary out. And I had signed us up for a distillery tour, but I think it's canceled. I got a call this morning about it, but the phone cut out. I think the wind is really bad."

"That's okay. We can find stuff to do. You said there's a movie theater, right?"

"And an indoor pool. Heated."

"See? We'll be fine."

"I know," she says. "It's important to me we all have fun. Especially Julie."

"We will. Don't stress about it."

"I know, I know," she says, pouring enough cream in her coffee to take the color out. She reaches for the sugar. She'll use it all.

"You don't like coffee," I tell her for the thousandth time.

"I like it," she says. "I like it how I like it."

She stirs with some of her charm school flair. She knows I'm watching her. She taps the spoon against the rim once.

"Blanche." We call her this sometimes when she's being a belle.

She ignores me.

"So, this girlfriend lady of yours. Taylor. You really into her?"

"Yeah," Mae says. "I mean, I am. It doesn't feel like it usually does. There's none of the 'does she like me back?' jitters. I know she does. And she's very sure of herself. I've never dated anyone like that before. I attract confused people. You know that. But Tay's not confused."

"Mae and Tay. Wow."

"I'm excited about it. Truly. But I'm still . . . You know. There's part of me that's hesitant. Worried it won't pan out."

"That's always a possibility, but you can't let it stop you from pursuing this relationship if it makes you happy. You have to allow yourself to live your life. Could be worth the risk."

"You're one to talk."

"Yeah?"

"I didn't mean it like that. I just think you should start dating. You don't need to keep punishing yourself, Lise."

"I'm not punishing myself."

"You are."

"Mae."

"You and Molly both. Impossible."

"I think Molly dates. She just doesn't tell us."

"You think?"

Maybe not. Molly had a high school sweetheart named Matt. He went into the military straight from graduation, and after two tours in Iraq, he wasn't the same. The distance didn't help, either. She tried to make it work, because she loved him, but also because she had convinced herself no one else would be able to accept where her leg stops. When the relationship was beyond saving, they broke up, and Molly didn't make an effort to date anyone else. She made an active effort not to date. She presented herself as one of the guys, friend zone only.

We knew boys who had crushes on her in college, but they were too intimidated to say anything. One thing about Molly is she doesn't know how beautiful she is, and she assumes any compliment is an act of charity. We stopped trying to tell her. Eventually everyone does. What's the point? She reacts with venom. No guy can pursue her; it's like trying to cuddle a porcupine.

I yawn, refill my coffee cup.

"You should go back to bed. Try to get more sleep. You could meet us later."

"No, no. I just drank my weight in coffee. I should be fine."

"Okay," she says. "Should we get mimosas?"

"Um, yes."

"We shouldn't wait for the others?"

"Order four."

"You're the smart one, honey."

"Order six. That way we can be on our second."

The waiter, an older guy with his gray hair pulled back in a low ponytail, gives us a curious look but doesn't ask any questions. He brings us six mimosas.

"Cheers!" we both say, and clink the other four glasses. It's good to be with Mae again. She's easy to be around. As she would say, "positive energy." I wish I could leach it off her, keep it for myself.

"Started without me?" Molly asks, standing above us with her hands on her hips. "Good for you."

She sits down next to Mae and grabs a mimosa.

"I'm assuming this is for me. Julie's not here yet?"

"No, just us," Mae says. "Elise didn't sleep last night."

"No? I didn't sleep great, either. The waterfall kept making me think I had to pee."

"Maybe this wasn't the best choice," Mae says.

"Don't get pouty," Molly says. "I would have an issue anywhere. I don't sleep well. I like it here. It's like a quaint Vegas, sans casinos. And that's for the best, because I think I have a gambling problem."

"Okay," Mae says, and takes a measured sip of her drink.

"Did you guys order yet?"

"No, we waited for you."

We browse the menu, engage in the great debate: pancakes or eggs. We're hungry, but we wait for Julie. Another five minutes go by, and just as Mae's about to call her, she comes skipping over. She looks better today. Her skin more like skin and less like whatever it looked like yesterday. Pudding with a film on top.

"Good morning," she says, cheery. "Late to the party, as per usual."

"Party doesn't start without you," I say, scooting in so she can sit next to me.

"Sorry if I kept you waiting. I slept in."

"Did you sleep okay?" Mae asks.

"Yeah. Took me a while to fall asleep, but once I did, I was out. Didn't wake up at all."

"Good," Mae says.

We signal the waiter and order. Julie asks for more coffee. At first, she says she's not hungry and doesn't want anything, but then she orders steak and eggs, hash browns. No toast.

"What's on the agenda for today?" Julie asks.

"The weather put a wrench in things," Mae says. "It's really windy, and it's supposed to rain all day. I thought we could go to the indoor pool for a morning swim. Have lunch. Then we can check out the movie theater. How does that sound?"

"Good, good," Julie says. She unwraps her napkin and her fork slips away, bouncing off the table and onto the seat between us.

We both reach for it, and when our hands touch, I gasp.

"Oh my God, Julie! Your hands are freezing!" I slip my fingers under my thigh to warm them up.

She responds with a hostile growl. That's the only way my brain can reckon the sound she makes.

"They're not. Yours are clammy," she says with a little too much malice. She inches away from me on the seat. "You have the clammiest hands."

I look to Mae and Molly for help, for sanity, but they're looking anywhere else. At anything but me. Their eyes are on the ceiling, on the floor, studying their nail beds.

Our food comes. It gives us something to do. The coffee hasn't done much for me except make me shaky. I can barely hold my silverware. My eyelids are itchy, tired, and this all doesn't seem quite real.

"I might nap after breakfast," I tell them.

"Okay," Mae says. "Did you want some chamomile?"

"Cute, Maebs. No, I think I'll pass out right away."

"I have to call Tristan," Julie says. "But I'll meet you for lunch."

"No pool?" Mae asks, her disappointment expanding her bottom lip.

"Maybe," Julie says.

The vibe among us is off. No one knows what to say next. Molly, who usually bails us out of ruts like this, seems to be more interested in her eggs Benedict. I hoover my pancakes and excuse myself.

"See you soon," I tell them.

I have a fear that this is what they've been waiting for. That they never wanted me around in the first place or that I've just provided them with the opportunity to discover that they don't miss me. It's a pesky insecurity. It's immature. I'm angry at myself for thinking about it.

I run into Patsy on the stairs.

"Good morning," I say.

She looks frazzled. Her hair is elevated with a layer of frizz, and she's got dark bags under her eyes. She gives me a half smile.

"Morning," she says.

Her enthusiasm from yesterday is gone. I wonder if she's got supersonic hearing and heard the four of us making fun of her.

She passes me, moving oddly, in a hurry she's trying to disguise.

"Did you find her?" she asks.

I turn around and realize she's not talking to me. She's talking to another staff member who looks equally flustered.

"No," he says.

"Okay, well, then call Alex, please. See if she can come in."

Patsy looks back at me, like she can sense I'm eavesdropping. I linger on the stairs, not bothering to pretend I wasn't.

My room is finally a decent temperature. The thermostat seems to be working. It's dark, but I'm not afraid. Something about knowing that it's daytime, that outside my door other people are around, awake. I'm optimistic. I'm about to have a superior nap. I change back into my pj's and hop into bed.

My head on the pillow, I close my eyes.

I open them again. Everything is still. It's just a room. I'm alone. I'm safe.

I keep asking myself if I'm scared, and the answer is no. I'm really not. Not anymore.

I wake up just shy of noon, well rested. It was a dense, dreamless sleep. Exactly what I needed. Outside, the rain beats against the window like war drums. I kick open the curtain with my foot, too lazy to get out of bed. I see nothing but white fog.

After I enjoy a few minutes of languid phone scrolling, there's a knock on my door. Three solid, standard knocks.

"It's me," I hear muffled through the door.

"Who?"

"Molly, asshole."

I wrap the covers around me and waddle over. The door is barely open when Molly pushes herself inside.

"I'm dying out here," she says.

"What?"

She throws herself onto the couch. "What in the world? This isn't real furniture! This is doll furniture. Literally."

She transfers onto my bed.

"It's so gloomy out," she says. "It's cold in here."

"What do you mean, you're dying?"

"Okay, so, we met up at the pool. Mae is there in, like, a mono-kini, ready to do fucking laps or whatever. Julie says she's calling Tristan and basically doesn't show up. She, like, meets us there to say she's not staying but she'll come back later? She was, like, 'I'll be back in an hour.' Mae is all depressed. And she's trying to get me to go swimming, and I'm not undressing when there's, like, one fucking random old dude lifeguard standing there who's gonna have all his attention on me and Esther Williams over here."

"Did Julie ever come back?"

"Nope."

"Did you try to reach her?"

"I texted, but she didn't answer. My service is shit up here anyway, so who knows if it went through? And I get what Mae is saying about not ambushing Julie or whatever, but she's acting super weird. That thing at breakfast when she snapped at you?"

"That's not so out of character. She gets like that toward me sometimes," I say. And it's true. Sometimes we're mean to each other out of nowhere, just because. Like sisters.

"I don't know, man. I can't shake it. Something doesn't feel right. And this *place*," she says, shivering. She reaches out for the blanket, which is still draped around my shoulders. I get in bed next to her so we can share. "I can't say this to Mae, obviously, but this hotel is creepy as shit. It reminds me of, like, a basement. Like when you walk into an unfinished basement and get that feeling. Don't look at me like that. You know what I'm talking about."

"What you're seeing is relief. I thought I was being paranoid and crazy."

"Why would you think that?"

"I don't know. I always assume it's me. And I've been having problems sleeping, but last night I felt different. It wasn't basic in-somnia. I couldn't sleep because I was scared."

"Me, either! I'm an adult woman, and I slept with the lights on."

"Me, too!" I say, pulling the covers over our heads so we're in a cocoon. "So you *do* think it's haunted? Oo-oo!"

She rolls her eyes. "No, Elise. I don't think it's haunted. I'm not twelve. It's more like I've seen this episode of *CSI*."

"*CSI: Cute Catskills Hotel*?"

"Exactly."

"This isn't even our biggest problem. What do we do about Jules?"

"Fuck if I know." She rolls over onto her stomach and yawns. "Mae went to go knock on her door and see what's up. I got to come find you."

"Lucky you."

She winks at me.

"So, what's new with you?" I ask her.

"Nothing, really. Happy to be working on the show, not bored of it yet." She works as a producer on a late-night talk show. She's always telling me it's more glamorous than it sounds. It's a bunch of people who haven't showered and haven't slept, eating junk food, sitting around with laptops, talking on the phone, sifting through scraps of papers and stacks of note cards. Sounds glamorous to me. Anything is more glamorous than my job. But I guess that's by design. I'm an office manager at an insurance agency.

"I like LA," she says. "California's dope. It's cold here. Look at this shit."

She gestures outside, where the wind whines and carries in rain on its back. It's hideous weather.

"You should move to California. Get out of your self-imposed exile. It's enough, Lise."

"I'm not in exile."

"If you say so. I'm not trying to have this argument with you again."

"So don't have it."

She sits up. "We should go."

"Go where?"

"Get lunch. See our friends."

"Ugh."

"Don't be an asshole. Get up."

I do, reluctantly. Molly goes back to her room to respond to some work e-mails. She says she'll meet me downstairs in fifteen.

I'm feeling much better than I was. Rested. At ease.

I put on different clothes. Tie my hair back. Brush my teeth. Go to the bathroom. Wash my hands.

The hotel soap smells amazing. Eucalyptus? I need to steal a thousand tiny bottles from the first cleaning cart I see. The towels are soft, too. Extravagantly soft. I press one to my cheek.

I hear a noise. A faint rattling.

I nudge the bathroom door open with my knee. It was never

fully shut. Bad habit. The door shrieks on its hinges; it doesn't go far. I give it another push, this time with my foot.

It opens, and it opens in time for me to catch a glimpse of a shadow crawling beside my bed. Only shadows don't have limbs. This dark mass, dark figure, is humanoid but not human. It moves, in this sliver of a moment, like an insect. It vanishes under my bed before I can ask myself if it's real.

Well.

It's not real.

I know it's not real.

I know what I just saw is not real. I reach for my phone, but who would I call? The front desk? What would I say? I just saw something inhuman crawl under my bed?

They'd think I'm crazy.

And they'd be right, because it's not real.

I'm too afraid to confirm this by checking under the bed. I'm also too afraid to turn around and leave. With my back turned, it could run after me, grab me by the hair as I'm trying to get out.

Was it under the bed this whole time? Were Molly and I on top of it, unwittingly shooting the shit while it listened in? This terrifying, obviously imaginary thing?

Overcome by some incarnation of foolishness or bravery, I run over to the bed and lift up the bed skirt. There's nothing underneath.

Right.

Of course.

I can't keep giving in to this anxiety. It's not normal.

I force myself out of the room, plaster a smile on my face and walk down to meet my friends.

. . .

"Hey! Wait up, sleepyhead." Julie's behind me as I'm about to walk into the dining room. She looks strikingly good. Even better than this morning. Her hair falls in fat, shiny curls. She's got on a long-sleeved black dress. It's loose, but she doesn't look frail in it. There's color in her cheeks. She looks healthy. She looks like Julie.

She smiles at me, and that's it. We're back. We slide into the booth, and she puts her arm around me and squeezes.

I don't look at Molly or Mae for a reaction, to check if they're seeing what I'm seeing. I don't need the validation. I've got my Julie.

"Do you feel better, hon?" Mae asks me.

"Yep!" I say, ignoring the knot lingering in my stomach. Everyone's in good spirits; I'm not going to say, "Hey, by the way, I know we're worrying about Julie right now, but actually, I might be losing my mind!" "Sorry to keep you waiting."

"What's for lunch?" Molly asks.

"I'm not that hungry. You want to split a sandwich?" Julie asks me. It sinks me into the warm, woolly euphoria of familiarity, of affection. We used to do this all the time.

"Sure," I say. I'm not hungry at all, but I won't ruin the moment by saying no. "You pick. You know I'll eat whatever."

"I know," she says. "You pick."

"Okay." I always end up picking.

"We're going to the theater after lunch," Mae says. "They're playing *Rebecca*."

"It's like they knew we were coming!" Julie says, hugging my arm.

"Kismet," I say.

She snaps her fingers like a beatnik. *Snap, snap, snap.*

We eat our lunch and make our way to the theater. It's down a set of narrow carpeted steps. We come to a small lobby that smells like butter and bleach. The floor is black-and-white-checkerboard vinyl. There's an array of vending machines and an old-timey popcorn stand, red with white script across the side that reads POPCORN, as if you couldn't figure it out on your own. There's a slot underneath with paper bags, and on the front, two metal scoops hang by their necks, tied with red ribbon. The walls are painted glittery gold behind old movie posters in garish silver frames: *Rebecca*, *Roman Holiday*, *Citizen Kane*, *City Lights*, *Casablanca*, *Gone with the Wind*, *Singin' in the Rain*. It's a cute room, but it lacks the production value of the rest of the hotel. They must have run out of money by the time they got down here.

We're all full after a lunch we weren't hungry for in the first place, but we get snacks anyway, shoving quarters and dollar bills into the vending machines in exchange for bags of Twizzlers and Peanut Butter M&M's.

We go through a set of double doors to get inside the theater, which is all black: black linoleum, black walls, a few rows of glorious black pleather loungers. We descend into them, and they form to us. Julie and I sit next to each other. I notice she smells a little. I noticed the smell upstairs in the dining room but thought it might have been the room, some old food rotting on the floor somewhere. I'm so happy we've fallen back into our old rhythm, I'm willing to ignore it. I hold a bag of popcorn up to my nose and inhale, override everything with butter.

"Laurence Olivier—now, that's a man," she says. "That mustache."

"It's a man's mustache," I say.

"Would you date a guy with a mustache?" she asks me.

"If he looked like Laurence Olivier."

"Ooh, it's starting!" Julie says. "*Shh*. Molly, *shh*."

"I wasn't talking!"

"It's preemptive."

"Fuck off. I'm well behaved."

Julie looks at me and mouths, "She's not."

"What happens in this movie?" Molly asks, obnoxious on purpose.

"Girls," Mae says, in her best mom voice.

It doesn't really matter if we're loud; we're the only ones here. But Mae has her rules, and Julie is very particular about her movie-viewing experience.

A minute passes, title card, title card, sweeping music. Julie leans over and whispers, "Who would you rather: Laurence Olivier or Cary Grant?"

"Olivier. You?"

"Probably Olivier, but Grant *is* charming."

"Cary Grant or Jimmy Stewart?"

"Oh, God."

"*Shh!*" Mae says. "I can hear you whispering."

"Seriously, what happens in this movie?" Molly asks.

"Watch it. It's good," Julie says, patting her on the knee.

It starts, and we're quiet for a while. Engrossed. Julie and I first watched this movie our freshman year, drunk after a bad party at a frat house. We huddled on the couch in our common room under layers of blankets. We shared a pint of mint chocolate chip ice cream. We stayed up until five a.m., talking about what a good movie it was and whether or not we'd ever date a widower. We theorized about the true weight of baggage in relationships we weren't mature enough to have or experienced enough to understand. As I watch the movie again with her now, there's a phantom taste of mint in my mouth.

Sometime after they search the shipwreck, I realize I'm falling asleep. Blinking infrequently, eyelids lingering shut. The actors become faceless. They speak a language my brain doesn't translate.

"Elise, wake up! Watch the movie," Julie says, nudging my arm. "You're missing prime Olivier hotness."

"Mm, sorry." I yawn. "I'm watching."

"You all right?" she asks. Big eyes. Lashes curled. She heats up the eyelash curler with a blow-dryer. It works better hot, she used to tell me. But not too hot. Don't want to burn your eyelids. That'd be misery.

When the music soars and end credits roll, Molly says, "Fucking exes, man."

"What did you think, Mae?" I ask her. She's making a funny face.

"It was good," she says, her voice too high.

"But?"

"Unpleasant."

"Aw, Maebs." Julie hugs her.

We leave the theater, step into the lobby. The light stings. We rub our adjusting eyes.

"I would have peaced out the minute I saw that house," Molly says. "No, thank you."

"I thought the house was beautiful," Mae says. "I loved the house. Manderley."

"Hard no for me on the house," Molly says. She comes to an abrupt stop. Her face scrunches.

"What?" I ask her.

She leans her head back, looks up at the ceiling. She's standing underneath an air vent. It's not an ordinary vent. Of course not—not in this hotel. All the vents here have different decorative covers. This one is antiqued brass with delicate swirls. She points up to it.

"It's a vent," Julie says.

"I can see that," Molly says. "I think it just dripped on—" Before she can finish the sentence, a fat drop lands on her forehead. She jerks back. "Uh!" She wipes it away with her hand.

None of us yells. None of us gasps or screams. None of us makes any sound at all, even though we see Molly's palm is red, even though there's a red smear across her forehead where she was dripped on.

It's a random shock that robs the room of air.

"It's rusty pipe water," Julie says, shrugging. She dances past Molly. "What should we do next, Maebs?"

"It's not fucking water," Molly says, shaking her hand. "It looks like blood! It feels like blood."

"It's not blood," Mae says. "It came from the vent."

Another drop falls, this time onto the floor. It lands with a crisp *tap*.

"See? It's leaky," Julie says.

"Lise?" Molly says. Her eyes are distressed, huge, inflated like balloons. I lift her hand up to the light. Along her palm is a thin layer of red. It kind of looks like lip gloss, with that assertive shine. There's no way to tell what it is.

"Condensation," I say. I really don't know what else it could be. "The grate is probably rusted on the other side, like Julie said. Mae, hand sanitizer?"

"On it," Mae says. She already has it out, squeezes some into Molly's hands.

"This is gross," Molly says, furiously rubbing her hands together.

"You're looking at me like I'm overreacting! If it were any one of you, you'd be having a fit."

"You're not?" Julie asks.

"Julie!" Mae says. "I'm sorry, Molly."

Molly groans. "I feel like I need a shower."

"Here," Julie says. She licks her thumb and uses it to remove the red residue on Molly's forehead.

"Get outta here with that," Molly says, pushing her away.

"Come back, my little lion cub," Julie says, chasing her through the lobby. "I will lick you clean!"

"Ew, Julie!" Mae says, clutching an invisible set of pearls.

"Help!" Molly says, hiding behind the popcorn machine. "Help me!"

"Sorry. I would, but I kind of want to watch this play out," I say. "Mae, popcorn?"

"All right, all right," Mae says. "Let's be nice to each other. What does everyone want to do next?"

"You know what? I could use a drink," Molly says. "Let's go back to one of our rooms and get trashed. We brought bottles. And we have snacks."

"Yeah?" Mae asks, looking at Julie for her approval.

"Sounds fun," Julie says.

"Lise?"

"Yep."

"Your room is the biggest," Mae says. She lilts like it's a question, but she isn't asking. My room was supposed to be Julie's. Joke's on me, because I hate my room. The thought of going back to it gives me pins and needles.

"Sure," I say. Maybe it won't be so bad if I'm not alone. "Let's go."

We head up the stairs.

"Did you bring chasers?" Julie asks.

"Who are you kidding?" Molly says. "I've watched you chug tequila out of the bottle. Multiple times, you monster."

"I don't have the slightest idea what you're talking about," Julie says.

"Really? No recollection of those nights? I'm shocked."

"I have pomegranate soda and ginger ale," Mae says. "Is that okay?"

"That's perfect," Julie says, reaching for Mae's face. Mae lets it happen, but when Julie's hand grazes her cheek, Mae's eyes twitch madly, and she reaches up to adjust her glasses, breaking contact.

We go to Mae's room to get the liquor. All I want is to stay here, in this pink paradise. It's warm and bright and smells like roses. She hands me a liter of soda and a deck of cards.

"Ready?"

It's the opportunity to ask, "Can we stay here?" The question bounces around my mouth. The urgency of it surges, and I'm afraid of how the words will sound if I let them out, so I don't.

My room is fine. It's me.

I repeat this to myself until we're there. When I open the door, I let my friends in first.

They fill the room with something different. Julie sits on the floor like a kindergartner, leans her head way back to look up at me. Mae sits on the couch, tucks one ankle under the other as she carefully unwraps the plastic from the neck of the bottle of gin.

After a thorough handwashing, Molly sits herself in one of the chairs, whiskey already open. She's drinking straight from the bottle. Molly, Molly, Molly.

"Hope none of you minds my cooties," she says.

"This takes me back," Julie says, "to the pregaming in our dorm room days."

"Except we'd be drinking Southern Comfort and Malibu," I say. "Ninety-nine Bananas."

"Stop," Molly says. "I'm going to throw up."

"Just the thought of Southern Comfort," Julie says.

"I had Southern Comfort ice cream last summer," Mae says. "There's a shop in the Village that makes all these boozy ice creams."

"And you didn't immediately *Exorcist*-style vomit?"

"It was good! I never got sloppy with it," she says with pride.

Molly raises her eyebrows. "You didn't, huh?"

We have our stories. Denial is fruitless. If one of our memories fails, the rest of us will pool ours together. We're witnesses to one another's triumphs and destruction. We're eager to reminisce, though we each have our own version of events.

The only time any of us has seen Mae genuinely drunk was the night we tried Southern Comfort for the first time. She ended up aggressively making out with a stranger who had a *Nightmare Before Christmas* neck tattoo and a rattail. It was unclear how old the stranger was, whether she went to our school, and if she didn't, why she was at a party thrown by our mediocre baseball team. Mae disappeared with her for a while, and we found them in an upstairs bathroom, snorting lines of cocaine off the back of a toilet.

We had to pry Mae from the house at three a.m., as she kept shouting, "But I love her. I love her."

"You don't even like Tim Burton!" Molly yelled, struggling to pull Mae out the door. "Or hard drugs!"

"You don't understand! She's my soul mate."

In the morning, she made us all swear we would never talk

about it again. So we didn't; we don't. But I wonder if when she had that ice cream, she thought about that night. I wonder if, for a moment, she never wanted to see us again, because she knew sometimes we thought about it, too.

You can't erase your past when there are pieces of it scattered inside other people.

"Sit," Mae tells me, patting the couch.

I walk over but land on the floor instead, next to Julie. She hands me a can of soda, and Mae passes me the bottle. I take a sip of the soda and pour some gin in the can, hand the gin to Julie. She does the same.

"Cheers!" she says.

We tap our cans together, take a sip, narrow our eyes. She knows. She gets the bottle and pours a little more for us.

"To us," Mae says, lifting a glass I'm guessing she brought from her own room.

"Should we put on music?" Julie asks.

"I think there's something wrong with my TV. But I'll try." I get the remote off the mantel and turn the TV on. I manage to navigate to a screen with music channels.

"What genre?" I ask. "Smooth jazz?"

"Hits!" Julie says.

"Hits isn't really a genre of music," Mae says. She's an intolerable music snob. That contributes to my motivation to select HITS.

The first song that comes on is by some whiny boy band. I leave it on because I've already made my choice. The sound is working fine.

"Like no time has gone by," Julie says.

"It has, though. I don't know this band," I say. "And I bet we're too old to date any of the members. That's old. We're getting old."

"Elise! Don't say that," Mae says.

"I don't think it's fair that I'm twenty-seven," Julie says. "The last two years shouldn't count."

The rest of us don't know what to say to that. Trying to save an awkward silence, I say, "If you don't remember them, they don't count."

"Thanks, Lise."

"We should all take a shot," Molly says. I know what she's doing. She thinks if we all get drunk, she can ask Julie the questions she wants without the repercussions. She can apologize tomorrow and blame the whiskey. Maybe she thinks there's a chance the alcohol will loosen Julie's lips, if Jules is actually hiding something.

I'm not opposed.

"Shots!" I say. We each gulp from the bottle as the others cheer us on. Well, Molly and I do. Mae doesn't take shots, and when the bottle gets to Julie, she pours it into her can and drinks from there.

"That's not a shot," Molly says.

"The can is empty! No mixer left."

"Okay. I'll allow it."

"God," Julie says, pulling a finger across her bottom lip, smudging her vibrant red lipstick. She wipes her lip again. "It's been a while since I've done that."

"Hm?"

"Taken a shot."

"Oh," I say. "Me, too."

"You're not taking shots all the time? Wake-up shot."

"Yeah. Morning shot. Midafternoon shot."

"Flask in your desk drawer."

"You know me."

Molly starts singing along to the music in a funny voice.

"Oh my God! This song!" Julie stands up and starts to dance. Mae joins her immediately. Positive reinforcement for normal behavior.

"Come on," Mae says, grabbing my arm. She gives me a look. This isn't optional. Dancing is required.

I take another drink out of the bottle and get up.

"Molls?"

"Fuck off," she says. Molly doesn't dance, not for anyone. She does keep singing along. Belting now. My neighbors must hate me. If I have any.

Huh. I don't like the idea of two empty rooms on either side of me. A memory surfaces; it speaks to me in a newscaster voice. A woman at a motel in Bumfuck, Indiana. Someone broke into her room, and she screamed and screamed but the rest of the hotel was vacant. No one could hear her. She tried to dial 911, but somehow ended up recording her own murder. The audio lives on the Internet. It's not hard to find.

I hope I have neighbors.

Mae grabs my hand and spins me around, pulling me back into the moment.

The three of us vibrate around the room, break into weirdo dance moves. Julie, the only one of us who can actually dance, tries to mask it. She's always done that. Maybe to make us feel better, or maybe because it's more fun.

"We're so cool," Julie says. "We're the coolest."

"Everyone in the world is jealous of how cool we are."

"I'm cooler than all of you," Mae says while attempting to moonwalk.

Molly is laughing so hard, whiskey drips out of her nose.

"Lost some good whiskey out there," she says before taking another sip.

We do this for a few more songs until we run out of gas. We collapse back into our positions. Mae sneezes.

"It's official!" Julie shouts. Mae sneezes a lot when she's tipsy. It's an adorable quirk.

"Mae's got the buzz," Molly says.

"I'm allowed to sneeze."

Julie opens another can. She's on her second or third. I've lost track. A new song is on, and I don't remember what came before it. I'm tipsy, too.

I don't know if Julie is. She doesn't have a tell like Mae. I watch how much she pours. If she isn't already, she'll be gone after this.

"What's Tristan up to?" Mae asks.

"Stuff around the house, keeping busy," Julie says. "I think he's worried about me being away. He wanted to drive me, but I told him no. Seven hours here, seven back. Twice! Crazy. And it was kind of nice to be alone with my thoughts."

"I love being in my car. That's how I survive in LA," Molly says.

"I don't miss driving," Mae says. "It makes me nervous."

"I don't mind driving, but I don't like having a car," I say. I stop myself from giving the reason. It's expensive. I'm broke. They already know.

"Move back to New York!" Mae says. By New York, she means Manhattan. "Please, please, please, please!"

I shake my head. "Mae."

"I could help you find a job."

"I'm not gonna argue with you about it. I can't."

"You're not still sleeping with him, are you?" Julie asks me.

A commercial comes on the music channel. I let it distract me from what just happened.

"I'm sorry. I know it's a sensitive subject. But I don't know what I missed."

"No," I say. "I'm not still sleeping with him."

"That's good! I'm proud of you," she says. "I'm glad it's finally behind you."

"Finally," I echo without emotion.

Julie's always been the most accepting of what I did, but that means she's also the most forward. She knows I don't like to talk about it, in general, ever. But she also knows if I'm going to talk to anyone about it, it's going to be her.

When I first told her I was sleeping with my professor, a semi-successful writer who had one of his books adapted into a very successful movie, she told me it was "life experience."

"You don't think I'm a cliché?"

"Oh, no, you totally are," she said. "But who cares?"

"He's married and has kids," I said. "Little kids."

"That's his problem, not yours."

When I told her I loved him and was following him to Buffalo, even though that was where his family lived, even though I knew not a soul there, and it was cold, and I was abandoning my master's, my scholarship, my life, she said if that was what I wanted, then she supported me.

"You have to do what makes you happy," she said. At the time, she was about to depart for Tokyo.

Molly and Mae told me it was a huge mistake, and I would regret it for the rest of my life. They were right, of course, but I didn't want to hear it.

"I don't understand," Mae said. "You've always had your head on straight. Why are you doing this now?"

"I don't know," I told her. "Maybe I'm tired of being good."

That was part of it, sure. Along with the fact I'd never really been in love before. And then there was the other thing, pointed out ever so gently by Molly.

"You've got some major daddy-issue shit surfacing," she said. "You need therapy."

The only person I could talk to about it, free of judgment, was Julie.

Toward the end of the relationship, when my resentment congealed and my love peeled like a sunburn to reveal the sneering face of reality underneath, I called her to confess.

"Then leave," she said. "I don't know what you're still doing there. You're miserable."

I was angry. I called for sympathy and wasn't getting any.

"I thought you of all people would understand."

"Why?" she asked. "I love you. I'll support you in everything you do. But you're playing the victim here."

"I'm not. You're not hearing what I'm saying."

"I am. I'm sorry if you're having a hard time or wish you'd done things differently. You can't change the past. But you can do something now. You can leave."

"I'm not like you, Jules. I can't just pick up and leave."

"I'm sorry, honey," she said. "That's the only advice I can give you."

I think that was the last time we spoke of it until now.

"Did something happen, or did you just stop?" she asks. Mae and Molly squirm, horrified that this conversation is still happening.

"Nothing happened. I told him I didn't want to see him anymore. He didn't object. That was it."

"Do you still talk?"

"Sometimes. Not really. Not like we used to."

"And he's still married?"

"Yep. Still married."

"All worked out," she says. She's drunk. She picks at her skin. Her bottom lip is raw. She rubs it, bites it. It must be painful, but she doesn't seem to feel it. "What's new with you, Mae? Are you going to stay in the city?"

"Yeah, I love it."

"I like your glasses," Julie says, slurring. "Can you wear contacts anymore?"

"Yeah," Mae says quietly.

"Hey, Julie," Molly says, sitting forward, "do you really not remember what happened to you?"

"Nope," she says, smirking either because she's drunk or because she's lying. "No clue."

"Huh," Molly says. "Does it bother you?"

"Does anyone want snacks?" Mae asks. "I brought a bagful of snacks. I have chips and cookies and I think crackers or something. Here, let's look at the spread."

"I have to live with it," Julie says. "What's the point of being bothered?"

"Aren't you curious?" Molly asks.

"I don't want to know," Julie says, and takes another swig from her can. She laughs. "We're not good at talking about things."

"I'll take some chips," Molly says.

Mae hands her a bag of organic potato chips. I don't know how potato chips can be organic, or what it matters when you're eating fucking potato chips, but all that is above me. I'm also trying to figure out how we went from having the best time to being severely uncomfortable in a matter of minutes.

I guess we forgot Julie gets like this when she drinks. Bold. She says things she wouldn't say sober. Things that upset people. It's funny, the selective memory we have when it comes to the people we love. I remember her dancing on tables, demanding attention from whoever she wanted it from and getting it. I remember her ordering us pizza we never paid for because she overtly flirted with the delivery guys, who stood in the doorway immobilized by awe and fear, like those antelopes you see videos of that try to stay still so the lions won't see them, then try to run when it's already too late.

"What else you got?" I ask Mae.

"Veggie straws," she says. "They don't taste like vegetables."

"I'm confused," I say, but I reach for them anyway. "You want some, Jules?"

"No, thanks," she says. "Not hungry."

She didn't eat much lunch, and she didn't have any candy or popcorn at the movie.

"No?" I press her.

"You want something else?" Mae asks.

I point the open bag toward her.

Julie shakes her head. "You try first."

"They kind of taste like vegetables," I say, letting one dissolve in my mouth. "A hint of vegetable."

"Sorry!" Mae says. She's getting worked up now, ultrasensitive to the soured atmosphere.

"I have to pee," Julie says, practically skipping to the bathroom. She doesn't seem aware of the irritation she's caused, or if she is, she doesn't care.

When the door closes, Mae looks at Molly. "I told you not to ask!"

"Wait. What? How are you mad at me?"

"She's not going to tell us anything if that's how we approach her."

"That's how she approached Elise."

"That's different."

"How?" I ask. I should let them fight it out, but the more I think about it, the more I'm annoyed.

"Because that's just Julie. It's not malicious."

"I wasn't malicious," Molly says.

We're whisper-yelling. I wonder whether Julie can hear us, or if she can't, whether she's suspicious of the supposed silence.

"She's drunk," Mae says. "She gets like this when she's drunk. It's nothing new."

"I'm over it," Molly says. "I'm over pretending nothing's wrong. Oh, we're back together again, sugar and rainbows. We went to her goddamn funeral."

"No one's pretending. We're not interrogating her."

"That's your excuse to avoid confrontation," Molly says. "And these chips taste like cardboard."

"You're being mean. I tried to do something nice for everyone and you're all being mean."

"What'd I do?" I ask.

"You hate it here. You all hate it here."

"That's not true," Molly says.

Mae's crossed the threshold. Her voice breaks. She blinks rapidly, eyelids flustered by the threat of tears. Molly's going to feel like an asshole, get all red and quiet. There's officially no salvaging the evening.

"Hey." I sit up on my knees and wave them in closer. "Mae, we appreciate you coordinating this. We do, and you know it. Molly, I get it. It's frustrating. But Julie isn't going to tell us anything until she wants to. Drunk or sober. We might as well let her come to us. And I'm sorry I'm such a fuckup that the mere mention of my ex ruined the whole evening."

"It didn't," Mae says. "You're not."

"You don't need to apologize," Molly says, because she agrees that I'm a fuckup.

"Truce?" I ask.

"Yes," Mae says.

"Okay."

"You really don't like those chips?" Mae asks.

"They're all right," Molly says. "Are we getting dinner at some point?"

"It's seven thirty now," Mae says. "We would have to go sooner rather than later. The kitchen closes at nine."

"It's after seven? Jesus Christ."

"I'm not that hungry," I say. "But we should probably eat something because we've been drinking."

Molly shrugs. "I'm not hungry, either. Maebs?"

"Not right now, but you're right. We should probably eat. We can see what Julie thinks when she gets out."

"She's been in there awhile," Molly says.

Three sets of eyes drift to the bathroom door. In the transition between songs, we can hear the water running. What might be dry heaving. An awful, hollow sound. A cat retching up hair.

"Should I knock?" Mae asks.

"Nah," Molly says. "She can handle herself."

"What if she's purging?"

"I don't think so," Molly says. "She just had too much to drink."

"Lise?" Mae asks, her hands clasped together as if she's in prayer.

"She wouldn't with us right here. She'd go back to her room," I say. Though it wasn't something the four of us openly discussed, Julie was always transparent with me about her disordered eating. It was the subject of one of the first real conversations we had freshman year, beyond "So, do you have a boyfriend?" and "What's your favorite movie?" We were drinking cappuccinos on our way to the library, and I made some self-deprecating comment, probably about my nose, and she started telling me about her history with food, eating. She said she had it under control, for the most part, but it was something she'd carry with her always, like a bad scar. She talked for a long time, until it was dark, the two of us roaming around campus, holding empty cups. Then she looked at me and said, "I never told anyone this stuff before."

Just like that, we were close.

I rub my eyes, fight a yawn. Lose.

"You're fading," Molly says.

"I'm messed up from not sleeping last night. Sleep deficient."

"I'm zonked, too. I'm about to pass out by nine p.m. We're old as fuck."

"It's fine," Mae says. "We can get some sleep tonight, recharge. Tomorrow we can walk the grounds in the morning, and then there's an outdoor wine-and-paint thing in the afternoon."

"Is the weather supposed to be nice?"

"Don't know." Mae frowns. She checks her phone. "Yes. Sunny and warm."

"There ya go," Molly says.

"There's a cooking class tomorrow, too. In the morning. Making crepes. If you guys don't want to walk."

"Either is fine with me," I say. "I'd make crepes."

"You would? It's at ten."

"Works for me."

"I would vote for walking, but it's probably too muddy for me," Molly says. "My culinary skills begin and end at the microwave, so I might burn the place down, but I'm here for the cooking thing."

"Yay! I'm so excited. It'll be fun," Mae says. "You think Julie will like it?"

Our eyes return to the bathroom door. I don't know how long she's been in there. Too long. It's my bathroom. I'm aggravated that whatever she's doing, she's doing it in my bathroom. I'm pissed at her in general. Maybe she thinks coming back from the dead gives her an excuse to say whatever she wants. I hear it again: "You're not still sleeping with him, are you?"

I tried to explain to her. He made me feel special. No man had ever done that before. He singled me out. Told me I was brilliant. Told me I was talented. Told me that I was funny and beautiful and that I had more power than I understood. He said he wanted me in his life in whatever form I was willing to give him. I took the form I wanted. Anything to be close to him, spend more time with him, continue to live as special.

And *he* was special. His books were on the shelves. People knew his name, sang his praises. He told me about how empty it all was, and I thought that made him perceptive, but really it was his way of telling me that he was a void, a bottomless pit, and I wasn't enough to fill it. Nothing was or would ever be. I didn't get that until much later.

My whole life leading up to meeting him, I did everything I was supposed to. I was a good student, an obedient daughter. When I was fourteen I got a part-time job busing tables at a restaurant, eventually moved up to hostess, then waitress. I saved up to buy my own car. I worked hard in school to get scholarships. I played soccer. I was in the honor society and did mock trial. I was editor in chief of the student newspaper. I got into my top-choice school and bought the twin XL sheets and bed risers myself. My first drink was halfway through first semester. Didn't touch the stuff in high school.

I dated. I lost my virginity at nineteen because I got impatient waiting for someone worthy. I liked the guys I thought I was supposed to like. Ones with crew cuts and sensible majors who were nerdy in high school but trying to start over. I never dated anyone for longer than a semester. I used the breaks as an excuse. Winter break. Summer break. Let's take a break. "I don't want you to feel obligated. You're free."

They thought I was cool, or maybe they were hurt but too proud to show it. I wondered if I would ever feel anything. I got anxious watching romantic movies or listening to ballads, thinking, *Is that real? Am I capable?*

Then there was him. It was a fluke that I ended up in his class. I was studying journalism, and he taught primarily fiction. But apparently I needed a fiction credit, and "Compelling Narratives" seemed the least painful option. In retrospect, he zeroed in on me pretty quickly. He probably sensed my discreet desperation. Feelings of inadequacy. Eagerness to please. Latent childhood trauma. All chum in the water.

He introduced me to want, the gateway drug. He introduced me to my body. Made me unafraid of it. I fell in love with him, with mornings making coffee in his small Chelsea apartment, days in plush bathrobes talking books and philosophy, going out to dinner at the best hole-in-the-wall spots (he knew them all) and taking long walks over the Brooklyn Bridge at night, eating truck ice cream on the waterfront. Kissing with rainbow sprinkles in our teeth.

He told me early on about his wife and two young kids. They lived in Buffalo, and he went there to visit some weekends. I think her job kept her there, but I don't remember what she did. He told me her name, but I forgot it. It's kind of amazing what you can choose to ignore and how successfully. Selectively lobotomize whatever doesn't serve you. I figured if it was that easy, it must be right.

I don't know. It's mostly a blur to me now. Another feat of the mind. I can't remember exactly how it started, aside from a hand on my thigh and a lightbulb over my head. *Oh. This!*

I can't remember how a drink after class turned into my practically moving in or how a semester turned into two or if he asked me to move to Buffalo or if I volunteered.

"I'll help you find a place," he said, kissing my forehead.

It wasn't as fun there. Right from the beginning, staying up waiting for him to come over, pacing around my apartment, I knew. I had already set my life on fire; going back wasn't an option. I committed. I bought furniture at yard sales. I painted. I hung art, nailed things to the walls. I inserted myself.

There was a lot more sneaking around, something I hated myself for enjoying. Driving to Grand Island to eat at some shitty pizza place where you had to get your own soda from the fountain, where the lids didn't quite fit the cups. Having sex in the backseat of his car, parked somewhere, like we were teenagers.

This went on for a little over two years.

I had nothing else there. No one else. I was isolated from my family and friends. I was lonely. I clung to him, but at the same time, I became detached. In retrospect, I fell out of love with him slowly, fragments of disappointments and harsh realities assembling over time. Promises he didn't keep. Showing up late or too early or not at all. Lines he repeated to me like he was quoting himself. The deepening of the wrinkles around his eyes, the gray at his temples spreading. I never had a future with him, something I knew from the beginning. I think that was part of the appeal, but it was like I was stuck in this waltz, waiting for someone else to stop the music. I wanted to be found out.

I started driving past his house. I'd never been inside it—a boundary he'd set and I'd accepted—but I knew where it was. My curiosity became this insatiable beast. I liked to see the bikes on the lawn, newspapers neglected at the end of the driveway. I liked to see the garage door open, shovels and rakes, canned goods, kayaks, a lawn mower. A peek into his other life.

I saw her one day, with her short suburban bob, slight frame, dragging the recycling out to the curb. She wore loose jeans tucked into rubber boots, a University of Buffalo sweatshirt. I thought I would pity her, envy her, hate her, but instead, all I wanted was to roll down my window and call out to her, strike up a conversation. I felt a compulsion to befriend her. I was certain we would get along, that we would drink sangria at her kitchen table, go to the gym and gossip from adjacent ellipticals, start a book club, trade recipes and clothes. Bond over our love for the same man.

The one look wasn't enough. I started driving by every day on my way home from work, at around five thirty. I would catch her occasionally, gathering deflated basketballs or watering plants or flipping through the mail.

I think I got addicted to that feeling, the sharp bliss of doing something I knew I shouldn't be doing. When it wore off with him, I got the buzz from driving past his house. When that wasn't enough, I needed to go inside.

I was still seeing him then, though less and less. He seemed surprised when I asked him to come by my place. He kissed me hard as soon as he walked through the door. We had sex on the kitchen counter, and afterward, he looked smug. He walked naked to the bathroom with some swagger, left the door open while he cleaned himself off. It was the first time I was actively unattracted to him.

"You're going to be late," I said. "You should go."

He told me he could stay a little longer and spread himself across my bed.

I sighed. "Are they ever not home?"

He scratched himself. Then he asked if that was what had been bothering me.

I deflected back. "They're always around. Waiting for you."

He said no. She was back to working full-time. And now that the kids were older, they were playing sports and hanging out with friends. They were out later. He had more time.

"When?"

Monday, Wednesday, Thursday.

"Don't you teach Mondays?"

"Yeah," he said. "Sorry."

I called out sick the next Monday. I parked down the street to watch the kids get on the bus, to watch their cars pull out of the driveway. I walked up to the house casually. I wondered if the neighbors were home. I wondered if they saw me. I wore a University of Buffalo sweatshirt. I figured from a distance I could pass for her. Her sister. A babysitter. They would assume something.

The front door was unlocked. I knew it would be. They weren't the kind of people to lock their doors. They weren't the kind of people to watch the news and think, *That could happen to me!* They thought, *How awful for them!*

I walked right in.

The thrill spun through my limbs, raved in my chest. My fingers and toes went tingly. I stepped into the foyer and closed the door behind me. It was basic-house America. She tried to keep it clean, but with the kids, she was fighting a losing battle. There were a pair of dirty socks on the bottom step, a balding Barbie sprawled out near the umbrella stand, a granola bar wrapper, the torso of a baby doll tattooed with black marker. There was a textbook leaning against the wall, its paper-bag jacket mostly torn away, a casualty of too many trips in the backpack, of getting shoved carelessly into a narrow locker.

The owners of that textbook, that Barbie, those socks, came from this person I'd been close to for years. They came from his body, a body I knew well, and they existed in the world. They had been abstract before, but they were real now. I saw their school pictures configured along the stairs. And another photo, posed, all of them together. He looked happy in it.

He had never told me the ages or genders of his children, and I had never asked. Two sons. Close in age. Maybe twins. The same haircut. Matching polos. Around ten? I can never tell how old kids are. Baby or teenager. Everything in between is a mystery.

His daughter was closer to a baby. She had sweet ringlets, large eyes. I wondered when she was born. Last year? Two years ago? Three? It should've disgusted me, but instead I was amazed. What a master he was. An omission of that scale. I thought back. Was there a time he hadn't been available, when he had seemed tired, when I had called and he hadn't answered?

Not that I could remember.

Maybe it was an old picture. Maybe she was already around before I met him, and he had just failed to mention her. Or maybe she was why he came back to Buffalo, instead of staying in Manhattan and living like he didn't have a family.

I wasn't interested in the pictures. I should have been. I should have stood there, studying their faces. Felt some kind of way. But they bored me. I was interested only in what they said about the person who chose to hang them. About the person who made the decision to go somewhere and have a family portrait taken. Dress up the kids in those clothes. Insist they brush their teeth and hair. Bribe good behavior with candy. I was interested in the placement of the pictures, in their arrangement. Displayed so they could be seen as one ascended the stairs. Was there any particular reason why? Who stops midway up the steps and thinks, "I wish I could look at a picture of me with the other people who live here"?

It signaled to me narcissism at worst, at best a lack of originality. The latter seemed to be a theme in the house. The beautiful dark wood floor of the foyer was covered by a big, generic Persian rug. The wainscoting was smudged with fingerprints. By the door there was a table with a bowl on it, for keys and whatnot. Inside it were two Matchbox cars and a tube of lipstick. Above it a mirror. I opened the lipstick. A nude shade skewing pink. I leaned forward and watched myself apply it in the mirror. There was a rush of adrenaline while I did it that faded afterward because the color didn't look good on me. I dropped the tube back into the bowl and it made a loud *clank*.

There was movement. I didn't have time to panic or to process relief when I saw it wasn't a person but a cat. It was one of the biggest cats I'd ever seen, tiger striped. It approached me and rubbed itself on my leg. I got a wave of pleasure out of knowing I was seen inside the house, but by a family pet. There was a witness, but it couldn't tell anyone. It couldn't recognize that I wasn't supposed to be there. It purred at my ankles. I decided to ignore it.

I moved into the dining room. A naked table, another area rug, a display cabinet full of plain white china. A print of an impressionist painting hung on the wall. The frame looked cheap. The room was painted a dull blue. The kitchen was the same color.

It was a big kitchen. White marble countertops, stainless steel, an island cluttered with sippy cups and plastic plates. Picked-over breakfasts of scrambled eggs and whole wheat toast, the crusts removed. I examined the size of the bite marks on the toast. Tiny jaws, tiny teeth.

I opened the fridge. It was a family fridge. Double doors, an ice maker. Inside there were cans of San Pellegrino soda, juice boxes, multiple cartons of milk, kids' yogurt with Rollerblading zebras on the packaging. Deli meats insufficiently wrapped in white paper and unsealed plastic bags, Tupperware containers full of leftovers, condiments. A few bottles of Rolling Rock. His. The freezer was overflowing with microwavable meals and bags of chicken nuggets and ice pops.

There was a bowl of fruit on the island. Apples. A lone banana. Oranges that had seen sunnier days.

The kitchen table was covered in mail, a laptop that wasn't his. Or maybe it was. Double life, double laptops.

I thought about leaving then, after the kitchen. I knew she could come back at any moment. Or he could. He would be mad, maybe. I didn't care so much about that.

Whatever the consequences were, they were hypothetical. They weren't enough of a deterrent. I was enjoying it too much.

The family room was carpeted. They had an unreasonably large TV. They must have watched it a lot. I counted four remotes on the ottoman. There was an L-shaped couch. A leather recliner, the classic dad chair. I had a hard time picturing him in it. I sat in it. It smelled like a person. Not specifically him. But someone spent a lot of time in that chair and allowed him- or herself to seep into it.

The rush began to wither as I went upstairs, past the stupid family photos. A memory wafted in. When I was really young, Lu took me to this church carnival. Cotton candy and funnel cakes, beanbag tosses, a Ferris wheel you didn't quite trust—that sort of thing. Paper tickets, proceeds go to Jesus. There was a fun house at the back of the lot. It was mostly ball pits and crazy mirrors, but one of the rooms was dark and narrow with low ceilings, even for a kid. Along the walls were these portraits of hideous people with obscene noses and humongous, wart-riddled chins. As you walked by, the eyes followed you.

I thought their eyes were following me, too. The cute little girl's, the boys', hers. His. As I walked up, they came with me.

What if there were cameras?

Logic began to nag, to tug at my sleeve. But the compulsion to keep going was stronger. I needed to see their rooms. Where did they sleep?

The upstairs hallway was a series of doors. The first one I went through was to the girl's room. Stereotypical little-princess room. I was over it in about two seconds. The boys' room was shared. Two beds, unmade. Shelves with sports trophies. No. *Participation* trophies. There weren't any books visible in either bedroom. Maybe they hadn't inherited their dad's love of reading. Maybe they were idiots.

As I left the boys' room, I thought about leaving the door wide-open. It had been almost closed when I went in. I thought maybe they would notice when they got home. If they didn't, maybe their mom would. And maybe she would wonder. Maybe it would make her afraid, strike up a fear. Maybe she would get some goddamn sense and start locking her front door.

I decided against it.

At the end of the hall, there was a home office: desk, desktop, landline. Naked walls. From the office window, I could see out onto the street. I could see the empty driveway. Leaning at a certain angle, I could see my car. Seeing how far away it was reawakened my concern. There would be no quick exit.

But I hadn't been in their bedroom yet, and leaving without getting a good look at it wasn't an option.

I reached back to shut the office door, almost expecting when I turned around again that someone would be there. A nanny, a cleaning lady. His wife.

The hallway was empty.

Their bedroom was boring. They had a king-sized bed with a brown comforter thrown haphazardly overtop, pillows askew. Someone had attempted to make it but did a half-assed job. On every surface there were glasses with about two fingers' worth of water left. The dresser drawers weren't shut all the way, and the closet was open with the light on, revealing a mess of clothes piled on the floor, some slouching off the hangers. The bathroom was an equal disaster.

A roll of toilet paper was unraveling across the floor. There was a thick layer of toothpaste hardened on the counter. Dual sinks clogged with hair. The Jacuzzi tub was full of toys: plastic whales, mermaids, starfish. Empty containers of soap bubbles with their lids missing.

It was underwhelming. I don't know what I thought I would find or what I expected to feel. I stood at the foot of their bed for a long time, wondering.

In a frame on the dresser there was a picture from their wedding. He looked young, and she looked happy. Her dress was ugly.

Above the bed was a Rothko. A print, of course. This told me that she was the kind of person who liked to give the impression she knew about art by name-dropping famous painters. I bet she had a Pollock hiding somewhere. I bet she'd had *Starry Night* tacked to her dorm room wall in college, or an Andy Warhol *Marilyn*.

A whirring rose in my ears.

The garage door.

I rushed to the window. There was no car in the driveway.

The sound died.

My heart thumped belligerently, and I knew it was time to go, but I still didn't want to.

Their photo albums. She was a scrapbooker, for sure. Where did she keep them? I wanted to look through their family photos. I wanted to see him holding his children when they were newborn babies. I wanted to see if they took pictures together, couple's photos. If they were posed or candid.

It wasn't because I cared, and I think that became more obvious to me the longer I lingered in their bedroom. It was curiosity. I wanted to crack open this family and see what it was like inside, how it functioned. It was like walking through a museum exhibit or going to the zoo. I was the observer. It was my favorite thing to be.

The whirring noise returned. I checked the driveway again. Empty. It was my ears' way of telling me to get out.

The reality of the situation clicked then. I hurried down the stairs, past the wandering eyes, out the front door. I closed the door behind me and walked to my car. The air was cold, and I remember how it made me blink fast, how it tricked me into crying.

I reached down into my pocket. What if I had dropped my keys somewhere inside the house? What if I had to go back?

I had my keys. I was surprised to find that my hand was steady and that I wasn't in any particular rush. I was cool. I wasn't acting like I'd just broken into someone's house. I wasn't acting like I'd done anything wrong. I didn't even feel like I had.

Driving home, I thought it was possible it hadn't sunk in yet, and that when it did, I would be filled with remorse.

But the rest of the day, that night, the next few weeks, went by and nothing.

I never told anyone about it. Julie was the only person I could tell, and she was gone.

I made up excuses not to see him in the weeks that followed my break-in, trying to sort out my feelings independently, though I already knew and had known for a long time.

He confronted me. He came over and sat on the edge of my bed, listening while I stood and said, "I don't think we should keep doing this." I told him I wasn't in love with him anymore. He nodded, kissed both my cheeks and left without much fanfare. That was it.

I cried but not because of him. I cried for what I had sacrificed and for how long and because if I had to do it over again, I would make the same choice, even though it was the wrong one. That scared me. I cried for the worry that I would never love anyone like that again or, if I did, what I would do for that love. What I would be willing to give up.

Or maybe it would be different. Maybe no one else would inspire me to be so stupid. Maybe I'd exhausted passion. Maybe I'd go on to live a boring, lonely, practical life. Maybe this was it, my only chance, or maybe it wasn't, but it ruined me. Maybe I was numb.

I continued to worry about all that. Until Tristan.

"Lise? You're zoning out," Molly says, waving a hand in front of my face.

"Sorry," I say, falling back into my body, returning to the present. My hand remembers the can in it and raises it to my lips. I finish what's in it, but there isn't much. I guess I'm drunk.

"She's been in there a long-ass time," Molly says, pointing to the bathroom door.

"Molly," Mae says in her mom tone.

Molly rolls her eyes. "I'm gonna go back to my room."

"Stay," I say. "Please."

"I'm tired. We'll start over tomorrow."

"It's still early," Mae says. "We could get a board game from the front desk."

"A board game?"

The bathroom door opens. I don't know how much time has passed since Julie went in, but it looks like years. She's lost color in her cheeks, her lips. Her eyes are sunken in. She smiles at us, probably because we're staring, and her teeth are sharp and yellow. It could be the lighting.

"What'd I miss?" she asks.

"I'm gonna head off to bed," Molly says, throwing in a theatrical yawn.

"Oh, me, too, I think. I know it's early, but I'm fading," Julie says.

Mae sighs. "Okay."

"Meet at our table in the morning? Nine?"

"All right," Mae says. Defeated.

"Night. Love you all." Julie blows a few kisses.

Molly rises.

"Wait," Mae says. "I'm coming, too."

Mae doesn't want Molly to have time alone with Jules. She can't trust Molly to keep her mouth shut. She needs to supervise.

She gathers up the cans and bottles, the open bags of chips.

"You can leave it," I say. "I'll clean up."

"No, no," she says.

Molly helps her carry. Julie holds the door open.

"Night, Lise," they say. They let the door slam.

"Night," I mumble to myself.

I get the remote and turn off the music. I send Mae a message.
You can come back.

I'm sorry. I'm grumpy now. I'm going to take a bath and sleep.

Not at the same time?

No. I'm not that upset. Dark for her.

Sorry about tonight.

You've got nothing to be sorry for.

I guess not. I wasn't the one to dredge up my past, but I'm the one with the past that makes everyone uncomfortable. That was my doing.

I lock the door, the dead bolt. I walk to the back wall to make sure the door out to the balcony is locked, too. It's not, which is weird, because I made sure it was locked last night, and I haven't unlocked it since then. Not that I remember.

But I can't trust my memory. I'm drunk. The edges of the room are frayed, and everything is hazy, like I'm looking through frosted glass.

I turn the music back on, low this time, dance around by myself as I clean up the few cans they missed. Two are empty. I crush them and put them in the garbage. The others still have liquid sloshing around inside. They aren't my cans, or maybe they are, but another shot and I'll be too drunk. I don't want to catch the spins.

I go to the bathroom to pour the cans out in the sink. I hit the light switch with my elbow.

Red. There's red everywhere. Red spattered against the tur-quoise, turquoise, turquoise of the bathroom. A thick red mass squirms down the sink drain. There's red bubbling, overflowing from the toilet. I back up out of shock and disgust and hit against something. A body. A chest. For a second, I hear its wheezing breath, and in the mirror, I see it. A dark creature towering behind me, its long arms slowly lifting, its spiderlike hands coiling around my shoulders.

A moment later, after I black out or come to or nothing, there's no one in the mirror but me, and behind me only ordinary shad-ows. The blood is still there. Not the crime scene I saw before, but it's there. Evidence of it in the sink, around the drain. A few splotches on the mirror. A bloody tissue floating in the toilet. I flush it. The toilet gurgles, takes it reluctantly.

I run the tap, splash some cold water on my face to sober up, to calm down. I'm at the point where I can't trust my own senses. I'm a drunk, paranoid mess, literally scared of my own shadow.

I take another look around the bathroom. It's Julie's blood. I don't question that. Maybe after two years of living God knows where, she forgot how to clean up after herself?

I lean over the trash, and there's a stack of tissues inside. I see blood on a few.

I don't want to use the bathroom, but I really have to pee. I hover over the toilet. Flush. Wash my hands hastily, an ephemeral lather.

I'm drunk enough that sleep should come easily. I fling myself face-first into bed. I'm desperate to get some rest and put a cork in a shit night.

I can feel myself falling asleep, my grip on consciousness loosening. My thoughts slow, and all sensation dies. I welcome the nothingness.

I don't know how long I'm asleep for. It's a deep, quality sleep. Total blackout. Must be loud to have woken me up.

I'm confused at first. Is it my alarm? I need to orient myself.

There's no light coming in through the curtains. It's still dark. Still night.

I hear it again. It's inside the walls. A knocking.

Pipes. It must be the pipes. It's an old building. Some of it, anyway.

I flop back against the pillow and close my eyes.

I don't know if I get to sleep again and it wakes me a second time or if I don't quite fall asleep because the sound won't allow me to.

It's traveling through the walls. It's behind me, ahead of me, at the window, underneath me. *Knock, knock, knock,* knock! The bed shakes, and I'm ripped into full awareness.

I left the bathroom light on and the door open. I guess I left the TV on, too, because it's glowing blue light and humming softly to itself.

There might be something in the bathroom. The light shifts as if it's accommodating a shape. There's a faint rustling noise. But maybe it's coming from under the bed. A sensation rolls up the backs of my legs, and it could be my blood flowing, or it could be a set of hands under the mattress, reaching up.

The pipes sing. A steady chorus of knocking. Is it the heat coming on?

It's cold. I blow into my hands, touch my face. Nervous sweat forms a damp crown at my forehead.

It must be the heat coming on.

There is nothing in the walls.

There is nothing in the bathroom.

There is nothing under my bed.

I get up, cross the room, peek inside the bathroom. Empty. I turn off the TV. Check the thermostat. It's at sixty again. This thing has been funky ever since I got here. It's busted.

I turn it up to seventy-two.

I yawn, fumble around for a bottle of water in the mini fridge. They'll charge me eight dollars for it, but I'm buzzed and thirsty, so I don't really care. I would pay twenty.

I slam back the water and put myself in bed.

The knocking hasn't stopped, though. It's even louder. More consistent. As I listen now, it's more of a scratching. I close my eyes and try to sleep, but it doesn't let up, and it's driving me crazy.

"Shut up," I tell the walls.

And they seem to listen. The scratching fades. Instead, I get a new sound. Like a door handle jiggling. Like a lock being jimmied. And I see it. I see the door handle move. Someone is on the other side of the door, out on the balcony, trying to get in. They're moving the handle. I'm watching it go. Up and down. Up and down. This isn't me being drunk or sleepy or paranoid; this isn't my overactive imagination. This is real. I'm seeing this.

If it's someone who has the wrong room, they'll figure it out. They'll leave.

I wait.

"Hey!" I say, but I don't know if they can hear me.

I grab my phone off the nightstand, and before I can change my mind, I pull back the curtains.

I'm met with darkness.

There are no lights outside on the balcony. It's completely black. I press my face up to the glass, use my hands to block out the light from the room. I look around in every direction until the fog from my breath obstructs my view. I wipe the window with my sleeve, look out at the bleak night, the dark sky void of stars.

There's no one there. The door handle is steady now, unmoving.

I take one final look outside, just to be sure, and close the curtains.

I exhale, climb back into bed. I'm not going to be able to sleep now, my heartbeat in total anarchy. I sit up with my back against the headboard, sheets gripped tightly in my hands. I look around the room, and it inspires a familiar feeling. It's like I'm back at his house, in his room. Back somewhere I shouldn't be.

V

I slept maybe an hour. My eyelids itch. My head is too heavy. I don't want to get up, but Mae will be expecting me to be on time and on my best behavior.

I pull back the curtains and am greeted by another dreary day. It's raining, despite the forecast last night showing no chance of rain. The wind is bad. I can see it bend the rain. It's foggy, too. Party, party.

I take a handful of Advil and drink from the other water bottle from the mini fridge. I put on lazy clothes. Leggings, a sweatshirt. I clip up my hair. I layer on concealer, attempting to hide the dark circles. Doesn't help. I hold each eye open to add a quick swipe of mascara. I can't stop yawning, and now my jaw aches.

I grab my room key and my phone. My anxiety stops me from leaving, forces me to go back and check the door to the balcony. Locked.

The hotel is bigger. It's grown overnight. Or I shrank. The hall seems to go on forever, and I'm so thankful when I finally get to the stairs, I nearly fall down them.

Mae is waiting for me in the dining room. She sits in our booth, scrolling through her phone or maybe taking a picture of her cappuccino.

"Hey," I say. "Look at me. Right on time."

"Morning," she says. She's at a fraction of her usual pep. We've enervated her.

I yawn; she frowns.

"Did you sleep?" she asks.

"Not really," I say. "It's okay."

"Did you take anything?"

"Couldn't. I was drunk."

She purses her lips. "Get some melatonin from Molly for tonight."

"I will."

"You look tired."

"I'm just not wearing a lot of makeup."

She adjusts her glasses and shakes her head. "Don't say that."

"It's true. Little eyeliner, some blush, and you'd never know." I yawn again.

"Never know," she repeats. I get a smile.

"How'd you sleep?"

"Not well," she says. I watch an internal struggle as she folds and refolds her napkin. Finally, she says, "I cried."

"Why?"

"Because," she says, "no one's having a good time."

"That's not true. We're having fun. It's just a different kind of situation, Maebs. We're all getting used to each other again. We haven't been together, all of us, in a long time. Not to mention we had a funeral for Julie, and now she's here," I say, looking around for the waiter. Coffee is top priority. "Cut us some slack. Cut *yourself* some slack."

"I know. Yes. I know."

"We'll have a fun day today. We had fun yesterday, right? For the most part."

"For the most part."

"Is there an echo in here?"

She giggles. "That's a dad joke."

"I am a dad. Didn't I mention that?"

"Must have slipped your mind."

Molly pushes into the booth. "I'm on time," she says. "I need fucking coffee." She's never been a morning person, but she's on a new level. She's wearing a baseball hat. "I didn't sleep at all. Not at all."

"Did you take melatonin?" Mae asks. She's suddenly obsessed with melatonin.

"Didn't work. Maybe I've built up an immunity after all these years. I was tossing and turning. I would be this close and then wake up. Like, completely awake. Like someone was screaming in my ear."

"Me, too!" I say.

Mae's bottom lip goes. She's going to cry. Here at the table. Delicate little Maeb tears.

"It's not the hotel," Molly says, lifting a hand. "It's not you. The hotel is baller. This weekend is great. It's something else."

"What?" Mae asks, weepy.

"You're not gonna like it," Molly says. She looks at me.

"Julie," I say. "It's Julie."

"Why can't we just say, 'Hey, what's going on with you?'" Molly asks.

"I've already explained," Mae says, folding her hands in her lap and lifting her chin. Superior Mae.

"Elise," Molly says, putting her hand on my shoulder. I'm literally in the middle. Mae's on my other side, her foot on my foot. "What do you think?"

I pause, considering my next sentence. But my words form and flee without my consent. "She left blood all over my bathroom."

"*What?*" Molly says, slapping her hand down on the table. "What?"

"There was blood. In my toilet. Bloody tissues. Blood in my sink. On the mirror. I think she tried to clean it up. But it was there."

"Blood from what?" Mae asks.

"Does it matter?" Molly says. "And have you seen her teeth?"

"She was gone, Molly. I doubt she was going to the dentist," Mae says.

"That's not the point," Molly says. "I swear, sometimes they're worse than others. I swear it."

I know she's right. I've noticed it, too. I want to tell her, but I'm afraid to say it out loud. If I give that confirmation, I can't take it back, and I don't know where this is leading.

"We have to confront her. We have to ask her, 'Do you really not remember the last two years? What's going on with you?'" Molly says. "At this point, I don't even give a shit if Jade was right and it was a hoax, or if Julie was off doing some, like, Rajneeshee-type shit. Maybe she volunteered for secret medical testing. I don't care. I just want the truth. She owes us that much, don't you think?"

Mae and I don't speak our answer, but of course it's yes.

"It's our responsibility as her friends to ask her these questions," Molly says. "I don't want to do it alone. You shouldn't make me. But I will."

"No one is making you do anything, Molly. It's not possible," Mae says with a hint of a smile.

"Correct," Molly says. "That is correct."

"Okay. All right. I'm open to the possibility if you both feel strongly. But I think we need to be very careful about what we say and how we say it."

"Fine."

"Maybe we should call Tristan," Mae says. "See if he noticed anything off about her since she got back."

"No," I say, too quick and too stern. "Why would we do that?"

"Why wouldn't we?" Molly asks.

"Don't know," I say, trying to play it off. "How would he help?"

"He's *married* to her," Molly says.

"I think we should call him," Mae says.

I shake my head. "What if he tells her? Wouldn't that be worse than her hearing it directly from us?"

"I don't think he would. Do you? Not if he was really concerned," Mae says.

"I wouldn't think so, but we barely know the guy," Molly says. "We only met him the once."

"I'll call him," I say. "I can talk to him."

"Do you guys talk?" Molly asks. I don't know how she knows all my secrets. How she sniffs them out. She knew when I cheated on my history final freshman year. She knew I was the one who puked on the carpet in Jordan Wheeler's room at his frat's Mardi Gras party. She knew about me and my professor before Mae did, and I lived with Mae at the time. Does she have a sixth sense specifically for my shame?

"I've checked in on him since the funeral," I say. It's not a lie. It's an understatement.

"Okay," Mae says. "You'll call him?"

"After breakfast. Unless we're on a schedule. Didn't you say we're doing something?"

"Crepes. Learning to make crepes. After that?" she asks.

"Yes."

"Coffee. Where's the fucking guy with the coffee?" Molly stands up. "Coffee? Does anybody work here?"

I look around. "Where's Julie?"

"Late," Mae says. "Remember? Always at least fifteen minutes late."

We don't wait for her. When the waiter finally comes by, we order our breakfast. Sure enough, twenty minutes later, Julie strolls in.

Her hair is pulled back like mine, and she's wearing the same thing I am. Her legs are rails. I examine her for signs. Of what, I don't know. On her face she has some blemishes that she's done a lazy job covering in makeup. A few of her nails are broken. One is a nibbled stump.

She smiles. Her teeth *are* different. We're just not used to them yet. It's not that they're getting better or worse as the weekend goes on; it's just now when we see them, it sets something off, a little voice in our heads shouting, "Those aren't Julie's teeth!" But they're not that bad. She can always have them fixed.

"Am I in trouble?" Julie asks. "I overslept."

"You sleep well?" I ask her.

"Pretty well," she says, reaching over and twirling one of my stray hairs. She seems herself today.

"We ordered," Molly says.

"That's fine. I'm not hungry."

Patsy bursts out of the kitchen and power walks across the floor.

"It's a rare Patsy sighting," Julie says, doing a bad Australian accent. "In her natural habitat."

"*Shh!*" Mae says. "She'll hear you."

"She won't. Look at her. She's on a mission," Molly says. "She looks stressed-out."

"I wonder what's going on," I say. "I saw her yesterday, and she was stressed then, too."

"It's a stressful job, I'd imagine," Mae says.

"Eight rooms," Julie says. "Our place only has eight rooms."

"That's enough to live off of?" Molly asks.

"Yeah," Julie says, but she's not paying attention anymore. She's spaced-out, staring off at nothing. She takes a deep breath. "What's the plan for today?"

"There's the cooking class at ten thirty. Then wine and painting. It's supposed to be outside by the pasture but . . ." Mae trails off.

"Pasture?" Molly asks. "Pasture?"

"That's what it says. There's an area behind the hotel. They have cows and pigs. There's a chicken coop. They're building a stable for horses, but they don't have any yet."

"Is this one of their pigs?" Molly asks, holding up a piece of her bacon, which just arrived.

"Molly!" Mae says. "No!"

"You don't know that," Molly says.

"They use the eggs from the chickens," Julie says.

"How do you know?" Molly asks.

Julie shrugs. "I'm assuming."

"Interesting."

"There's this documentary—," Julie starts.

"No," Molly interrupts. She makes a show of finishing her bacon.

157

I'm no longer interested in my breakfast. I sip my coffee and force myself to have some toast. I slather it with apple butter to make it easier to swallow. I can't tell if I lost my appetite completely or if it's hiding, if it plans on reappearing in an hour, stomping its feet.

I add more cream to my coffee to make it last longer.

Mae clears her throat. "As I was saying, I think they'll move the wine and painting inside."

"This is an afternoon activity?" Molly asks.

"I think it's at two. We can check with the front desk after the crepe class."

"I love crepes. I literally only ate crepes when I was in France," Julie says.

"Oh, you went to France?" Molly asks. Her sarcasm is warranted. When Julie got back from Europe it was all she talked about. Everything was better somewhere else. "I had the best beer in Brussels, the most amazing marzipan in Switzerland." It got old fast.

"Mae will make the best crepes," I say. "Out of the four of us, at least."

"No, no. Oh, please. That's not true," Mae says, doing an adorably bad job of denying it.

"What were those cookies you sent us for the holidays?" Molly asks. "They were white with, like, that stuff in the middle?"

"Oh my God. I ate them all in one sitting, and I'm not even ashamed to admit it." It's true. They arrived on my doorstep on a Friday afternoon. I watched reruns of nineties sitcoms and ate every last cookie in the tin. There must have been two dozen. "I have no regrets."

"I want these cookies," Julie says.

"I'll make them again this year."

Things are good. Last night is fading. The unpleasantnesses

shrink and slip inside the folds of my brain to reemerge later when I'm mad about something else, when they decide to pile on top like tag-teaming wrestlers.

We finish our coffee, reminiscing about an adventure we took at the end of freshman year, trying to find a combined Taco Bell KFC. We got horribly lost in a shady neighborhood, and at one point, we ran out of sidewalk and were walking along the curb in a single-file line. We passed hypodermic needles, rosary beads, old newspapers and eleven condoms (Molly counted). None of us remembers why we were on such a mission or whose idea it was to go in the first place or what we ate when we finally got there.

I don't even remember who brought it up. It might have been Julie. Sometimes when we're all together, I get confused about who is who. Where one of us stops and the others start. We overlap, bleed together.

I love it.

We misbehave making crepes.

The instructor is a guy who is almost definitely from Staten Island but is trying to convince everyone he's from Europe, using a bad accent and a skinny mustache. He calls himself "Jean."

"John?" Molly asks.

"Jean," he repeats.

"John."

We snicker like cruel schoolgirls, even Mae. We can't help ourselves. He takes himself so seriously.

Molly starts snacking on the fillings, eating slices of ham and Gruyère, quartered strawberries.

"You won't have any left for your crepe," Jean says.

"You have more in the back," Molly says. "Can I have more, please?"

There's a couple taking the class with us. A handsome suburban dad in head-to-toe athleisure and his lawyer or executive husband. Executive lawyer. He's wearing khakis and a button-down shirt with cuff links and keeps adjusting a tie that isn't there. He has rich-person posture and designer glasses. He says early on he's "more of a spectator." Code for shy or lazy. Afraid of failure. He doesn't actively participate. He looks over his husband's shoulder, occasionally contributing something useless, like passing a measuring cup. They don't seem to mind our antics.

We arrange a taste test for our completed crepes. It's supposed to be judged blind, but there're only four of us, and Mae's looks perfect while Molly's looks like an omelet.

When Julie tells her as much, Molly responds, "That's because it is an omelet."

"You guys can be the judges," Julie says. "I'm not hungry."

"Don't be a square," Molly says.

"It's hip to be square."

"Don't you Huey Lewis and the News me. It's a bite. You can have a bite of a fucking crepe."

"I thought you said it was an omelet."

"Miss," Molly says.

"Okay, okay," Julie says. "But Elise goes first."

I try Molly's. "Solid omelet." Mae's is delicious. "Perfect. But I also think I prefer a sweet crepe to a savory crepe." I get to Julie's. It looks fine. It looks a lot like mine, but I don't want to eat it.

The reluctance storms up my throat. It digs a picket sign into my tongue. DO. NOT. EAT.

I take a deep breath; the fork begins to slip from my clammy hand. Why are my hands always so clammy? What's wrong with me?

I hold the fork more tightly. My heart rate spikes.

"Am I the only one?" I ask them. "Where are my other judges?"

"Here!" Mae says.

The idea of her and Molly also eating Julie's crepe intensifies my aversion. Something's not right. Something's not right. The feeling is so strong. It's like watching a scary movie when the teenagers stand at the door of that old, abandoned house plagued by urban legend, and they reach for the knob slowly, and you think, *I wouldn't do that. I would go home.* It's the screaming intuition you suffer but they lack.

Here I am, staring down the door.

It's too late. Mae's got a mouthful of Julie's crepe. "Mm, it's delicious!" She makes a show of taking another bite. She's trying to make Julie feel good.

"I'll go," Julie says, her wafer-thin patience coming in for the save. She reaches across me for a forkful of Molly's omelet.

I think I hear it after she says, "Ow." Or the "Ow" reminds me of the sound. A muffled crack. Julie reaches for a napkin and spits out her bite.

"Hey!" Molly says.

But then we see she didn't spit out just omelet. There's blood. There's a tooth.

Mae gasps.

Molly says, "Fuck!"

I lunge to a nearby table for a glass of water. I hand it to Julie.

"Thanks," she says, a spray of blood coming out of her mouth and hitting me square on the chin. I wipe it off immediately because it's gross and because it feels like acid. I know it's my imagination, but it burns.

"Are you okay?" Mae asks. "Do you need anything?"

"It's okay," Julie says, trying to keep her mouth closed to contain the blood. "It happens."

Molly's eyes bulge.

"I've lost two since I got back," she says, moving her hands to illustrate her stifled words.

"Have you seen a dentist?" Molly asks.

Julie nods.

"Do you need to see one now?"

She shakes her head. "I'll see him when I get back."

She plucks her bloody tooth from the napkin full of chewed omelet. It's in the palm of her hand now, and she looks at it curiously. I can't tell which tooth it is. None of the front ones.

"How much you think the tooth fairy will bring you for that?" I ask her, taking up the mantle of tension breaker.

She smiles. "I should take care of this."

"Do you need help? I can go with you," Mae offers.

"Aw, thanks, Maebs," Julie says. She pulls Mae in for a hug. Mae goes stiff but allows it to happen. Then Julie turns her face toward Mae's and kisses her on the cheek. Mae tries to tilt her head back to get away from it, but it's too late. Julie catches her on the corner of the mouth. It's not unlike Julie to go overboard with her displays of affection, but considering what just happened, it shows a frightening lack of awareness. "I'll be okay. I'll text you."

She closes a fist around the tooth and heads out. We watch her until she's gone.

We don't have anything to say at first. Molly stares at the bloody napkin that Julie placed on top of her omelet. The husbands leave, understandably disturbed. It's just us three and Jean, who is some-where nearby but out of sight, likely sulking and stroking his thin little mustache.

"What the actual fuck?" Molly says. "I knew something was wrong with her teeth."

"Like I said earlier, she hadn't been to a dentist in two years," Mae says. She dabs at her mouth with a napkin. "We don't know what she's been through."

"She needs to be somewhere where she can be supervised."

"Like where?"

"I don't know."

"What are you insinuating?"

"I'm not insinuating anything. She's not okay."

Molly and Mae have never argued like this before. They're usu-ally pretty in sync.

It's the situation, I know. But there could be something else at play here. Mae's become a lot more comfortable standing her ground over the past few years. Maybe that damaged their dynamic. Threw off the equilibrium. I picture their friendship, all of our friendships, as a jellyfish-like creature. Stretching and expanding, shriveling and shrinking, taking on new shapes as it travels forward. A living or-ganism not entirely in our control.

"Hey," I say. "Us arguing about it isn't going to help."

"Okay, John Lennon. What do you suggest?" Molly's turned her anger to me, and now I wish I hadn't gotten involved.

"Why don't you call Tristan? Let him know what's going on. See what he says. That was the plan, right?" Mae asks.

"Yeah," I say. "I can go call him."

"Okay, let's go," Molly says.

"You want to call him, too?"

I see her suspicion. Narrowed eyes, flaring nostrils.

"I want to hear what he has to say," she says.

"I'll tell you."

"Okay, fine. I'm going to my room." She takes off walking.

"Molly. Molly!" Mae calls after her, but ultimately lets her go. "This is a disaster."

"Everyone's on edge. We haven't been getting a lot of sleep."

"I'm so tired," she says. "But it's more than that. I'm drained. I feel drained."

"Yeah, same. Why don't we go back to our rooms? You can rest. I'll make the call. We can figure out when that painting thing is."

"I'm going to stop by the front desk and ask. I'll walk out with you."

"All right."

"Thanks, Jean!" Mae calls out to the empty room. She drops her head. "Poor Jean."

"If men aren't teased, their egos get too big. We did society a favor."

We walk out of the bar and are about to part ways when she asks, "Why didn't you tell us you were in contact with Tristan?"

My stomach contorts. "Why would I?"

"I don't know."

"I assumed you guys talked to him, too. You both have his number."

"Did he reach out to you?"

"I don't remember. It's not a big thing. We talked occasionally while she was gone. Mostly about her. Sometimes about other random stuff. I figured it was probably good for him to feel like he had a tie to her life. Talk to someone else who knew her. I don't know why you guys are so scandalized by it."

"We're not scandalized."

"Then what? You think I have a thing for married men?"

"I didn't say that."

"Then what is it?"

"Well," she says, "we noticed you guys hit it off at the funeral."

The hotel warps into something unrecognizable. I've lost my sense of place. I'm angry, and it has erased my surroundings.

"Hit it off at the funeral? What are you talking about?" I ask, my voice doing that thing where I sound mean, where I'm yelling without raising the volume. "It was a funeral. I wasn't sitting on his lap."

"Then maybe it was him looking at you."

"He was devastated when we were there."

"Still."

"That's bullshit. You guys want to cast me in a certain light because of my past. You think I'm a career mistress or something? Is that it?"

"No, Lise. I wasn't trying to—" She stops, switches tracks. "This weekend keeps getting worse. I don't know why I bother."

"Don't do that."

"Do what?"

"Feel sorry for yourself while I'm mad at you."

She searches my face. "Are you serious?"

I don't know.

She adjusts her glasses. "I'm sorry, Elise. None of that came out right."

"All right. I'm sorry, too."

"We don't think that about you. I hope you know that."

"I don't. But thanks."

"I'll let you know about the painting."

"And I'll let you know what he says. After our phone sex."

"You're worse than Molly sometimes—you know that?"

The guilt sets in immediately. I'm a liar. I lied.

"The smell is absolutely horrendous," some woman is yelling at Patsy at the foot of the stairs.

"I'm sorry to hear that," Patsy says, looking mortified. "As I explained, we're short staffed and do apologize for the inconvenience. We could move you to one of our suites."

"It's not just the room. It's the whole goddamn hallway!"

The hotel does have kind of a funny smell, especially down here. I can't identify what it is.

"I'll see you later," Mae says calmly, pretending to be unbothered by what we just heard. "You go call Tristan."

She marches toward the lobby, leaving me alone to navigate around this altercation to get up the stairs. I put my head down and rush by.

I don't remember there being so many stairs. Too many stairs. And the hallways are infinite. It takes ten years to get back to my room.

I kick off my shoes and take a few jumps on the bed to release some tension. The bed whimpers in protest.

I go to the mini fridge and, knowing what it'll cost me, remove a tiny blue bottle of gin. I twist it open before I can change my mind. I take the vodka, too.

I take my phone, my room key and the liquor out onto the balcony. It's cold. Freezing, actually. I go inside and layer a sweater under my sweatshirt, steal the throw blanket from the foot of the bed and wrap myself inside it.

Before I go back outside, before I call, I should think about what I need to say, how to broach the subject.

I imagine Julie in her room, somewhere below me, holding her tooth. The *third* tooth she's lost since she got back. I think about her reaction. She wasn't surprised or upset. It was "Oh, lost another tooth." Like she chipped a nail.

That's not like Julie. I lived with her for four years. Every zit elicited the same reaction as Jack not fitting on the door in *Titanic*. She was obsessive about her appearance, about her body in general. I spent hours upon hours of my life reassuring her in our cramped dorm bathroom as she straightened her hair, as she did and redid her makeup, as she changed her outfit a million times.

"You look great," I would tell her.

"You're just being nice. I'm a troll."

It's possible that she's mellowed over the years. That she's finally happy and comfortable in her own skin. But looking through the wider lens of the situation, I'm skeptical that newfound confidence is responsible for her casual reaction.

Anyone would be freaked out losing a tooth.

Come to think of it, the tooth might have been the culprit of the bloody bathroom incident. It could have been loose. Do loose teeth bleed? The gums, I mean.

What else could the blood have been from? And why wouldn't she tell us? Why wouldn't she ask us for help?

I'm stalling. I open the door to the balcony and step outside. I can't get over how cold it is. It's October. It feels like January. The wind hisses, and the rain falls in an ambiguous direction. The fog is patchy, and where it lacks, I can see the grass. It's overgrown and coils into itself. If I squint, I can see the trees. They lean forward into the fog with their branches outstretched, like they made a mad dash for the hotel but forgot about their roots. It's miserable out. The weather couldn't be worse.

I should go inside, but I don't want to make this call in the room. What if the walls are thin? What if someone's listening?

It's stupid, but it's one of those stupid things I can't be bothered to talk myself out of.

I wish I could smoke. I can't risk Molly smelling it on me.

I hover my finger over his name. I press. It rings.

Rings, rings, rings, rings.

No answer.

He could be busy. Or he could just not want to talk to me. We've spoken only once since Julie got back, a five-minute call for him to tell me how she was doing. We'd been talking on the phone at least twice a week in the months leading up to her return. Texting a lot. I hope he deleted his call history and our conversations. They were basically harmless, but the sheer volume was enough to raise eyebrows.

There was no spark at the funeral, no chemistry or whatever Mae thought she picked up on. Yes, I saw that he was attractive. He's objectively attractive. He's tall and sandy haired, with the build of someone who does manual labor, who was skinny in high school but is a man now. It's not like his appearance was a surprise. I'd seen his picture.

Mostly, I was fascinated by how different he was from anyone Julie had ever dated and how different he was from Julie herself.

His suit didn't fit him right. Julie wouldn't have liked that. Julie liked someone well dressed, someone well put together. Refined. Laurence Olivier. She liked ambitious men. Men who wanted to live in New York or LA, who had lofty career goals, who were money hungry. She saw herself as the charming half of a power couple who hosted the best parties with fun themes and lots of liquor. All of this came straight from her mouth during one of our late-night conversations. This isn't me projecting or exaggerating or making excuses.

Tristan's uniform was a Red Sox hat, paint-splattered jeans and a sweatshirt with his high school mascot on it (the Silverton Wolves, *owwooooo*). He drank beer during the day and listened to hair metal while he cooked us breakfast the morning after the funeral.

He's blue-collar. That's not what Julie wanted. Because it reminded her of her dad or her childhood or something, or because she thought having a lot of money meant having a better life. I don't know.

She always came back from winter or spring break ripping into townies.

"There's this guy Charlie I was in love with in high school. He was a senior when I was a freshman. So gorgeous. Wouldn't give me the time of day. So, while I was home, I went to get gas, and I'm inside the store grabbing a granola bar, and he's there behind the counter. Can you believe that? I was in love with him, and now he's working at a gas station."

"So?" I said, trolling her snobbery.

"I thought he was going to be a hockey star. Play in the NHL."

"Maybe he's happier working at the gas station. Fewer concussions. More teeth."

"Yeah," she said. "I bet he's thrilled."

She judged the girls who retained their high school boyfriends past graduation, who were excited to buy houses across the street from their parents. In hindsight, these criticisms probably stemmed from jealousy. Maybe she wanted to want a simpler life, instead of acting or music or whatever, anything involving attention and potentially fame, buckets of money. Maybe she wished she could be happy with the basics: a good partner, a functional home, getting the same coffee at the same shop every morning and seeing the same people at the grocery store. Maybe Tristan was some subconscious wish fulfillment.

The morning after the funeral, Molly and Mae left for the airport together. Pretty early. I drove because I couldn't afford airfare, so I stuck around. Had another cup of coffee. Part of it, I think, was that I had crowned myself the best friend. The most important person in Julie's life. I wanted to impress that upon Tristan. Make sure he knew. And I felt sorry for him. He was sad and alone, like me. Isolated.

"Can I help you with anything?" I asked him.

He shook his head. "Thanks, but I got it. I appreciate you coming."

"Of course."

"She talked about you all the time. Them, too. But mostly you."

"Good things, I hope."

"Oh, yeah, yeah. You want a beer?"

It was ten a.m., and I had to be on the road within the hour, but I said yes. We drank sitting on the porch steps.

"Are you going to keep this place?" I asked him.

"Yeah. For a while, anyway. Don't know what else to do with myself."

"Good to keep busy."

"What's funny is, everyone was telling me that having a funeral would bring me closure. Everyone was saying that. That word. 'Closure.'"

"Do you feel it?"

"No," he said, laughing a little. "No."

"Me, either," I said. Then for some reason, I added, "But I don't believe she's dead. Molly and Mae think I'm crazy. They're probably right. If it's too hard for me to accept, then I guess it is what it is."

He laughed again, but this time it was a nervous laugh. "I feel the same. About Julie not really being gone. I haven't told anyone. They would definitely think I'm crazy."

"You could be," I said.

"Yeah," he said. "Maybe."

"Maybe not."

He insisted on carrying my bag out to my car. He gave me a bottle of water and a good-looking sandwich. Lettuce, tomato. Cheese.

"Drive safe, all right?"

"I will."

"You have directions?"

"I have GPS."

"Right," he said, looking down. I caught his cheeks going red. He seemed like the kind of guy who used a map on principle, who believed everyone should know how to read one. I bet he could point north no matter where he was. In a basement. Blindfolded.

"Thanks for coming," he said. "It was good to have someone to talk to about it. Have an honest conversation."

"You can always call me if you want to talk. Say what you really think instead of what you think other people want to hear."

"I appreciate that. Let me know when you get home."

"I don't have your number."

"Oh," he said. I gave him my phone. I looked away while he put himself in it. "There you go."

"Thanks. This was nice. She would have liked it."

"Really?"

"Really."

We stood a few feet apart, not knowing if a hug was appropriate. We decided it was at the same time and fell into each other in a way that was comfortable, that was safe and familiar. I thought we fit together nicely. I didn't want to let go.

I spent most of the ride home in silence, wading through a bog of thoughts. I had never liked any of Julie's boyfriends. The only exception was Luke, a guy she dated first semester junior year. He had a dry sense of humor I appreciated, and he was always considerate of me, asking me questions about myself and later circling back. "How was your philosophy test?" or "Did they kill that big gator by your aunt's house?"

It was a nice change of pace, considering all her other boyfriends either ignored me or treated me like I was a nuisance, a hurdle they had to clear to get Julie alone.

Only Julie didn't take well to my friendship with Luke. At first, she kept saying how great it was that we got along. But it quickly turned into comments like "Your new BFF is coming over" and eventually "My boyfriend likes you better than me."

"He's just being nice," I would say. What was the alternative? Have him not like me? Have him be a dick to me like the others? She cared only because I was single.

I complained about it to Molly, who deemed it trivial, and Mae, who said, "Why don't you talk to her about it?"

I never got a chance. She broke up with Luke.

She's matured since college—we all have—but I knew she wouldn't approve of what I did next.

I let Tristan know I got home all right. I called him. I asked how the rest of his day went. I listened to his voice while I unpacked my black funeral dress, while I changed into my pajamas and got into bed. I asked him about the bed-and-breakfast, about what he'd done so far and what he planned to do next. I put the phone on speaker and set it on the pillow next to me. I closed my eyes, and it was like he was there.

"I miss her," he said about an hour and a half into our conversation. "Lately, I—I think I'm used to her being gone. I don't want to be, but it's better than being sad or pissed off like I was. Like, I don't want to move past it or accept what happened, but I'm starting to, and I'm confused if that's messed up or not."

"There's no right answer," I told him. "She would want you to be happy."

It was a nice sentiment, a nice thing to say, but of course it wasn't the truth. The lie was thorny, and it hurt to speak it. It scratched the roof of my mouth. Julie wouldn't want anyone to be happy or move on. She would expect perpetual mourning. But how could I say that to him? I thought if he didn't already know, I shouldn't tell him. He should get the gift of this ignorance. Some peace.

He was a good guy. Uncomplicated. Pure, honest, direct. Not Julie's type at all. It just didn't make any sense to me.

"I'm not happy," he said. "Not even close. The funeral didn't help. It's the day-to-day I'm getting used to. Getting up alone. Brushing my teeth alone. Making one cup of coffee. Cooking for one. That kind of thing. That stuff killed me at first."

"Humans are resilient. We're designed that way."

"I don't know if I am," he said. "I think I've got a bad memory. I'm forgetting what it was like before."

"What's the alternative?"

"Sorry?"

"What I mean is, you shouldn't feel guilty or conflicted over trying to get past it and move on with your life. It's been a year.

What's your other option? You sit around depressed? You're doing the best you can. Don't beat yourself up about it. Don't worry so much about how you think you should be feeling or what you think you should be doing. Don't add that stress. Let things happen. Feel what you feel."

"You're good at this."

I laughed. "I'm good at giving other people advice. I'm terrible at taking it."

"Don't take your own advice?"

"Nope."

"Here I was thinking you were an expert."

"No. Just trying to help. We're in the same boat here. Kind of."

"Yeah. Kind of."

"Well, it's past my bedtime. Long drive really takes it out of you."

"Yeah. Hope I didn't keep you up."

"No, it was nice talking to you."

"Yeah. Thanks. Thanks again for coming yesterday. Good night."

"Night."

I hung up and buried the phone under my pillow, like I was planting a seed. Like in the morning I'd wake up and he'd be there, grown overnight. Then he wouldn't be alone, and I wouldn't be alone. I was so tired of being alone. Of getting up alone. Brushing my teeth alone. Making one cup of coffee.

My phone rings, and I return to the present. It's him.

"Hey," he says. The sound of his voice reminds me how much I loved talking to him, something I've been working to forget. "How are you? Everything okay?"

"I'm all right. How are you?"

"I'm good," he says. "Well, okay. What's going on?"

"I'm calling about Julie."

"Oh," he says.

I'd been waiting for him to call me. For him to reach out first. Now I've got him on the phone, and we're talking about her.

"What?" I ask him.

"Nothing," he says. "What about Julie?"

"Um." I don't know what to say. I'm too nervous to be articulate. The wind spits at my feet, wets my socks. I push myself back against the window.

"What's that noise?" he asks.

"The wind," I tell him. "I'm on the balcony outside my hotel room. Weather's garbage."

"It's been pretty bad here, too," he says. "But today's nice."

"Look at us. Talking about the weather."

He offers a soft laugh. This is worse than awkward. "It's . . . ," he says. "It's been weird."

"It's not a normal situation."

"Any advice?" he asks me.

"No," I say. "Sorry."

"Yeah. Me, either."

I don't know what we're talking about. Us. Julie. Both.

There's a lull. Silence.

But the silence isn't really silence. The wind is relentless. It consumes the quiet, chomps on it, breaks its bones. Snap, crackle, pop.

"Yeah, so . . . ," I start. How do I put it?

"Elise?"

"Yeah?"

Please.

"You said you called to talk about Julie."

"Mm."

"I . . . ," he says. "I don't think it's Julie. It's not Julie."

The words burn through me. "What?"

"I don't know how else to say it. Please don't tell anyone. I haven't been able to talk to anyone about this. I can't."

"You can talk to me."

"I know."

I wait for him to continue but he doesn't.

"Did something happen?"

Nothing.

"Tristan?"

"Yeah."

"You still there?"

"Yeah. This is—" He stops.

"It'll stay between us, I promise."

"It's not that. I mean, it is, but it isn't. It's just . . . I don't know if you'll believe me. No, actually, I think you will. It's . . . it's . . . I don't know if I want to say it out loud."

"Say what?"

"There have been things," he says, and takes a breath, "since she got back. I noticed she was acting different. She wouldn't let me touch her."

Why would he want to touch her?

"When she was in the hospital, I tried to take her hand. She was freezing, Elise. Not like anything I ever felt before. I can't describe it. I offered to get her a blanket or make her tea, but she didn't want any. I told the nurse, but he said he'd just taken her temperature, and it was fine. I didn't know what else to do. I let it go."

"What else?"

"When . . ." He's deteriorating. His voice keeps breaking. "When she came back, she started sleeping in one of the guest rooms. She insisted on sleeping alone. She said the doctors warned her about night terrors, but when I asked them, they didn't know what the hell I was talking about. One night I wake up to go to the bathroom, and the guest room door is wide-open. The window is open. She's gone. I freak the fuck out. I'm calling her name. Running around. I search the whole damn house, run outside. I find her sleeping on the lawn. No blanket. No pillow. Curled up on the lawn down by the bushes. I don't know if you remember, but the bushes are down at the end of the footpath. And I call her name, but she doesn't wake up. I'm too afraid to touch her. God, I'm an asshole. I just left her there."

"You're not an asshole."

"I didn't know what else to do."

"You don't need to keep saying that. I know."

"Next morning, I ask her how she slept, and she says fine. I don't like to confront people. I'm not like that. I didn't say anything. And then I couldn't say anything because I got sick. Some bug or virus or something. I couldn't get out of bed for weeks. Couldn't keep my eyes open, couldn't keep food down. I only started feeling better in the last few days. I don't know what it was. I was exhausted. My mom thought it was everything catching up to me."

"Maybe."

"I don't know. There's been other stuff, too."

"Like what?"

"Fuck, I don't even want to talk about it. I don't even want to say, Elise. I don't know if I can."

"It's me. You can tell me."

"God." He's crying now. "I lock my door at night. I'm fucking ashamed. I lock my door. I'm scared of what she is."

"What is she?"

"I don't know!"

"Okay, take a breath. Talk to me. Maybe I can help."

"I'm sorry. I'm sorry."

"It's okay. It's me. You can talk to me about anything. We've talked about pretty much everything under the sun. I still think Green Lantern is cooler than Batman."

"You're wrong, but okay," he says, regaining control of himself. "Okay."

It was mid-July, a few days after he had found her sleeping outside. He was too afraid to confront her or to reach out for help. What would he say? She was acting funny? The doctors told him to expect as much and to be on the lookout for certain "red flag" behaviors. Being cold and sleeping separately or outside weren't red flags. Not really. They warned him about self-harm and short-term memory loss. They warned him about massive mood swings and gave him a list of signs of depression and post-traumatic stress.

"I thought it was PTSD. It made sense. The cold thing didn't, but since I couldn't explain it, I tried to put it out of my mind. But the thing is, even when she wasn't doing anything different, even when she was being normal, it was like she was different. She wasn't the same."

He tested her memory. He would bring up things they had done before she disappeared, and she remembered. She would return a specific detail that only she could know.

"Remember that diner we went to on Christmas Eve? What was it called?"

"Jerry's," she said. *"Best apple pie in the world, but we can never go back there because you forgot to tip."*

"I don't know what I was expecting. Her to trip up and then I'd have my proof?"

If he was after proof, he never got it. She had all of her memories from before. Still none from the time that she had been missing. He didn't press her on doctors' orders.

"They said the memories should surface naturally, or she should be working with a psychiatrist to help bring them up safely or something. Like, they wanted a doctor around in case the memories are bad? I mean, we know they must be bad, or she would remember. Right? She wouldn't have blocked them out. She wasn't upset about it or anything. She didn't care that she didn't remember. She didn't want to see a psychiatrist. She said whatever happened was in the past, and she didn't want to dig anything up," he says. He's speaking quickly, tripping over his words, and he stops to catch his breath.

He goes on. "That reminds me. This is going to come off like a dick thing to say, but she had dirt under her nails. Ever since she got back. Like, a lot of it. I could see it. And she would bite them, her nails. She never did that before. What I'm trying to say is, there were changes. Her nails. Her skin. She didn't look healthy, and she was either starving or not interested in food at all."

"You're not a dick for paying attention," I say. I want to ask about her teeth, but I don't want to get him off track. "I asked you to tell me."

"She started eating meat. I didn't think twice about it at first. I almost forgot she was a vegetarian. It'd been two years. I made breakfast, and I look over and she's eating bacon. It didn't click until later that day, when I walk into the kitchen and she's eating slices of roast beef out of the packaging. Just the meat. Not a sandwich. I realized. I was about to say something, and then she asked me if I wanted to go for a walk. I didn't want to make it a thing. From then on, she was eating meat. A lot of meat. At the store she would fill up the cart with ground beef and steaks, sausages, bacon, pork ribs.

Everything. She's so thin, I thought it was good she was getting the protein. I thought maybe the doctors told her something they didn't tell me. They did give her these powder-based shake things, but she wouldn't drink them."

"Did you tell the doctors?"

"No. I didn't think it was a big deal," he says.

"I'm not judging. I'm asking."

"I'm sorry. I just," he says. "I'm sorry."

"It's okay. Go on," I say. It's not raining anymore but the fog lingers like a playground bully, relentless and vindictive. I stretch my legs out in front of me to see if it will take my feet. It does. I'm gone past my ankles.

"One night, after I caught her outside, I woke up at, like, two a.m. I was in bad shape. I'd sweat through my sheets. I stripped the bed and went to the linen closet for new ones. I saw her door was open. I thought she might be outside again. I couldn't really walk. I thought I was gonna pass out. I needed water. I called out her name. No answer. I went downstairs. I fell on the bottom two steps—that's how weak I was. It was bad. I called for her again. She didn't say anything, but I could hear her. I could hear something. Breathing. But not really. Not like normal breathing. It was more intense than that. Like, heavy breathing. I thought an animal had gotten in the house. That's what it sounded like."

I could picture him there at the bottom of the stairs. It was an old, stately staircase. The thick spine of the house. That big house with too many windows and too many rooms. I didn't sleep when I crashed there after the funeral. I stayed awake, sitting on the bench built into the bay window, my arms around my knees. I watched the line of the trees, the pale silver moon, the path down to the beach with the kind of sand that clings to your ankles like magnets. I watched because I thought she might appear, that maybe I could summon her. I watched because she would know I was watching. She had to.

"I pulled myself up and saw the light was on in the kitchen. That's where the noise was coming from. I didn't know what to do. If it was an animal, I couldn't catch it myself. I was seeing double. I couldn't breathe."

I can see him. He takes slow, stumbling steps down the hall toward the kitchen, his approach muffled by the rug beneath him. She bought that rug at an estate sale shortly after moving in. She sent me a picture.

"First find for the house! Twenty bucks. Can you believe it?"

It was pretty, brown and green, patterned with flowers and little birds.

I see his bare man feet come down on those birds.

"When I got closer, the sound was really loud. I can't describe it. Like, a slurping? And I get to the doorway, and I look into the kitchen and . . . Jesus, Elise. I can't."

"Tristan, you have to tell me."

"God," he says. He's back to crying. He's not very good at hiding it, even though I can tell he's pulling the phone away from his mouth. I can hear him. He's hyperventilating.

"Tristan."

"And I see her standing there. She's hunched over. The fridge is open so the light is on her, and I can see what she's doing. She's got the meat out—" He stops. He sobs and starts again. "She's eating the meat raw."

Over his shoulder, I see her, too. Her skeletal frame in loose pajamas, one of Tristan's old baseball T-shirts, long enough to wear as a dress. I see her ravenous mouth unhinge. I see what's inside it.

I pull my feet in from the fog. I need to see them. I need to escape my vision of Tristan's story. I attempt to move my toes. I can't. I'm detached from my body. I don't feel it at all. I might not even have one.

"Elise?"

"I'm here."

"She was eating ground beef. Raw. She was using her hands. There was a piece . . . God, it was hanging out of her mouth. And then she reached for a steak and took a bite of it. The blood was all over her chin."

"What'd you do?"

"Nothing. I couldn't move. And then," he says, "she saw me. She looked at me. Her head was down, and she didn't lift it. She just looked up at me with her eyes. I couldn't see her that well in the light from the fridge, but she wasn't blinking. She saw me, but she didn't see me. Or she didn't care. She kept eating. Then she looked away. She was looking at the meat."

"Then?"

"I went back upstairs. I kept looking over my shoulder to see if she was following me. I locked my door. I pushed our dresser in front of it. I was afraid she would come in while I was sleeping. I didn't know what she'd do."

"Why didn't you tell anyone?"

"I thought it was a fever dream. I told myself that until I believed it."

"It doesn't sound like you believe it."

"Why are you asking me?"

"She's not acting like herself."

He's quiet.

"Why did you let her come here this weekend? So you could have witnesses?" I ask.

"She wanted to go. I tried to talk her out of it. She wouldn't listen." He's not sniffling anymore. I like him better this way.

"Okay."

"You don't believe me."

"I didn't say that."

"The way she looked at me that night, Elise."

"You said it's not Julie. Who is it, then?"

"That's not what I meant. It's not someone else. It's her. But she's not the same."

"She's sick, Tristan."

"I think it's more than that."

"More how? Do you think she's dangerous?" I can't believe I'm asking this question. About the person I slept next to for four years, who used to buy me yogurt raisins during exams because she knew I liked to snack on them while I studied.

"I don't know. I don't think so."

"What do you think we should do?"

"I was hoping you'd tell me."

"I don't always have the answers."

"Damn."

The rain returns without warning. Drops the size of my fists spill onto the balcony and resoak my socks.

"Hey, I've got to go," I tell him.

"Are you going to talk to her?"

"I guess. Someone has to say something, right?"

Lightning bleaches the sky. I hate the anticipation of thunder.

"Elise?"

"I need to think. I'll call you later."

"Okay," he says. "Thank you."

"Yeah," I tell him. "Bye."

I hang up. I should go inside. Take shelter from the storm before I'm ripped into it, but I can't move. The only sensation I've got is from the army of goose bumps gathering across my skin.

It's the image of her standing in the kitchen eating raw meat. I can see the strings of ground beef falling through her fingers. The red smudge of her mouth, the dark caves of her eyes.

What happened to her?

If I ask, will she tell me?

I need to ask. I need to talk to her. I need to help her.

My skin marches over my bones. My heart slams against my rib cage. Someone's knocking on the glass behind me. In my room.

Someone's in my room.

I'm afraid to turn around. I'm afraid it's Julie.

The door swings open. "Elise, get the fuck inside. It's a monsoon."

Molly.

"How'd you get into my room?"

"It was unlocked."

"Really?"

She closes the door behind us and locks it. "Safety first, Lise. Safety first."

I toss my phone onto the bed and take off my wet socks.

"What were you doing out there?"

"I called Tristan."

"Couldn't do that in the comfort of your hotel room?"

"I hate this room."

"Fair," she says, looking around with her hands on her hips. "What'd he say?"

If I tell her, she'll want to break down Julie's door with torches and pitchforks. She's a geyser. She'll lose it. I need to talk to Julie first. It needs to be me.

"Pretty much what we already know. She eats meat now. She doesn't look well. He said they don't sleep in the same bed anymore. She wants to sleep alone in case she has night terrors."

"What about her teeth?"

I dig a pair of clean socks out of my bag. "Didn't come up."

"What do you mean, it didn't come up? Wasn't that the point of calling?"

"No. At least, that wasn't clear to me. I thought I was supposed to figure out what her behavior was like at home. I did that."

"What else did he say?"

I decide to go down this road. "I know you and Mae think I was flirting with him at the funeral."

She's on my bed now, hugging a throw pillow, fidgeting with its loose threads. "I think you have a repetition compulsion."

"What?"

"Because of your dad. You go after unavailable men."

"This is why I don't go to therapy. You leave psychoanalyzing everyone like you're a fucking expert. I made a mistake in my early twenties. It wasn't Freudian. It was me being human. Why am I not allowed? Why can you be too afraid to date, and Mae serial date models, and why can Julie get married on a whim, but I can't have my thing?"

"Because your thing hurts other people," she says. "It was wrong, and what gets me, to this day, is I don't think you know that."

Molly is a black-and-white thinker. There's no room for nuance. I could try explaining to her the complexities of life and morality and relationships, but it'd be like shouting into a plastic bag.

Or maybe she's right, and I'm a terrible person.

"Do you talk to Tristan a lot?" she asks.

"Every night. I wait by the phone in lingerie."

She throws the pillow at me. "I'm serious."

"We talk every once in a while. We're friends. We check in on each other. I didn't realize it was a criminal offense." In college, Molly and I went through a brief phase when we would get high and watch Court TV. "Guilty!" she would say, banging an imaginary gavel. She always made up her mind early, a few minutes in. Plaintiff. Defendant. Both, usually. "You can see it. You can hear it in their voice." She was so sure. I would ask, "Yeah, but do they believe they're guilty? Do they know they did something wrong?" She wouldn't miss a beat. "Oh, they know," she would say. "They know."

It's not lost on me, why this memory is surfacing now. I swat it away.

"Don't you get where we're coming from?" she asks me.

"No. I really don't," I tell her, doubling down. "And I think it's mean."

"Sorry," she says, like a sibling on parent mandate.

"I haven't even talked to him since Julie got home," I tell her.

"See," she says. "That makes me think something's up."

"Molly, please. I'm so done. I'm done with this conversation. I'm done with this whole trip."

"What do you mean, you're done with the trip?"

The lamp flickers in the other room.

She turns to me. "The hotel doesn't want you to leave."

"You're the worst."

"I'm sorry. I love you. Don't leave me."

"Love you, too."

"If the power goes out, I'm gonna lose my shit."

"If the power goes out, Mae is actually going to lose it," I tell her. "Besides, they've probably got backup generators."

"Paaaattsy," Molly whines, "help us."

I think about Patsy getting reamed out by that woman downstairs. She's got her hands full.

"Can we talk about this weather?" Molly asks. "I haven't been on the East Coast for a while. Is this normal?"

"It's just rain."

"It's straight up hailing," she says. "Look."

Through the veil of fog, I catch shimmers spiraling downward. They announce themselves when they arrive in violently loud thwacks.

"It's not normal for October," I say. "But it's not unheard-of."

"I'm never leaving California again."

"You were looking for an excuse." I nudge her with my toes. They've defrosted.

"You know," she says, still staring out the window, "I'm not afraid to date. I choose not to."

"I know. I'm sorry."

"Not everything is about my leg. Does it factor in? Yeah, in ways you and Mae and Jules will never understand, and that's fine. But it's not the reason," she says. "Believe it or not, I'm good on my own."

"I believe it."

"If I come home to dishes in the sink, they're *my* dishes. I watch TV, it's whatever *I* want. I go wherever I want, do whatever I want. I've got a lot going on. I'm not some lonely sad sack out there. I've got a good life."

"Molly," I say. It's rare for her to be vulnerable like this. I want to tell her now. About what a lonely sad sack I am. About Tristan. Maybe she'll understand, be more receptive than I assumed.

She clears her throat, shakes her head. Snaps out of her vulnerability. Moment's over.

"Look," she says. "We need to focus on what we're going to say to Julie."

I shrug.

"Lise. I thought you were with me on this."

"I am. I'm going to talk to her. I'll talk to her."

"You don't want us there?"

"I think it's better if it's just me."

"Okay, fine. Whatever. But you need to do it soon. We're her best friends. We're basically lying to her face right now."

"How?"

"We're in here talking about her and not saying any of this shit to her face," she says. She adjusts the pillows and lies on her side. "I have one leg. Listen to me."

"Thought you'd pepper that in," I say. I love her so much right now, lounging on my bed, helping herself to all my pillows, being serious but never too serious. That classic smirk. I want to spread this moment on a cracker and eat it.

"Oh, wait till Mae comes in here with her sweet Southern belle routine," she says. "You know she dials up the accent when she wants something. You'll be back on her side in a second."

"And you're lecturing me about morality."

"Fuck right off," she says. "But seriously. Something has to be said. Even if it's, like, convincing her she needs to see new doctors. She should go to New York. How good are doctors in Maine?"

I shrug. "Considering the situation, I'm thinking not very."

"You think she was honest with them?"

Of course she wasn't. She didn't stroll in for a checkup and tell them she was sleeping outside and eating raw meat. That wouldn't have gone over well. Maybe I can go with her next time. Maybe she needs me there. She's sick. She just needs some help.

"When are you going to talk to her? Tonight? After paint by numbers or whatever?"

"Yeah, I guess I could do it then," I say, but the dread breeding in my stomach disagrees.

"All right. Good. This is good. We need to do something. She clearly needs some kind of professional help."

Molly has got herself all amped up. This is why she can't know about the raw meat. This is why she can't be there when I talk to Julie.

"Shit." Molly looks down at her phone. "We should go down for lunch."

"Already?"

"Mae said painting is at two, and she wanted to meet for lunch at one. It's twelve fifty-eight."

"Let me change and pee."

"At the same time?" she asks with false enthusiasm.

"It's my cool new trick."

"It's freezing in your room."

"I think the thermostat's broken."

"California, man," I hear her say as I close the bathroom door.

VI

When we get to the table, Mae isn't there, but Julie is. She gives us a big smile. "Surprise! I'm early."

She looks about the same as she did this morning, except I can spy the dark gap where her tooth used to be.

"Don't start being early," Molly says. "I thought I could rely on you to always be later than me."

"Sorry for letting you down," Julie says. "Sit. The look on Mae's face when she sees we're all here and *she's* late . . ."

"I don't know. She's never been late before. She might be dead," Molly says.

"You all thought I was dead, and here I am," Julie says, winking.

"You're making jokes now?" Molly asks.

"I'm pursuing a career in stand-up. Didn't I tell you?"

Molly opens her mouth to say something, then changes her mind and closes it. I've never seen her stumped before.

Julie's perky. She's in a good mood. Maybe the tooth was holding her back.

"How're you feeling?" Molly asks. "How's your tooth?"

"Emancipated."

"Are you going to go to the dentist?"

"Yeah, I called Tristan. He'll make an appointment for me when I get back."

Molly's not so subtle. She's confused.

I'm not. Julie's lying. I was on the phone with Tristan. He would have mentioned if they had talked before I called. He would have mentioned the tooth. There's no way they talked after. He would have called me back. Texted.

"What?" Julie asks, catching on.

"Nothing," Molly says. "Sorry. Teeth stuff freaks me out."

"Didn't mean to traumatize you."

"Should I have my therapist bill you directly, or . . ."

Mae comes in. She's not surprised to see us all here. She's not anything but tired. She rubs her eyes.

"Hey, guys," she says, sitting next to me.

"You okay?" Molly asks.

"I'm not feeling well."

"What's wrong?" I ask her, sliding her a glass of water.

"Tired. My stomach is acting up," she says.

"I'm sorry, sweetheart," I say. "You want ginger ale?"

"Yeah," she says. "I ordered some at the bar. He's bringing it over. I'm sorry."

"Don't be sorry," I tell her.

"We can still paint," she says. "I asked the front desk. They've got a small reception hall for weddings and events. They'll have it in there."

"If you're not up to it, we can just hang," Molly says.

"I'm up to it."

When the waiter comes, she orders plain white toast. Molly, Julie and I get sandwiches. Mae takes the tiniest sip of her ginger ale. She pats at her temples. She's sweating.

"Don't worry," she insists. "I'm fine. Let's talk about something else."

"How about this weather?" Molly says.

"Not that."

"Talk fashion to us, Maebs. Give us the scoop."

"Ooh," she says, looking alive again. "Okay."

She tells us about celebrities she's worked with, who's nice or mean. She tells us about colors and cuts and designers.

"Are capri pants ever coming back? I hope not," Julie says. "I hate my ankles."

I think about what Tristan said, about Julie not being Julie. I watch her closely, waiting for some evidence. An unfamiliar mannerism, a new tic. But she moves the way she's always moved. She smiles the same; one side of her mouth goes before the other. It's Julie. It's my best friend. I can't deny her.

Maybe part of me wanted to so I could step out of my life and into the one she built. I'm jealous of that life. I'm jealous of her. I always have been.

And I'm jealous of Mae, her passion, her career, her apartment. The cute plants she has in hanging terrariums that she can keep alive and thriving while all my plants shrivel and die within days.

I'm jealous of Molly and her zero fucks given. Of her stress-free existence out in Los Angeles. Of how she knows the place, how she speaks about the streets and the neighborhoods, maps out this other world with a lightness in her voice that can be only love.

I wonder what it's like to love where you live, to wake up in the morning and feel lucky to be there.

It's shameful to admit this jealousy. You're not supposed to be jealous of your friends.

"I do think three-quarter-length sleeves will come back in a big way," Mae says, "and . . ." She grabs the table with one hand and puts the other over her mouth.

"Maebs?"

She reaches for a napkin and vomits into it. "Oh, God," she says.

I hand her another napkin. "Here."

"Oh my God."

"I'm sorry," Molly says, tapping Julie's shoulder. They slide out of the booth. "The smell will make me . . ." Molly wretches.

"No, no, no," Mae hums to herself.

"Here," I say. "We'll get you cleaned up. Don't cry, honey. *Shh.*"

Julie tosses me another napkin. I wipe Mae's chin and leave the soaked wad on the table. Some leaked down onto her shirt; there's some in her hair.

"We'll go up to your room," I say. "Get you showered and changed."

"Okay," she whimpers.

"Can you guys have them send more toast and ginger ale to Mae's room?"

"Sure," Julie says.

"Yeah," Molly says. "Sorry. I can't deal with that."

"I've got it," I say. "Come on, Maebs."

I put my arm around her waist, and she leans on me. I try to ignore the smell, breathe through my mouth.

"I don't know what's wrong with me," she says.

"Could have eaten something bad. Could be a stomach bug."

"I can't be sick," she says. "What else could go wrong?"

"Not a thing," I tell her.

The staircase is Everest. Mae can barely support her own weight. She's not heavy. It's just awkward dragging an extra set of limbs up the stairs.

"I'm so sorry," she says.

"Don't apologize for being sick."

"I'm sorry."

"One more time and I'll drop you."

"Please don't."

"You know I'd never."

She hands me the key, and I open the door to her room. I forgot how comically pink it is.

"I'm going to shower," she says. "You don't have to stay."

"I'm staying."

"The remote is on the table if you want to watch TV. I've also got some magazines in my suitcase."

"Don't worry about me. Do you need anything?"

She shakes her head. "I'll feel better after I shower."

She closes the door to the bathroom, turns the fan on. I can still hear her getting sick. She flushes the toilet twice. The shower comes on. She probably hates that I'm here. Mae doesn't like people to see her sick. She likes to quarantine herself until she's better, to give the illusion she's immune. It's all about appearances with that one.

I put something on TV, turn the volume way up to give her some semblance of privacy.

I like this room. It's much smaller than mine. It feels safer. I appreciate how girlie it is. Maybe it's meant to be romantic, all the hearts and flowers. Valentine's Day in room form. I wouldn't want a man in here. I like it alone, where I can pretend I'm a princess or a movie star or both. Grace Kelly.

It's like I'm inside a Barbie Dreamhouse.

I never played with Barbies, but I understood their appeal. Every once in a while, when I was a kid, I'd be at Walmart with Lu, and she'd walk me down the toy aisle. She'd tell me I could pick something out, whatever I wanted. I'd look at the Barbies, with their thick synthetic hair and forever smiles, and think, *Maybe*. I liked their outfits, the variety of options. But I never ended up getting one. Not because they were expensive, and I knew we didn't have a lot of money, though that might have had something to do with it. I never really wanted one. What would I *do* with it? I couldn't perceive any enjoyment beyond standing in the aisle, looking.

I pace around. I check in with my reflection in the heart-shaped mirror. I don't look so good. My hair's sloppy. My eyes are puffy and bloodshot.

I should be doing something productive, like searching for a medical condition that makes you crave raw meat. It's too hard to think about with the enduring smell of Mae's puke in the air.

There's a knock at the door. I open it, expecting Molly or Julie, but it's Patsy. She's carrying a tray.

"Room service," she says with a big fake smile. She's blinking a lot.

"Thank you," I say, taking the tray.

"I hear your friend is sick. Is she doing okay?"

"She's fine. Showering. Could be a stomach bug. Maybe something she ate."

Patsy's smile descends. Then it falls away entirely. Her eyes widen. I turn around to look behind me, assuming she's reacting to some alien swamp monster in my blind spot.

"What?" I ask her.

"I'm very sorry she's not feeling well. Please let us know if you need anything."

I don't know who this "us" is. I feel like Patsy is the only one who works here.

"We want our guests to have the best possible experience," she says. "For me, this place is home. It's important to me our guests enjoy their time here."

"Yeah," I say, hoping she'll leave.

"Anyway. Will you let us know when she's feeling better?"

"Sure. Thanks." I let the door shut. It slams. I'm holding the tray, so I couldn't stop it. I'm not sure I feel bad. I set the tray down on the foot of Mae's bed. They sent up the sandwich I ordered at the table. I eye it suspiciously. There's no way this isn't a food-poisoning situation.

It hits me like a baseball bat. The crepe. Mae was the only person to try Julie's crepe. Not to mention Julie kissed her on the mouth.

Tristan said he got sick, too. He said he was tired, couldn't keep food down. Just like Mae.

What if Julie carries some kind of sickness? What if she has a parasite? Worms? Would that explain the raw meat?

If so, wouldn't the doctors have caught it?

I take my head in my hands and squeeze. Mae had only two tiny bites of Julie's crepe. It couldn't be that. Not possible. I'm making up stories, trying to connect random dots, and for what?

Julie has the answers. I just need to suck it up and ask. Have a conversation.

I wonder if I'm in denial, if the situation with Julie is more severe than I'm allowing myself to acknowledge or willing to accept. But the last time I questioned whether I was in denial, I wasn't. I was right. Everyone thought Julie was dead, but I knew she wasn't. I knew she would come back, and she's back. She's here.

Light-headed, I peel the bread off of my sandwich and peck at the crust. I turn off the TV so I can concentrate, figure out what exactly I should say to Julie and how to get her alone to say it. But with the TV off, I can hear Mae getting sick again. I can hear her over the shower. I get up and knock on the door.

"Maebs? You all right?"

No response.

I knock again. "Maebs?"

Another knock.

"Mae? Mae, I'm coming in, okay? I'm going to come in."

I count to five, giving her another chance to answer, then open the door.

She's on the floor in the fetal position, her body barely covered with a towel.

"Honey." I drop down on my knees. "Mae?"

She groans. "I'm sorry."

"What's going on?"

"I'm so sick," she whispers.

"Is it just nausea?"

She shakes her head. "I'm tired. My whole body aches."

"Okay, Maebs. I think we're going to have to get you to a doctor."

"No, no. I'm fine."

"You're not fine. It could be something serious."

"It's not. Touch of food poisoning," she says. She tries to sit up and realizes she's exposed. She pulls the towel around herself.

"I'm going to bring you some water. Let's see if you can keep it down, okay?"

"Okay."

I get the water Patsy brought up. Mae sips at it.

"How's that?"

She nods.

"You've got to finish that glass. Take your time, but I need you to finish it."

"You're good at this," Mae says.

"Not as good as you. You used to take care of me when I got sloppy drunk."

"A few times."

"I'd take care of Julie. You'd take care of me. Molly can hold her liquor."

"Molly doesn't need to be taken care of," she says, between sips and deep breaths.

"You didn't get hammered in college. Except for the Southern Comfort incident." I catch myself. "Which, of course, never happened."

She manages a feeble laugh. "I never broke my rule."

"Rule?"

"My maximum."

"Oh, right! The self-imposed two-drink maximum. Class act, you are."

She shakes her head. "It was because of Alice."

I forgot about Alice. She was Mae's best friend when she was growing up. They met on the first day of preschool and became inseparable. Everything they did, they did together. Girl Scouts, ballet class, homework, sleepaway camp, manicures with their allowance money. Their parents bought bunk beds because they slept over at each other's houses so often. They went to the same preppy private schools. At the end of their sophomore year, they went to a party.

These rich kids didn't have normal drinking-in-the-basement

high school parties. They had parties in their absentee parents' mansions. They drank top-shelf liquor out of glassware instead of cheap beer out of Solo cups. Alice got wasted. Mae tried to stop her. Tried to drag her home. But Alice was three sheets, and apparently, she was a mean drunk. She said something completely, soul-crushingly awful to Mae, so Mae left without her.

Later that night, Alice stripped naked in the middle of this big party. She walked around naked. Danced naked. Drank naked. Took pictures naked. The pictures went up online. Circulated around school. Someone printed them out and taped them to Alice's locker. She was harassed so badly she transferred schools. Her mom had to drive her an hour each way to a private school in another county.

Mae stuck by her in the aftermath. She defended her at school, took the pictures off of her locker and got in early every day to make sure no one put them back up. Mae felt guilty that she hadn't been there for Alice that night, that she hadn't tried harder to get her to leave the party. But she was conflicted because Alice said this horrible thing to her, and she couldn't confront her about it. At least, she felt Alice was in too fragile a state to be confronted. Alice claimed to have no recollection of that night. She likely didn't remember what she said. Or she did, and a lapsed memory was a convenient excuse. The wound festered. Their friendship was never the same, and since they didn't go to the same school anymore, they saw less and less of each other. They drifted apart. They're not in touch at all anymore.

That experience hatched Mae's two-drink limit. She stuck to it all through college, and to this day, she never gets out of control.

I think that's why she takes such good care of us, why she worries so much about our good time, our feelings. Why she's so afraid of alienating Julie. She knows what it's like to lose a friend.

"That's the last of it. I promise," she says to me as I hold back her hair.

"Don't tell me that to get out of seeing a doctor. Tell me the truth."

Tell me the truth. This is practice for what comes next with Julie.

"That is the truth," Mae says. She points to the robe on the back of the door. It's hot pink with red hearts. I hand it to her, turn around so she can change into it. When I lived with Julie, there was no turning around. For someone who was so self-critical about her body, Julie wasn't shy about getting naked. So I wasn't shy, either. We saw each other's bodies all the time. It wasn't a big deal. Maybe other people would think it was weird. It wasn't weird to us.

"I don't think I got a robe in my room," I say.

"Did you look in the closet?"

"I don't think there is a closet."

If there is, I haven't noticed it. I map out my room in my head. Where could it be? And if it's there, what's inside it?

"I'm decent," Mae says. She's leaning against the sink for support.

"You want to lie down?"

She nods. I help her to the bed.

"They brought food?" she asks, pointing to the tray.

"Patsy." I pull back the covers, clear a path between the pillows. I bring over the garbage bin and the water.

"I ruined the whole weekend. I should have picked somewhere else. I just thought . . ." She puts a hand over her mouth. I lift up the garbage bin and offer it to her. She shakes her head. "No, I'm okay."

"You didn't ruin this weekend. We love it here. Though it doesn't seem to like us much."

"We don't get to be together anymore. Not just because of Julie going missing. Because we live so far apart. We have separate lives now."

"I don't have a life," I tell her.

"Yes, you do, Lise. I know it's not exactly what you want, but it's a life. You're healthy."

That's the trump card. I can't complain about my life, my situation, when Mae has to live with strangers gawking at her. When Molly stared down death as a kid. It's supposed to give me perspective, but there's the nagging inch of me that resents it. My problems aren't invalid. Not to me. Just because they aren't life altering, life-threatening, doesn't mean they don't make me feel bad. I wake up with them every morning, carry them around all day like a lead backpack, and I fall asleep with them at night. They're real, and they're mine. I know I'm lucky. I know that. But it doesn't change how I feel.

I guess that makes me a shit person. My shittyness seems to be a recurring theme today.

"You're going to figure it out," she tells me. "You're smart and strong willed. Once you put your mind to something, it's on. You go after it. You'll end up where you want to be."

"We'll see," I tell her.

"It's a struggle for everyone. You know that, don't you?"

"I know."

"Do you?" she asks. She sighs, lets her head fall to the side. "What I'm trying to say is, I struggle, too, sometimes. It's hard for me, too."

"I'm sorry."

She raises a hand up. "I don't need you to be sorry. I need you to understand. That's why I started seeing a therapist. Sometimes I wake up in the morning and I feel completely untethered. I know you guys make fun of me, or think I'm shallow, but my clothes are so important to me. It's how I control how other people see me. They're part of my identity."

"Maebs," I say. She never talks like this. I can't tell if it's fever ramblings or if she's trying to open up to me. I push back her bangs to feel her forehead. "You're warm."

"I've got the chills," she says.

I give her the glass of water, and she takes a series of mini sips.

"Maybe I can sleep it off," she says.

"You think?"

There's a knock at the door. This time I look through the peephole. It's Molly and Julie.

"Hey, guys."

"I don't want an audience," I hear Mae say behind me, her voice hoarse.

I step out into the hall. I leave the door open a crack. If I close it completely, I might lock myself out.

"How is she?" Molly asks. Her eyes are wide and worried.

"She's fine," I tell her. "She'll be fine."

"What's wrong?"

"I'm not sure," I say. "Maybe something she ate."

"Great," Molly says.

"We need to put on happy faces for Mae. She's upset about everything."

"Is she still barfing?"

"It's been a few minutes. She's in bed now."

"I want to say hi," Molly says, and the way she says it, I know she's not asking. I open the door to let her in.

I stand out in the hall with Jules.

"What're you guys up to?" I ask her.

"We just finished our lunch. We sat for a while, had a drink. The painting thing starts in a bit, but I don't think Molly wants to do it."

"Arts and crafts aren't really Molly's thing."

Julie laughs. "No, not really."

I look down and notice Julie's arm. The sleeve of her sweatshirt is up, revealing a sequence of scratches on her forearm. They're pink and thick as ribbons. Fresh.

She catches me staring.

"What happened?" I ask.

She shrugs, goes to pull down her sleeve. I move to stop her, but she takes my wrist in her other hand.

"It's embarrassing," she says.

"What is?"

She slides her hand down, puts her palm in my palm, injects her fingers between mine. Her skin is ice, but I can't pull away. I think she's about to tell me something, something important.

But then she giggles. "It's nothing."

I've got two hands on my shoulders. There's a flare of white-hot panic before I realize it's Molly behind me. "Jesus!"

"Sorry."

"You startled me. Ninja."

"World's first and only one-legged ninja," she says. "Mae's barfing again."

I turn around to go in, but Julie stops me.

"I'm up," she says. The door shuts.

Molly grabs my arm. "You can't leave me alone with her."

"You went into the room."

"Not Mae. Julie!"

"What now?"

"It's awkward, first of all. Because I know something's up, and she knows that I know. I can tell. And then she's, like, eating the meat off her sandwich. She's, like, picking out pieces of turkey and eating them with her fingers. It's all stuck in her teeth. And I'm grossed out by it, and so I'm not eating, and then she asks me if I'm going to finish mine. I tell her no, and then she eats the meat off my sandwich. What the fucking fuck?"

"Maybe she's paleo."

Molly puts a hand on her hip. "I appreciate the joke, but also, fuck you. I'm being serious."

"I told you I'll talk to her."

"When?"

"Later. Tonight," I tell her. "Mae might need to see a doctor."

"I'll take her," she says. "Give you a chance to be alone with Julie. I'm telling you, you should have seen the way she was eating."

She tripped a wire. Why is she so repulsed by her? We don't know what she's been through.

"Don't you have any compassion?"

It's a gut punch of a question. Molly's body takes it like one. She teeters back, then slumps forward. Her face expands with shock.

I wait for her to say something back, something mean and ruthless, or something to make me feel guilty. But she doesn't get a chance to say anything. The door swings open.

"Are you guys just gonna stand out in the hallway or what?" Julie asks, poking me.

I look back at Molly.

"After you," she says.

I turn around, and suddenly I'm so dizzy, I need to lean against the doorframe to stop myself from falling. It smells like pencil shavings. "Wow," I say, taking a deep breath. "I almost just passed out."

"What's wrong?" Julie asks. "Not you, too."

"No, not my stomach." I stagger into the room and sit down on the love seat. Molly stands in the corner with her arms crossed. She's probably pissed at me. I don't know if I care, even though it was too harsh, what I said to her. She's only saying what we're all thinking, and she's saying it because Mae and I aren't. If both of them were acting like nothing was wrong, I'd be up in arms.

"You okay?" Molly asks, her voice flat.

"I'm fine. Dizzy spell."

She hands me the plate with my picked-over sandwich on it, without making eye contact, without really acknowledging me at all.

Remembering the food here is potentially poisonous, I gnaw on the pickle. Safe out of the jar.

"Thanks," I say to Molly.

She won't look at me. "We should get Mae to a doctor."

Mae is still and doll-like. Her eyes peel open at the mention of her name. The covers slither around her. Her hands are so delicate and so white, they look like bones.

"No," Mae says, and weakly takes another sip of water. "Give me a few hours, and I'll bounce back. I'm good—I promise. You should go to the wine and painting."

"I'm not going to that," Molly says.

"Come on," Mae says. "Please. *That* would make me feel better."

"We'll stay here with you," Julie says.

Mae shakes her head. "I love y'all, but I should be alone. This isn't pretty."

"We got a 'y'all'!" I say, clapping. Julie and Molly join in.

"A 'y'all'!" Molly repeats. In a hillbilly accent, she adds, "A real, gen-u-ine 'y'all'!"

"My defenses are down," Mae mumbles.

"Yeah, we're not going anywhere," I say, moving to the foot of her bed.

She takes a deep breath and lifts a hand to her head. "Oh."

"You can't be alone," I tell her.

She's crying now.

"Aw, Maebs." Julie sits next to me. She's so light, the mattress doesn't sink under her weight. "If you don't want us here, we'll leave."

"This weekend is a disaster," she says. "I wanted us all to be together."

"We are," Molly says.

"Not like this." Her sobs yank her chest in, spit it back out. She's convulsing.

"Mae, please. Calm down. You're going to make yourself sicker," I tell her, putting a hand over her chest.

"Don't take advantage of the poor girl!" Molly says.

This gets me and Julie but not Mae. She's still beside herself. Or something. She's got a funny look on her face.

"*Shh,*" she says. "Do you hear that?"

The four of us go still as statues. There's a screaming. Distant, obscure, but there. It's more like a wail, a howl. Pure agony.

"What *is* that?" Molly asks, her eyebrows pinching together. She's scared.

Suddenly, the room gets smaller. It bears down on us. The door begins to clatter, rebel against its frame. The walls shake, the chandelier.

"You're seeing this?" Molly asks, slipping behind me, her new human shield.

The lights flicker, submerging us in moments of total darkness.

They come back on long enough for us to see Julie step toward the door.

"No," Molly says. "Don't open it."

Julie doesn't listen. She's at the door, hand on the knob. Even now, after everything she's been through, she can't help herself. She and I are the same that way. You could tell us, "Don't touch the stove. It's hot," but we'd have to see for ourselves. We'd need our palms burned to believe.

The door slams shut, sending a cold whoosh of air toward me. The lights are back, but the sound doesn't cease.

"What the hell is happening?" Molly asks. Mae lets another sob escape, but then she quiets, her lips puckered like a bad hem.

"There's no one out there," Julie says, coming back inside a second later. She covers her mouth to hide a yawn. "It's just the wind."

"The wind? No way," Molly says. "There's no fucking way."

"It sounds like that sometimes. When it gets really intense. It's like that up in Maine."

There's no window in Mae's room to look out of. We can't witness the brutality of the weather.

Julie grabs the remote and turns on the TV. She flips to the weather channel. "Weather advisory," she says. "See?"

A dark, menacing shape hovers over the Northeast. It's darkest over New York, above us. It begins to travel up the coast, eventually disappearing around Nova Scotia.

We're warned of rain. Hail. Winds up to sixty miles per hour.

"Power line might have gone down or something," Julie says, kicking off her shoes.

"It's October," Mae cries. I've never seen her like this.

"*Shh*, Maebs. *Shh*. It's okay. We're all happy to be here. We're having a good time. We can hang out in here. Play cards like old ladies," I tell her. "I've got a deck back in my room. I'll go get it, yeah? You up to it?"

She nods.

"Okay. I'll be right back."

"I'll go with you," Julie says.

I'm relieved I'm not going alone. There's a wicked voice in the back of my head telling me that it wasn't the wind, that Julie was wrong and that whatever was screaming, or whatever caused the screaming, is still out in the hall. Didn't sound like the wind to me.

I catch Molly's gaze and remember what being alone with Julie means. What I need to do. The anxiety spreads, quick and belligerent as a rash. "All right, after you."

"I feel like such a lady," Julie says, curtsying.

"You *are* a lady."

As soon as the door closes, Julie grabs me.

"Ah!"

She laughs. "Oh my God, you're so jumpy!"

"You grabbed me!"

"Not hard," she says. "Don't tell me you, too."

"What?"

"Molly is afraid of me."

"What do you mean?"

"Don't act like you haven't noticed," she says.

It's an invitation to have the talk. I should do it now. But her eyes are big and pretty and shining with mischief, and I love it when they get this way. I forgot how much I love being special to Julie, how good it feels to be on her team. She wouldn't talk to Mae about this. Not Molly, either, obviously. Just me.

"I mean, I'm used to people being weird toward me, but come on."

"Am I being weird?" I ask her.

"No more than usual," she says. "You and Mae are fine, but Molly can barely look at me. And when she does, it's like I'm disgusting to her."

"Really?"

"Yup."

"Are you going to talk to her about it?" I ask. I can't get my door to open. "I get that this key is supposed to be charming, but I miss key cards. *Boop.* That's it."

It's intensely cold in my room. I check the thermostat. It's at fifty.

"Great. The thermostat is officially busted. Look at it. It's a piece of shit. It's older than the hotel. I'm going to have to call Patsy."

"Let me see." Julie steps up to it. She turns the dial. "Why was it at fifty?"

"No idea. It's been doing that the whole time I've been here."

"Going to fifty?"

"No. Moving on its own."

"For sure a ghost," she says.

"Sorry. You were talking about Molls?"

"I don't have anything to add. I kind of expected her to be like this. Mae I thought would overcompensate, which she is, but, like, she always does, don't you think?"

"Agree, agree."

"You're you."

"Thank you."

"You're welcome," she says. "Hey, can I borrow your phone charger? Mine isn't working. It's definitely because it's terrible and stupid and not because I keep tripping over it and ripping it out of the socket."

"Sure." I unplug my charger and hand it to her.

"You're a dream," she says.

I find the cards in my bag. "What do you want to play?" I ask her.

"Uno."

"Crazy eights?"

"Jenga."

"Oh, I get it."

"Monopoly!"

"Jules."

"But I get to be the shoe."

"You can be whatever you want to be."

"I'm inspired."

"Should I call Patsy? About the thermostat?"

"I was gonna go downstairs to my room real quick to plug my phone in. I'll stop by the front desk."

"Really?"

"Yeah."

"Thanks, Julesy."

"For you, anything."

Molly opens the door for me. "Mae's in the bathroom again," she says. "What do we do?"

"How long has she been in there?"

"I don't know—like, five minutes? Where's Julie?"

"She went back to her room to plug her phone in."

"She couldn't do that here?"

"I dunno."

"Did you talk to her?"

"Didn't get a window. Listen, I'm sorry about what I said."

She raises an eyebrow. "Apology accepted."

"That was easy."

"Well, you're the only normal, nonpuking friend I have left! At least in this hotel."

"Aw, thanks!"

"I've been looking up walk-in clinics. There's one forty-five minutes away. Should I take her there?"

"That's the closest one?"

"Yeah," she says. "Better than nothing, though, right?"

"I'm not sure what they'll do for her there."

"She's really sick."

"I know. But there's no cure for food poisoning, and I don't know if all that time in the car is a good idea."

I want to add that if she wants out of here so badly, she shouldn't wait for an excuse to leave, but I bite my tongue.

Mae slogs out of the bathroom and gets back in bed. She's too weak to pull up the covers, so Molly and I help.

"Did you get the cards?" she asks.

"I got them."

"Good," she says, closing her eyes.

Molly puts a hand on her hip like a mom about to count to three. "Mae."

"That was the last of it," she says. "I'm fine. Promise."

Julie knocks. I let her in.

"I got ice for Maebs," she says, presenting me with a full bucket. She's winded, like she ran back up here. "What'd I miss?"

"Nothing at all," Molly says, sighing.

Instead of playing cards, we decide to watch TV. A marathon of bad reality shows. I sit next to Mae so I can apply a cold washcloth to her forehead. Julie curls up at the foot of the bed. Molly sits on the floor with a pillow behind her back and one under her legs.

Everything's fine. The mood has calmed. The wind has died down, or we can't hear it over the whining of the women on-screen.

I welcome their whining; it's like a strange lullaby. I was anxious before, but my brain's docile now. I've beaten it into submission with stupid TV.

"Do you think she knows what other people think about him, or is she not that insightful?" Julie asks about one of the women on the show.

"If she does know, she doesn't care. She paid a premium for the lifestyle," I say. Postulating about reality TV stars and celebrities is one of our favorite pastimes.

"I bet he's the kind of guy where at first she was really into him, but then she realized it was just the idea of him, but she stays because he's great *most* of the time. You know what I mean?" Julie asks.

"You guys are giving these people way too much credit," Molly says. "They're idiots."

Julie and I look at each other. We're smug. We know the truth about these strangers! No one else could possibly understand.

"Mae, you alive?"

She moans.

"What do you think, Maebs?"

"It's about her personal brand," she says, her voice scratchy from vomiting.

"Ughhhhh." Molly flops over.

This is the happiest I've been since I got here. I've got the new-crush giddiness but with old friends. I'm so happy to be with them and to be the version of myself I am when I'm around them.

I know this happiness is temporary. I think we all know that. This is borrowed time.

But it's how we operate. We run fast from the hard truths, and when they get close, grab at our ankles, we just kick them away, kick them away. But whatever's happening now with Julie, it's going to catch up to us. It's going to grab us by the ankles and bring us down, not let us go. It's going to change us.

So I don't care about anything but this moment. I'm going to let myself have it, this afternoon with them, because who knows when we'll be together again? And who knows if it will ever be the same?

"Mae, you should know I'm having a good time," I tell her. The washcloth has lost its chill. I sink it back into the ice bucket, which is now just a cold-water bucket.

"Me, too," Julie says. "This is all I need."

"Me, three," Molly says unconvincingly. She's fluffing her back pillow by punching it repeatedly. She's uncomfortable on the floor.

"You want the bed?" I ask her.

"I'm fine," she says.

"Hey, if you had to watch a reality show about someone we know, who would you pick?" Julie asks.

"In what world would I be forced to watch a reality TV show?" Molly asks.

Julie laughs. "Other than this one? Right now?"

"Fair enough."

"Everyone we know is too boring," says the lump of covers formerly known as Mae.

"Sassy, Mae."

She hasn't thrown up in two hours, which means we've been watching bad TV for two hours, and I regret nothing.

"More water?" I offer her the glass, and she drinks it down, no problem.

"I'm much better," she says. "You've nursed me back to health."

"Do you want anything? Ginger ale? Toast?"

"No, thank you. I'm good. But I don't think I'll be able to rally tonight," she says. "You guys should go down to the bar. Don't feel obligated to stay with me."

"Nowhere else I'd rather be," Julie says.

"Same," I say.

"Ditto," Molly says. "Love you, mean it."

"Next time we'll go somewhere warm," Mae says.

Julie shakes her head. "Heat is overrated."

"Speak for yourself!" Molly's got a blanket around her shoulders. She pulls it tight. It looks like a fuzzy straitjacket.

We continue watching TV. We add our color commentary. Molly and Julie have whiskey. I have gin. We order room service, and Mae offers to pay. She claims she's got a hint of an appetite. When we call down, they say they don't have a menu tonight; they just have pizza. We think that's weird, but we don't care. Pizza is pizza is pizza, cheese and bread. Can't go wrong with that.

"Maybe the kitchen is contaminated," Molly says.

Mae raises her hands to her face in horror. "Don't say that!"

Julie shrugs.

The pizzas (we got two, pepperoni and extra cheese) come in boxes. They were ordered from somewhere, some localish pizzeria. They're cold.

"Don't," Mae says before Molly can offer up the boxes as proof that something's awry in the kitchen.

"Pizza in bed," Julie says, picking the pepperoni off of her slice and eating it. "Like we're nineteen again."

"Do they have good pizza in LA?" I ask Molly.

"They have good everything in LA," she says. "Do they have good anything in Buffalo?"

"You're so funny, Molls. So hilarious," I tell her flatly. I feel compelled to answer, "Wings."

"Only teasing," she says.

"You can't beat Maine lobster," Julie announces with a splash of pride. "That's our thing."

"I don't like lobster. I don't like seafood in general, but lobster bothers me. Cooked alive in a pot of boiling water? Yikes." I remember being awed by the lobsters at the grocery store as a kid. Trapped in dirty, overcrowded tanks. Crawling over one another. Those blue bands that held their claws together, handicapping their God-given defense mechanisms. The water was always murky, a shade of brown or gray-green, and through it, they seemed to be nothing but legs, sadly awaiting execution and an afterlife of being slathered in butter and eaten by people who would talk about the quality and texture of their bodies.

I felt sorry for them, but they scared me. I thought they were ugly.

"Do you eat sushi?" Molly asks me.

"No. Does that make me uncool?"

"Yes."

We enter a long debate about which foods are cool. We discover we have staggeringly different views on this topic. The debate gets heated.

"A decade of friendship, and this is how it ends," Molly says. "Over Grape-Nuts and rice cakes."

After the few remaining slices of pizza have gone cold and dry, we abandon the food debate for one about music, then for one about which sides we would take in famous feuds, and then we fall down a dark rabbit hole that starts with a survey of the biggest dicks we've ever seen, turns to John Holmes, a hard left to the Wonderland murders, the Manson murders, Roman Polanski, Mia Farrow, Woody Allen, Diane Keaton, *The First Wives Club*, and ends with a sing-along of "You Don't Own Me."

After that, we're out of breath and out of steam. Mae's falling asleep.

"Mae, you need anything else? More water?"

She shakes her head no.

"Are you going to be all right?"

"Yeah," she mumbles.

"Make sure you sleep on your side," I tell her, propping a pillow behind her.

"Should someone stay with her?" Molly asks me.

"I'm fine," Mae says. "I'm going right to sleep."

"Want to come back to my room?" Julie asks us.

Molly shakes her head. "I think I'm going to turn in. I'm tired."

She might be lying. She might not want to be the third wheel with me and Julie. Sometimes Julie and I get on the same frequency, and it's hard for anyone else to join in.

Or she's trying to give me the opportunity to be alone with Julie so I can initiate "the talk."

"Lise, you want to come?"

"Yeah," I tell her. "I'll be up for a while. Haven't been able to sleep."

"You want melatonin?" Molly offers.

"Nah," I say. "I've got the good stuff."

"Oof. I don't fuck with that. I took Lunesta for a minute, and it wrecked me. You can sleepwalk off a bridge. For real! It happens."

Julie laughs. "That doesn't happen."

"I'm not going to sleepwalk off a bridge, Molly," I say. "Jules, I'm just going to change into my pj's real quick."

"Meet you downstairs?"

"Yep!"

"Night, Mae! Night, Molly." Julie reaches out to hug Molly. Molly leans back to avoid it, and Julie falls forward slightly. Her sweatshirt comes up, and underneath it her skin has a bluish tint, like a bad bruise, except it would have to be a massive bruise.

"Sorry," Molly says. "Lost my footing. I'm really tired."

Julie doesn't give up on the hug. Molly relents.

"Night, Julie," she says, patting her on the back. Tapping out of the embrace.

"You remember how to get to my room?" Jules asks me. I nod. She shoots me a thumbs-up. Then she leaves, closing the door carefully behind her.

Molly and I are quiet for a while. We listen to Mae's sweet little snores.

"You'll talk to her now?" Molly asks me.

"Mm."

"You need to."

"I know, Molly. I'm going to," I say. Her hounding me about it isn't the best motivation. "She knows, by the way. She knows you don't want to be around her."

"That's bullshit. I do want to be around her. But not like this. There's something wrong, and I don't know how to fix it. You know I'm bad with this kind of thing," she says. "You know that."

"I know." I wonder why she's allowed her flaws. Because her

problems stem from the trauma of childhood illness? I should be more understanding. I guess after almost ten years of excusing certain behaviors, I don't have as much sympathy as I used to. It's not good.

"I'm bad with feelings and emotions and articulating. I come off as aggressive," she says. "You can be honest without being harsh. But you're not soft, like this one."

She gestures to Mae, who furrows her brow. She's not entirely asleep. She's listening.

When I look back at Molly, it bubbles up. "It hurts me," I tell her, "that you think so low of me because of my past relationship."

She's surprised I'm bringing this up now. I don't blame her. We've danced around it for years.

She chooses her words carefully. Speaks them slowly. "You think I look down on you because of it. I don't. I just wish you wanted better for yourself."

"Okay."

"It frustrates me. I don't know what to do with that frustration. It breaks my heart."

"See, you're good at talking feelings."

"Shut up."

"I make a lot of mistakes, Molly. I have in the past, and I will in the future. Will you love me anyway?"

"Don't be an idiot," she says. That's her answer.

"I have to tell you something. And I need you not to judge me."

"Okay," she says. "You can tell me."

"You were right. About me, with Tristan. I mean, nothing's happened. We just talk."

"You just talk?"

"Yes, just talk. It started after the funeral. We both felt like she was still out there, and we sort of bonded over that, over missing Julie but not being able to mourn her."

"Did you talk about being together?"

"No, it wasn't like that," I say. "Not really."

"What do you mean, 'not really'? Do you have feelings for him?"

"Yes," I say. "But I can't tell if I want him or if I just want someone."

And there it is. Sometimes I surprise myself with the truth. I guess it's been there this whole time, living inside me, rent-free.

"Why didn't you tell us?" Molly asks. I have to give her credit; she's being very gentle with me.

"Because . . . it's not a good look. And with my past, I just . . . I knew you'd be mad."

"I'm not mad," she says. "This is a different situation. Is it fucked-up? Yeah, a little bit. All I want is for you to be honest with me and honest with yourself. Okay? You need to face reality here, Lise."

"I have."

"Yeah? You know that nothing can ever happen between you two, right? You get that? You've accepted that?"

"Yes, I know I will never be with Tristan," I say, and I mean it. "I know, Molly. There's nothing there. It's over. It's done."

"Okay. Good. Look, I'm not mad. Swear it. I am legit exhausted, though," she says. "We'll revisit this unsavory subject tomorrow. Preferably with alcohol."

"Yes."

"Do we have to hug now or something?"

"No, Molls. You're free to go," I say.

"Love you. You're a complete mess, but I love you," she says, shaking her head. "See you in the morning? I'll come by your room. You can tell me what happens with Julie."

"Sounds good."

We make sure that Mae is propped up by enough pillows and that her phone is handy.

"Call us if you need anything," I say.

"Mm, 'kay."

We realize we don't have any way of locking the door; it can be locked only with the key or from the inside. We shrug it off.

"Night, Lise. Godspeed."

"Night, Molls."

The thermostat appears to be fixed. It's at a comfortable seventy-two degrees. I change into a pair of joggers and a waffle knit. Hang uniform.

Before I leave, I check the door to the balcony. It's locked. For some reason, I get the idea that the tall, dark figure I've been seeing glimpses of ever since I got here is standing outside my room. Not on the balcony, but across the lawn, at the edge of the woods. If I pull back the curtains enough so I can fit my eyeball inside the opening, I would see it there. A gangly shadow thing. Waiting. Waiting for me.

The hotel is dead. There aren't many people around. In the hallway I pass a couple dressed in bathing suits and cover-ups, their hair damp and chlorine frizzed. I forgot this place has a pool. I see a stressed-out maid gathering towels while balancing a spray bottle of cleaner on her elbow. I smile at her, but she doesn't notice me.

I need to focus. Strategize. How can I talk to Julie about what

Tristan told me without raising any questions about my relationship with him?

I called him as a concerned friend. That's the truth.

I wonder how she'll react when I bring it up. Maybe it's what she
wants. Maybe it's all been a cry for help.

Busy contemplating my approach to the impending conversation, I seem to have gotten myself lost. I thought Julie's room was
down this hall, but this might actually be where Molly's room is.
There's a series of doors with strange names. There are no room
numbers or arrows or maps.

I backtrack. I ask the maid, "Excuse me—I'm looking for the
Lenore room?"

When she looks up at me, I feel sorry for her. She looks utterly
beat. She doesn't verbalize her answer. She points.

"Back there? Left?"

She nods.

"Thank you."

The second hallway looks identical to the first, but this time I
find Lenore. I knock twice.

"It's open."

The room smells horrific. Putrid. I remember the decor being
more playful than bleak, but it's oppressive. It's also freezing cold
in here.

Julie is in one of the armchairs. She's got an open bag of beef
jerky in her lap. Her legs are up on a small accent table.

"Come sit," she says.

In this light, I see nothing of the Julie from fifteen minutes ago.
Her skin looks like putty chaotically molded onto her bones. Like
underneath her face there's another face eating its way out. Her

eyes are sunken again, so deep she looks completely different. I can see her scalp through her hair, dry and patchy, like it survived a fire.

"What's wrong?" she asks innocently enough.

"Nothing," I say, realizing my left hand is still on the doorknob. I let it go. My right hand was in so tight a fist, my nails dug into my skin. I look down and see little crescent moons along my palm.

"Jerky?" she offers.

"No, thanks."

"I poured you a whiskey," she says, pointing to a glass on the nightstand. "What'd Molly say about me?"

"Nothing," I tell her. "Why?"

"Did you see how she refused to hug me?"

"She's bad with intimacy."

"She hugs you."

The air in the room is so foul, I'm afraid to inhale. Bizarre shadows skulk in corners. The ceiling is high, but the walls are too close and it's claustrophobic. It's crowded. It doesn't feel like it's just the two of us in here. It's like it's packed. Shoulder to shoulder with invisible people. I feel their breath. The grandfather clock *tick-tick*s. The pendulum swings.

I sit down on the bed, take a swig of whiskey.

"Molly is Molly. You can't take it personally," I say. "I confronted her about some of the stuff between us. How she's acted toward me since I moved to Buffalo."

"What'd she say?" Julie doesn't stop chewing. She spits out a tooth, gives it a careless glance before setting it down on the table. She pops another piece of jerky into her mouth. Unfazed.

"She said she was sorry." I don't remember if that's what she said. I have no idea what she said. I can't believe what just happened. "Did you lose another tooth?"

"Yeah," she says. "That's it? She was sorry?"

"Are you okay?"

"I'm fine," she says in a tone that lets me know she's not going to entertain any more questions. "That's it?"

"She said she wanted me to want better for myself."

"And what do you think?"

"I'm not sure."

"Elise, it's me."

And for a second, it is. It's Julie. If I don't look at her, if I just listen, it's her. I pick at my cuticles and pretend we're back in our dorm, back in our twin XL beds, surrounded by cinder block walls and vents leaking secondhand marijuana smoke.

"I don't know. I did what made me happy. I did something for myself. Before then, any decision I made was motivated by what I thought other people wanted or expected of me. I didn't want to disappoint anyone. Lu, Rick, my dad. Lu isn't my mom. Rick isn't my dad. They didn't have to take care of me. And I guess with my real dad, I thought I had something to prove."

"Makes sense," she says, tossing aside the empty bag of jerky.

"When I moved to Buffalo, it was for love. It wasn't because of the affair. It was in spite of it, if that makes sense. I wasn't in it for the drama. I loved him. And he made me feel loved. It wasn't conventional, and maybe it wasn't right, but it was love. I liked to be around him. He made me feel good. I wasn't punishing myself. It wasn't because I didn't think I deserved better. If anything, it's because I thought I deserved too much."

"How do you mean?" she says. She gets up, gets another bag of jerky out of her suitcase. I'm not sure she's listening to me. It's the first time I'm talking about this, and she's more interested in dried meat.

"Um," I say. "I don't know. I thought I deserved to be happy."

"You think that? Not just because the Bible tells us so?"

"Does it?"

"Fuck if I know. Clearly I've never read it."

I fake laugh. My eyes refuse to look at her. I can hear her chewing, teeth scraping together, the swish of saliva. I keep talking, mostly to distract myself from the sounds she's making,

"I mean, in retrospect, I thought I deserved happiness more than other people because of my past. Losing my mom, my dad being an asshole. I thought I had a right to happiness. It was owed to me. I didn't care about the logistics, who I was hurting. I felt entitled to it. And I'm not. No one is."

"You don't think happiness is a right?"

"No. It's a bonus."

"Huh."

"Do you?"

"Think I'm entitled to it? I've never really thought about it. I never felt deserving of anything."

"Jules."

"It's true. I wanted things very badly, but I didn't feel like I deserved them. Even if I became a famous actress or singer, or if I worked my way up at the label, whatever, I would feel like an impostor. I want things, and I'm sad if I don't get them or if it doesn't work out, but I'm also relieved. When I get what I want, it doesn't make me happy. It makes me feel guilty," she says. "Like with Tristan."

"What about Tristan?"

"I wanted him. I had a crush on him in high school. Not a big one, but when I saw him again, I was, like, overwhelmed by him. I needed to be with him. And it was easy. He wanted me, too. He wanted to get married. And when we did, I was standing there across from him, like, completely . . . I can't think of any other word but 'revolted.' It's too strong for what I'm trying to say, but you get it. I almost ran out midceremony. I thought, *How can I do this to this person I care about? He doesn't want to be with me. He doesn't know it yet, but he will soon. And when he does, it'll be too late. He's too good of a guy to ever leave me. He'll be stuck with me and be unhappy. And I'll be unhappy, too, because I'll feel guilty, because I'll get bored. I'll decide I want something else, and he'll bore me.*"

"Do you feel like that now?"

"Can't say with the whole disappearing for two years. I don't know if it's improved our relationship or if we're completely screwed. I haven't had time to parse out my feelings, you know?"

"Yeah. It'll take time." I wish I hadn't said that. I wish I'd said, "I have to tell you something." If I let this opportunity pass and don't tell her what happened between me and him while she was gone, I never will.

"Molly can be so judgmental," Julie says. "Not like she dates."

"She doesn't want to. She's happy alone."

Julie snorts. "No one's happy alone."

"Molly is."

"I don't know what her problem is. She thought I was dead, and here I am, and she treats me like this?"

I make the mistake of looking at her. Her eyes are so bloodshot, they're almost completely red. Her lips are covered in thick flakes of dead skin.

"You, too," she says. "And Mae. I come back, and you don't treat me the same."

"How?"

"If you could see your face right now."

I play dumb. "What?"

Her shadow fans out behind her on the wall, making her seem bigger than she is. She licks her teeth, so sharp and uneven I worry she'll cut her tongue. "I love you all. You're the loves of my life. You especially. You're like a sister to me. You're more my sister than Jade is."

"I feel the same, Jules. I love you so, so much. You know that, don't you?"

"I know," she says. "But you should be careful."

"What?"

She leans forward, puts a hand on my knee. "The more you love someone, the more you make yourself vulnerable to them, and it's easier for them to hurt you. Because you care so much, and because their love will inevitably fall short of your love. Your love is too big. And then, when it doesn't measure up, you're hurt. And that hurt turns to hate. To love someone is to hate them, a little bit. We hate everyone we really love."

"I don't know what you're trying to tell me."

"Nothing," she says. "You look tired. Did you take your sleeping pill?"

"Uh, no, not yet."

"I got some serious pills when I got back. They refilled my prescriptions no questions asked. Everyone knows my deal," she says, laughing. "I think they're afraid of me."

"The girl who lived."

She winks at me. She loses eyelashes in the process.

The days of us standing hip to hip at the bathroom counter sharing mascara and mindless gossip, they're gone. I'm looking at her now, seeing her now, and it can't wait any longer.

"Jules, I know it's a hard subject," I say, wrestling with each word. "But I think we need to talk about what's going on with you."

"What do you mean?"

"You're losing your teeth. You don't . . . you don't look well."

"It's sweet of you to worry, Lise. But I'm good. I feel good. Honest."

"You were gone for two years. Do you really not remember anything?"

"I already told you I don't," she says, lips curling.

"I know, Jules. But you have to understand what that time was like for me, for all of us. I watched Molly and Mae cry at your funeral."

"Did *you* cry?"

"I missed you every day you were gone," I say. "I want to help you, but you have to be honest with me."

She lifts her chin. "Don't you trust me?"

Having to say it makes me nauseated, expel an aggressive sweat. My throat tightens the way it does before I cry, and when I speak, I sound like a stranger. "I talked to Tristan. I know you were eating raw meat."

"Tristan told you that?" she asks. I can't read her. I can't tell if she's surprised or upset or couldn't care less. "That I was eating raw meat?"

"He saw you."

"He's been really struggling, poor guy. I worry about him."

"Jules, there's something I need to be honest with you about," I say, and down the rest of my whiskey. If I'm honest with her, maybe she'll be honest with me.

Or maybe she'll hate me.

"After your funeral," I say, "he and I started talking. As friends. We got pretty close. It was platonic, of course. We never saw each other. But we talked a lot. I don't know if I crossed a line."

I wait for her to interject, to react, but she doesn't. I take a deep breath. "I'd be lying if I said I didn't feel some type of way about him. I don't know if I ever would have acted on it. I don't think he would ever, even if he felt the same. I don't think he did. We were both lonely. We relied on each other to get through our grief. That's it, really. I needed you to know. I'm sorry."

"Grief? But you knew I wasn't gone," she says. She seems more bored than upset. Like she's waiting in line somewhere, and it's taking too long.

"I knew, yes. In my gut, in my heart, I believed you were still here. But it didn't make sense. Everyone thought I was crazy. Sometimes I thought I was crazy. Holding on to something because I couldn't accept the truth. Tristan understood in a way that Molly and Mae didn't. That's why it was so good to talk to him. We could say to each other what we couldn't say to anyone else."

"Okay," she says.

"Part of it, honestly . . . I think your life appealed to me. You had something good going. A home, a business, a partner. I wanted some of what you had. Or to know what it was like. I was lonely. I'm sorry. I know how messed up it is. I feel so guilty. I don't want you to think I was trying to steal your husband. I know what it looks like, with my track record. But I swear that's not what it was."

"If you say so," she says, licking her fingers. She appears unaffected.

"Julie," I start, not knowing how to finish. I shift. My foot hits something.

There's a pair of glasses on the floor, poking out from under the bed. Vintage cat-eye frames.

The glasses the girl at reception was wearing. The one who checked me in.

"Jules, why do you have these glasses?"

"You look really tired, Elise. Maybe you should lie down. You can sleep here with me. It'll be like old times."

"No, that's okay," I say. I feel ill. "Why do you have these glasses?"

She shrugs. "Girl must have dropped them."

"When?"

"When she brought me up to the room. I don't know," she says, irritated. "Are you sure you don't want to sleep over?"

"Yeah, I'm gonna go upstairs," I say. "I should get to bed. We can talk more in the morning, okay?"

"Stay here."

"No," I say too harshly. "I'm not feeling great."

"Let me walk you upstairs," she says, standing.

"I'm all right. Really. I think we should both take the night. Talk tomorrow."

"I'll come up in the morning." She hugs me, pressing against me so hard, I'm sure her bones will puncture my skin. I can't identify the smell. It's like spoiled milk, hot garbage. It's so bad, I'm embarrassed.

The clock gives a raucous cry. My shoulders shoot to my ears.

"Don't let the clock scare you," she says. "It's only time."

I make sure the door latches behind me. What the hell just happened?

Why would she have those glasses?

I don't have the energy to berate myself for giving up on the confrontation. Right now I'm so disturbed, so drained, all I want to do is get back to my room. I shouldn't have had that whiskey. My head is spinning.

There's toile wallpaper in this hallway. Since when? I must not have been paying attention before. It's a drastic deviation in style from the rest of the hotel, but I guess it's not entirely surprising. The Red Honey Inn is an amalgam of different styles and colors and patterns. Why not throw in some French country? Next hall over is Art Deco. Here, you time travel when you turn the corner. You're in different places all at once.

The wallpaper is the classic cream color with dark navy outlining various scenes. Colonialish men and women picnicking under a tree, children dancing with their hands clasped together, a rooster, a man chopping wood outside a farmhouse, a lady on a swing, a lamb nestled in the grass.

My vision blurs as I inspect the wallpaper as I hurry past. I have to stop and close my eyes to prevent a dizzy spell like the one I had earlier in Mae's room. I'm on the brink. I'm about to pass out. I take a deep breath. As I exhale, I hear a soft tap.

I open my eyes. There's no one else in the hallway.

Another deep breath.

There it is again!

Tap. Tap.

I stand sideways so I can see the whole length of the hall. There's no one around. I step forward, split my stance to steady myself, but it's not enough. The floor beneath me skews. I lean into the wall, rest my forehead against it with both palms flat.

I battle for each breath.

Tap, tap.

My eyes register movement. In front of me. On the wall.

The wallpaper is moving. The figures slowly distort. The picnic guests turn toward one another; the lamb stirs. The lady on the swing soars through the air. The children go round and round. They shrink and expand, double, warp.

I close my eyes, concentrate on my breath.

The tapping is more frequent, more intense. I press my ear to the wall. The sound is coming from inside. The sound is coming from inside the wall.

I step back, and I see it. A vent. It's low, long and wide, with an intricate white cover.

I crouch down. And through the narrow gaps in the pattern, I see nothing but total darkness. I lean closer.

There's a smell. Like the smell in Julie's room. Like something rotten.

I get the feeling, the one I'm so familiar with. The one I torture myself with. The feeling that someone is watching me.

Tap, tap. It's dripping. Something's dripping. But it's more than that. I hear breathing. Deep, wheezing breaths. For a brief moment, I swear there's a third sound. Chewing.

I turn onto my hands and knees, stumble to stand. I'm too dizzy to run, but I go as fast as I can.

I hit a fork at the end of the hall. I thought Julie's room was at the back of the hotel, but there's an adjacent hallway to the right. And across from it there's another hallway, marked with a sign for the pool and an arrow.

I go the opposite direction, toward the lobby, toward the stairs. I feel so weak, I'm going to have to climb up them on all fours.

I don't hear any voices drifting out of the bar or the lounge. I don't hear anything at all.

I'm alone. I'm totally alone.

I lean on the banister. A hostile nausea raids my whole body. I can barely walk. My legs, my feet—they're cast in iron. There's a fog rolling in my head.

I need to get back to my room. I need my car keys. I need to get out of this hotel.

I'm sweating. It's streaming down, soaking my clothes. It takes all of my energy to lift the key, to open the door. To lock it behind me.

I have to lie down for a minute. Close my eyes, just for a minute. I feel so heavy, I think I might sink through the mattress. I think it might swallow me up.

VII

My eyes are open. There's nothing to see. I pick at the crust settled in my tear ducts, the residue of yesterday's mascara stuck to my lashes. I've been asleep for a long time. I yawn and turn over onto my stomach. I've leaned into a cloud of my own morning breath, and it's lethal. I'm awake now.

I wish I wasn't. I feel like I've been hit by a truck.

I fumble around for my phone on the nightstand. It's dead. I reach for my charger.

Where the hell did I put it?

The outbreak of goose bumps tips me off on what my brain is slow to process. Then comes the sinking feeling, an anchor dropping, dropping, finding no bottom, no place to rest.

Last night.

Whatever's happening here, whatever's happening with Julie, it's worse than we thought or could have ever imagined.

I shove my face into the pillow. "Fuck!"

I have to find Molly and Mae. I have to tell them about last night, about what Tristan told me. Anticipating the looks on their faces, I can't stand it.

What time is it? Must be midmorning at least. Gray light fills the gaps between the window frame and the curtains. I reach over to open the curtains.

I hesitate.

What if someone's there? What if I pull back the curtains and there's a figure standing there, looking down on me with dark, hollow eyes?

I open the curtains, and no one's there to greet me. Just another rainy day.

The trees are stiff and naked. The wind must have seized the leaves yesterday during its tantrum, while it was running around screaming its head off. There's a layer of frost over the grass, icy spines holding it at attention. Thanks for nothing, October.

When I was little, five or six, I got lost at the mall. I was a pretty spacey kid, and I wasn't paying attention to where I was going. I got distracted people watching or peering into store windows, and when it eventually became clear I had wandered off, I saw Lu, ran to her, touched her leg, and when she looked back at me, she had a different face. It wasn't Lu, just another tall woman in jeans. She had the same hair. Long, thick and dark, in a ponytail that swiped the small of her back. When that woman looked at me, I started to cry.

She didn't stop to ask me why. She kept walking. I had to find the security kiosk on my own. I remember telling myself, *Don't look lost. Don't look lost.* If a stranger saw me and realized I was lost, realized I was alone, he might take me. Lu had warned me about strangers. So had Ms. Chantel, my kindergarten teacher. I was incredulous. I never thought it could happen to me, getting lost, getting taken. It happened to other kids. Stupid kids. Loud kids with overbites who didn't listen in class.

I saw a man in a security uniform and approached him. He walked me to the kiosk, and Lu was there waiting. She was biting her nails, her nervous habit, but when she saw how upset I was, she relaxed. She was good at that, at adapting her mood to fit my needs.

"Hey, kiddo," she said. "Too cool to shop with me?"

I sobbed and hugged her legs. She took me to the food court, and we ate Nathan's hot dogs and crinkle-cut fries covered in soupy orange cheese.

It was the first time in my life I had felt like I was in danger. I realized I'd taken my safety for granted. I realized it was possible to get lost and not know how to get back. I learned what it was like to feel helpless.

That's exactly how I feel now. Like I'm helpless. Like I'm in danger.

I'm wearing yesterday's clothes. I don't bother to change. I'm torn between a powerful sense of urgency and an even more powerful sense of dread. Between accepting what's happening and refusing to accept what's happening. Or refusing to do anything about it.

I'm scared.

I dig for the version of myself who broke into her lover's family's house. I need that version right now. I'm not brave, but I can detach from reality enough not to be as scared as I should be.

I open the door.

I go down the hall to Mae's room. I knock. No answer. They're probably in the dining room.

There are actually people out and about today. People walking with their suitcases rolling at their heels. There's a crowd at the bottom of the stairs. The hotel has been pretty empty since we got here, so it's a little weird. They're all talking in hushed voices. I hear *s*'s and *p*'s.

My chest tightens.

Maybe it's just a big group all checking out at once.

The lounge is empty. The fireplace is dark. It coughed up some ash onto the hearth no one bothered to sweep up. There's an open book on one of the couches. I close it to look at the cover. *The Magic of the Catskills: Images.* I set it on a nearby end table, next to a lonely mug with pink lipstick smudged around the rim. It's three-quarters full of a black liquid that's either coffee or tea. I hold my hand over it. Whatever it is, it's cold.

On the floor there's a used napkin marked with the same pink lipstick.

I leave it, even though its presence there makes me itch. I don't like a mess. The slight disorder of the scene isn't sitting right with me. But whoever left the lipstick might have spit into that napkin. Sneezed into it. I don't know.

"Elise!" Molly is rushing toward me. "Elise, what the fuck? I've been calling you for hours."

"My phone is dead. Why? What's up?"

"What's up? Hello! Everyone's leaving! They're closing the hotel. Something weird is going on," she says. She's in a frenzy. Her hair's disheveled, her eyes dark and wild. "Mae is still sick. And I don't feel so hot, either."

"What do you mean? Why? Where's Mae?"

"Mae's in my room. I went to check on her this morning and just . . ." She pauses, puts her hand over her mouth. She takes a deep breath. "She sweat through her sheets, and she's, like, completely out of it. It's scaring me."

"Where's Julie?"

"Straight to voice mail. I figured you were together."

"No. I just woke up," I say. "Molly, I have to tell you something."

"Not now, Lise. I need, like, toast or crackers or something for Mae. A bottle of water or, like, a Gatorade or something with electrolytes. I have to get back to my room. I left her alone. Can you get something and meet us there? Get your bags and shit, too. We need to get out of here."

"Okay, yeah."

"What a fucking nightmare," she says, hurrying away. "Fucking nightmare!"

If she thinks things are bad now, wait until I tell her about Julie. Spitting out teeth. The raw meat. The smell.

The hotel is closing. We're leaving. I would be relieved, if I could only get past the horrible nag of why.

The bar is empty. There's no one behind it. There are glasses out. Most still have some drink left in them, a few with a stray maraschino cherry or orange rind. They sweat onto thin multicolored coasters monogramed with "RH" in a romantic font. The Red Honey Inn.

Not knowing what else to do, I walk behind the bar. There's a bucket of melting ice on the floor. A scoop floats idly inside on its back. Beside the bucket, there are a pile of dirty dishrags and a lone bar spoon. I've always thought bar spoons look like weapons, with their long, twisted handles. The placement of this particular spoon isn't helping to convince me otherwise.

There's a mini fridge full of Red Bull. No water. No Gatorade.

I leave the bar and step onto the carpet in the dining room. There's a web of booths in front of me, too many to count. They're all empty. My eyes travel back and forth, back and forth until they catch on each other.

"Hello?" I hear myself say. The word echoes in this vault of a room. My heart turns elastic. It's expanding, filling my whole body. My forehead, my gut, down to my littlest toes. It's flooding my ears with its mounting thumps.

"Hello?" I say, more loudly this time, hoping to make the walls shake. I take a glass off a table just to prove that I can, to prove that this isn't a dream, that I'm real. I hold it in my hand, and it's not a relief. "Can someone help me?"

Some of the tables are clean set, but most haven't been cleared. Plates linger. Food picked over. There are flies devouring stacks of pancakes and scrambled eggs. There's toast covered in jam with a single bite taken out. More cups of cold coffee. Overflows of cream curdling in shallow saucers.

When is this from?

Some chairs are turned over. On their sides, their backs, their fronts. It almost looks intentional, like an abstract art exhibit at MoMA that people would call "provocative" because they think it makes them sound insightful.

Something about this feels like an elaborate prank. It looks staged.

"Hello?"

Somewhere, a pan drops on the floor, making the sound of a church bell.

I make my way through the obstacle course of chairs and booths, push open the kitchen door.

"Hello? I'm looking for . . ."

I'm crossing the threshold into the kitchen when it occurs to me that maybe I shouldn't be heading toward the noise. Maybe I should be running from it.

My shoes squeak against the linoleum. I slide. I look down at what's slippery. It's very red.

The kitchen is drenched in blood. There are slaughtered body parts strewn across the floor. Unraveled intestines. Pulsing, spongy chunks. There's a detached pink head at my feet, with fuzzy flesh-colored ears. A pig's. It's a pig's.

The scene is so gruesome, so grisly. I'm caught seizing in a fit of panicked dry heaves. I can feel none of my body. I'm a convulsing chest.

There are two hulking double fridges to my left, and directly in front of me is the window, with incomplete tickets hanging down, spaced like adolescent teeth. Through it I can see the line, a series of ovens and stove tops. There are pots and pans on the stove, the contents filmy, spotted, deformed.

I get sick in my mouth and spit it away from me.

The sharp ringing in my ears gives way to a frantic thrashing. I assume it's my organs rioting from the inside, but soon it's clear it's not coming from me. It's coming from somewhere in the kitchen. To the right, there's a short hallway. More fridges. More ovens. There's probably a freezer back there. A nook for fresh produce or racks of baked goods. There must be a person hiding, making this horrible noise.

But it's not a person noise. It's a thick, slimy sound. I've never heard anything like it.

I look down, down at the pig's head, as its mouth falls open, tongue bobs. As it begins to glide around, glide toward me on a river of its own blood.

I stumble backward.

I get the fuck out of the kitchen.

A butchering accident?

A bear attack?

What other possible explanation?

How was it moving its mouth like that? I swear I saw it blink. Do pigs keep on living after their heads get cut off? Like chickens? Is that just a rumor? Something the class bully tells girls during recess to make them shriek?

How long do our bodies go on without us? Twitching, free of thought.

Is this why the hotel is closing?

I have to get back to my room, get my car keys. I have to get back to Molly and Mae. My phone is dead and useless in my back pocket. I have to go.

I trip over my feet running through the dining room, past the bar, out of the lounge. I bang my shins falling up the staircase. I'm sprinting down the hall, room key in hand. But it's that thing, isn't it? My body is so panicked, it can't do anything right. It can't even open a goddamn door.

I finally get it open, slip inside, lock it behind me.

Car keys. I need my car keys. I grab them and my wallet out of my purse and put them in my pockets. I toss my bag onto the bed and start packing. My hands are shaking so badly, I have to stop. I take a deep breath, attempt to make fists. When I look up, I notice that the sliver of light on the right-hand side of the window, where the curtain falls just shy of meeting the frame, is missing. Mostly. There's still light coming in from above. From the top. But it stops, at the height of a very tall person.

There's a very tall person standing outside my window. I don't know how long they've been there. They're watching me—this I'm sure of. Because when I see them, they bang on the glass.

I fall backward like there's a string tied around my spine being pulled by some almighty force, like I'm a marionette. My limbs extend at odd angles, swinging around my joints unrestrained.

There's more banging on the window. The glass is on the verge of cracking. I hear it squealing.

My body is now working without me. I'm out in the hall, my room door shut behind me. I'm on alien legs. They're not mine. I've never seen my legs move this way, this efficiently.

I visualize myself running past reception, through the lobby, out the front doors, onto the lawn, leaving garden gnomes in my dust as I hurl myself across the parking lot to my car. I'll start the engine, lock the doors, peel out of here.

But I can't. I need Molly and Mae.

I turn a corner and nearly smash into someone.

It's Patsy. Her hair's insane; she's wearing ripped khakis and a ratty gift shop T-shirt that reads HILTON HEAD.

"Pardon me," she says. "I need you to please head to the lobby for checkout."

I can't articulate. I can't catch my breath.

She clears her throat. "We're closing the hotel."

"Why?"

She clears her throat again. "I'm sorry, miss. We're closing the hotel due to a staffing issue."

"Staffing issue?"

"Yes. Now, if I can please ask you to gather your luggage and sign out in the lobby . . ."

"Is this about the pig?" I ask.

She frowns. "The pig?"

If she doesn't know, I'm not going to be the one to tell her.

"What do you mean, staffing issues?" I ask.

She sighs. "We're having trouble . . . locating some of the staff. We want our guests to have the best possible experience, and unfortunately—"

"The receptionist? The girl who checked me in—she wore vintage glasses. Where is she?"

Patsy takes the question like a big pill, with a hard swallow, her head back. She pauses, and it's long enough for me to know she's not going to give me an answer. "We do not currently have enough staff to run the hotel properly. We're very sorry for the inconvenience," she says. She looks like she hasn't slept in days. "You will be issued a full refund for the duration of your stay. We hope that you understand and that you'll come visit us again soon."

"Someone just tried to break into my room," I tell her. "There's something else going on here."

No one's ever looked at me the way she's looking at me, with what might be pity or disdain. "Where's your luggage?"

"It's still in my room."

"I can assist you. Cassandra suite, yes?"

"Yeah."

She puts her hand on the small of my back to direct me toward the stairs. I don't want to go back up there.

"Actually, I need to meet my friends. I'll get my stuff later."

"I can get it for you. You can pick it up when you check out."

"No. I'll get it. Later," I say. "It's fine."

"I insist. It's the least I can do."

I lean into her. "I don't think you should go upstairs."

"I'm going to bring your things to reception. They'll be here when you check out. And please, do check out as soon as possible."

She's not going to listen to me. She's not going to take no for an answer. She doesn't understand.

"Be careful," I tell her.

She nods, lingers, looks at me funny for an excess of seconds.

Her brows sink, and her lips snap together. I can see the wiry gray hairs at her temples, not long enough to be confined by her giant hair clip, which looks like some kind of crustacean adhered to the side of her head. I can smell her BO and the gardenia perfume she slathered on her pulse points this morning.

"Will do," she says. She jingles the set of keys she's wearing around her wrist like a gaudy bracelet. The sound fades as she walks away.

I sprint to Molly's room. She's got the door open before I finish knocking. She looks me up and down. "Where are the crackers?"

"I couldn't find any," I say. I don't see the point in telling her about the pig or what just happened in my room. It will only make things worse, more chaotic. "The kitchen was locked."

She lets out an exasperated breath. "I've got all our shit packed. I'll need your help getting Mae out to the car."

Mae is folded delicately on the bed. Her opalescent hair is set in a neat bun at the top of her head. She's wearing silk pants and a matching blouse. Forever chic.

She sits up. "Lise."

"Mae, relax. You're making yourself sicker," Molly says.

"Hey, honey." I kneel at the edge of the bed. "Hanging in?"

"This weekend," she says. "It's on me."

"It's not, Maebs. Don't worry about it, okay?"

"Oh, God." Molly's patience is up.

"We have to get you to a doctor, miss," I tell Mae. "You ready?" She slowly swings her legs around.

"Wait," she says, patting my hand. "Where's Julie?"

I look down at my hands. I see they're shaking. I see my nails bitten into jagged stubs. I wanted to get a manicure before this trip, but I couldn't afford it. I wanted to pick a fun color and have Mae say something nice. A compliment from her means something more. It just does.

"Julie?" Mae asks again.

"She's not here," Molly says. "She probably left an hour ago. Like, when we should have left. Come on, Mae. Elise, help her." Molly's got the bags hanging off her shoulders.

"Did you talk to Tristan?" Mae asks me.

I don't know what it is. Her hand perched on mine, small and fragile like a baby bird, or maybe it's her eyes. She's not wearing her glasses. There's no barrier between us, and her eyes are so beautiful, an ancient blue.

It's exhuming the guilt, the shame of what I've omitted, to them and to myself. I should have told them last night. I should have told them as soon as I got off the phone with Tristan. What do I say now?

"What is it?" Mae asks me.

"What?" Molly shifts her weight and sets the bags down. "Did you have the conversation with Julie last night?"

"What conversation?" Mae asks.

"I tried. She said she was fine. But she looked . . . I don't know. Unwell. She was eating beef jerky, and she . . . she lost another tooth," I say. "When I talked to Tristan, he said some things. I should have told you."

"Told me what?" Molly asks.

I put my palms over my eyes. "He saw her sleeping outside. And eating raw meat."

I imagine this is what it's like in the immediate aftermath of an explosion. A moment suspended in shock. I understand now the truth of why I didn't tell them. We might never come back from this. This might be the end of us.

"What the fuck is wrong with you? How could you not tell us? What the hell were you thinking?"

"Molly," Mae says.

"Elise, I love you—you know I do—but I swear to God you need to wake the fuck up! Wake up! Both of you!"

"Molls," I say, begging.

"Raw meat? Jesus Christ. Jesus. Why didn't he take her to a fucking doctor? Why can't anyone step up and *do* something?" I've never seen her this angry. She's crying. The tears sizzle on her cheeks. She paces, punching at the air. "You know why? Because none of us can talk about anything. No one can be honest. Everyone's too fucking afraid."

"Elise," Mae says, "what exactly did he say?"

"It doesn't matter," Molly says, leaning down to pick up the bags. "We're leaving. We can call nine-one-one from the car."

"Nine-one-one?" I ask.

"Yeah. Have any better ideas." It's not a question.

"Come on, Maebs." I stand up, slip my arm under hers and lift. She's not deadweight. She's helium. I'm not worried she'll fall if I let go. I'm worried she'll float away.

Molly gets the door, propping it open for us with her foot. She's shaking her head at me, taking erratic breaths, muttering. Seeing her this upset is devastation I was not prepared for.

"I'm sorry," I whisper in Mae's ear.

"We were doing our best," she says. "We *are* doing our best."

The hotel is different now. Hollow. It spits our sounds back at us. Every footstep, every sigh.

"What do we do about Julie? We just leave her here?" I ask Mae. She doesn't respond.

"Mae?"

"I don't know, Lise."

We turn the corner to the lobby. There's no one there. Everyone's gone.

There's something unsettling about seeing a room like this empty. There's too much space for it not to be occupied. Light reflects between the mirrors on the walls. I can see dust particles swimming, delicate cobwebs in the corners.

Molly lets the bags go. They smack against the ground like fallen bodies.

"Hello?" Molly says, leaning over the reception desk. "Hello?"

"Is there a bag back there?" I ask.

"Don't see one."

"Patsy should be back soon with my bag," I say. "Here. You take Mae out to the car. I'll wait for Patsy."

Mae clings to me. "I love you."

"Love you, too."

Molly's taller than both of us. She hunches over to take Mae's weight. I notice she's looking beyond me, over my shoulder.

"Stop," she says. "Don't."

"What?"

She brings a finger to her lips. *Shh.*

Footsteps approaching.

"Is it Patsy?"

Molly's eyes widen. They get bigger and bigger. They're her whole face. Mae makes a sound like a siren.

There's something terrible behind me.

"What is it?" I ask.

Molly sinks her nails into my wrist. She mouths, "Don't move."

I catch a bad scent. Rotten, acidic, sickening.

"Where are you going?" A chill grabs me by the throat. It's Julie.

"Jules?" I say.

"Where are you going?"

"We have to leave," I tell her. It's her. She's what's behind me. I don't look at her. I'm too afraid.

"Why?"

"They're closing. See? There's no one around. We're the last ones here."

She laughs. It's punctured by wheezing breaths.

"You okay, Jules?"

"Elise, we need to leave," Molly says. "We need to leave now."

"Go on, Molly. Go," Julie says. There's a strain in her voice, same as with an old heavy smoker's. It's difficult for her to talk and breathe at the same time. When she finishes speaking she takes a desperate, rasping inhale. The exhale that follows is a dull scream. "You, too, Mae. You want to leave? Leave."

Molly and Mae back up, back away from me.

"What is it?" I ask them.

"You won't look at me, Lise?" Jules asks.

"Don't!" Molly says. "Don't turn around. Come with us. Let's go."

I don't know how far Julie is behind me, but I hear her take a step forward. There's the unmistakable sound of cracking bones.

"Jules, we need to get out of here. We have to leave."

She laughs again—this time it's marked by sporadic gurgling, like she's got too much saliva or something stubborn is caught in her esophagus.

I can't listen to that laugh anymore. I ask her, "What is it?"

"Don't you know? I'm not going anywhere."

Molly and Mae are slowly stepping backward toward the front door.

"Elise, we're leaving. Come with us," Molly says.

"Mae?" I say.

She doesn't hear me. Her eyes are fixed on Julie.

"I should have said something. I should have asked," she says. She's talking to Julie. "I'm sorry."

"Don't be sorry, Maeby," Julie says. "It's not a good look for you."

"Elise, we're leaving," Molly says. "Let's go."

"Good-bye, Molly," Julie says.

Molly ignores her. "Elise. Now!"

"It's fine," Julie says. "I didn't come back for them. I came back for you."

"Aw, Jules." I'm laughing now. Nervous, polite. Local-news-anchor laugh. "You didn't have to do that."

"I didn't have a choice," she says. "You wouldn't let me go."

"I'm not sure what you're talking about," I say. A vicious cold sweeps over me. If she were close, I would feel the warmth of another human body. Like when she used to sleep in my bed. I remember the extravagance of the extra heat. "Come back to the hotel?"

"No, not to the hotel," she says. "I'm not talking about the hotel. What's the matter with you?"

"With me?"

"You're smarter than this. You already know."

"Julie, trust me. I'm lost."

"You're choosing to be lost. It's frustrating me."

"I'm sorry."

"You don't know what I had to do to get here. What I have to do to stay here."

"Stay where?"

"And to be treated like . . . like a freak! By my best friends!" she says, anguished.

"Enough!" Molly's got the door open. "Elise, come on!"

"Go," I tell her. "Get Mae to a doctor. I'll meet you."

"I'm not fucking around. Come with us."

"Elise," Mae says. I wish she wouldn't say my name like that.

"Let them go," Julie says.

"We're right behind you," I say. "Promise."

"We?" Molly asks.

"I'm not leaving without Julie," I say, and when I hear it, I know it's true. Despite everything, I can't leave her. I just can't.

"You won't leave without me?" Julie says. "You won't even look at me!"

Moved by her pain, I turn around.

She's much, much closer than I anticipated.

Her skin isn't skin. It's a cratered, broken membrane stretched over her bones. It's got a weak sheen. The color of metal.

Her lips have dried out, split, scabbed over. Her teeth—it seems she's got a fresh row of them—are yellow, too long. Pointy. Red things dangle between them. The whites of her eyes are marbled, murky, her irises bleeding. The tip of her nose is gone. I can see the bone there. Her hair—the hair I once brushed, braided, straightened—is falling out in clumps.

Her body is frail and thin, but her presence is domineering. She's taller. She's grown.

As I take in the sight of her, the sudden ascent of terror overwhelms me, and I can't help but scream.

"What?" She might be offended. She leans away from me. "It's not so bad."

"Jules."

"Aren't you glad I'm *here*? Aren't you glad I'm not dead?"

"Of course."

"Then why are you looking at me like that?"

"Julie. Jules." I need to repeat her name. I need to call her by it, confirm it out loud, because the thing in front of me bears little resemblance to my best friend. "You don't look well."

"I'm *not* well."

"Elise!" Molly keeps screaming. "Elise, now!"

I turn to her. "I'm not leaving. I'm not leaving her like this."

Julie laughs. "Like what?"

"Jules."

"Okay," Molly says. She exchanges a look with Mae. "Okay. I can't make your decisions for you. I need to get Mae out of here."

"Elise, come with us," Mae says, but she's already out the door. Molly, too.

"Don't" is the last thing I hear Molly say. The door closes.

It's quiet for a moment. Then Julie laughs.

"Those two," she says, sighing. "It's just us now. Just us."

"Julie, can I help you? Can we go see a doctor?"

"I went to see doctors. All kinds of doctors. None of them could figure out what was wrong with me. They said I was fine."

"Julie, I love you. Please. I don't think you're fine."

"You think I don't know that? I know. I'm aware."

"What happened?"

"You judge me."

"I don't. I'm not. Tell me what happened." Behind her, I notice a trail of muddy footprints.

"You don't care. None of you cares. You all look at me differently now. I can't take it." She starts to cough, an intense hacking cough that grinds on and on. She curls over, grasping at her side.

"Jules?"

She coughs up blood. She catches it in her palm. She sighs, wipes her hand against her thigh, smudging crimson across her loose jeans.

"Julie, are you okay?"

"You want to know what happened to me?"

"You said you didn't remember."

She laughs. "I lied."

"Are you going to tell me now? The truth?"

"You won't believe me."

"I will. I promise."

"Cross your heart?"

I cross it.

"Okay. I'll tell you. But let's go sit down somewhere. It's a long story. You want to go to the lounge?"

I nod.

"Come on," she says, walking ahead of me. From behind, I can see the steep slope of her shoulders. She's hunching over. Her gait is off, like her legs hurt to walk on. She has to swing them to the sides to lift her feet.

She sits on one of the big leather sofas. I sit near her but not next to her. I hug a pillow just to have something between us.

"Remember," she says. "You promised."

"I know," I say, picking at the pillow, avoiding eye contact.

She coughs again, spits. Her breathing evens out. I've always been a curious person. I've finally come across a mystery I don't want solved, and here I am.

What Julie remembers is this:

He left wrappers in the sink again. There they were, floating in disgusting dishwater. The drain was blocked up by bits of beets and lettuce and walnuts from the salad she had made the night before. The beets gave the water a sinister red tint. Scene of the crime.

How many times did she have to ask him?

And why did she have to ask in the first place? Who puts wrappers in the sink? What grown man eats a candy bar and puts the wrapper in the sink? Why not throw it in the garbage?

When it first happened, shortly after they moved in, she shrugged and threw the wrapper out herself. But then it happened again the next night. And the night after that. He had to have a candy bar after dinner; he'd been that way since he was a kid. His mother used to give him candy bars as a reward for good behavior. Julie realized she was basically married to Pavlov's dog.

She was hyperaware of becoming a nag. Her mother was Queen Nag of Complain-a-lot. That was probably why her dad left and why she never got a stepfather who stuck around. It was probably why her sister turned to pot, desperate to chill the fuck out while living under their mother's roof, and why the pot, in the end, wasn't enough. In a tragic twist of events, after getting kicked out of the house for the zillionth time, her sister pursued a different tyrant. She moved in with a powerful drug dealer. He had face tattoos and a scar across his neck. He beat her up on a regular basis. He might have actually been her pimp.

Julie, on the other hand, refused to follow any type of predictable pattern that would land her in a therapist's office, the therapist crossing their legs and asking if she saw the parallel between X and her mother, Y and her father, Z and her childhood.

She had eluded it this long. Her greatest test of all had been taking care of her mother before she died. The fussiest, most high-maintenance woman she'd ever known, sick and helpless and dying. Julie stayed patient through it all. She got her mother whatever she wanted, whenever she wanted it. Julie never snapped. She never asked the selfish questions like "How come when I was six you told me I was fat?" or "What did you love about my father?" She had proved to herself that she had transcended her circumstances.

She didn't have any intention of being broken by a stupid Snickers wrapper.

But it wasn't just a Snickers wrapper. There were Milky Way and 100 Grand and Reese's Peanut Butter Cups. Every night something different. She thought about asking to change their original arrangement, which was that she would cook and do dishes and do the laundry, and he would clean the rest of the house, bathrooms included, and do all the outside stuff. Mow the lawn. Garden. He was a contractor, a landscaper. He had the skills. It seemed like a fair deal. After taking care of her mother, she was grateful not to have to clean any bathrooms.

She was happy with the deal at first, but as she stood over the sink each night, with him drinking a beer in another room, listening to records or watching TV or tinkering with something in the house, her suspicion grew that she'd actually gotten the shit end of the stick.

The bottle caps, too. From the beers. They would appear randomly around the house. At the foot of the stairs. On the bookshelf. On the vanity in the downstairs bathroom. Was it so hard to put a bottle cap in the recycling bin?

After weeks of holding her tongue on principle, she gave in. "How come you throw your wrappers in the sink instead of in the garbage?"

"Don't know" was his answer.

"Can you put them in the garbage instead?"

"Yeah, okay."

But he didn't. Next night, same thing.

That was when she began to ask herself questions. Why did the wrappers bother her so much? And the bottle caps? And how come he was always going on about missing socks in the laundry, like she'd lost them on purpose? What about all this got her so angry? Not annoyed but angry. Scream-into-a-pillow angry. Pull-out-her-hair angry.

Why was she putting up with this domestic shit? It was never what she wanted. She wanted to be famous. She wanted to be successful. Live in LA or New York, not small-town Maine. Not own a bed-and-breakfast. Not be married to a hard-core Patriots fan who drank Sam Adams and didn't own dress shoes.

What had happened?

She was happy in the day-to-day, got swept up in it or the idea of it. It was picturesque. Their house was beautiful, the kind of house other people walked by and wished they lived in. It was peaceful where they were, and you got a view of the ocean from some of the rooms on the third floor. The beach was good for sitting on and reading. Not so much for swimming, but she didn't like swimming in the ocean anyway. Too many variables.

Everyone in town was friendly. She knew them by name, and they knew her. She got the sense that all of the men were in love with her and all of the women were jealous. It could have been a lie she told herself to feel good. But most of the people had lived there their whole lives, and she was an outsider. There was an allure to that.

She loved Tristan. He was gorgeous and made her laugh and was good to her. Checked all the boxes. He was the polar opposite of her in so many ways, it was fascinating. Initially. She couldn't tell if she loved him but wasn't in love with him or was in love with him but didn't love him. She knew something was missing. Something had gone wrong. And her getting so worked up about the wrappers was just a symptom of a deeper problem.

The beet water left her hands pinkish. She washed them and washed them until her knuckles were raw.

She went into the living room, where Tristan was drinking a beer and watching the news, and she said, "I'm going hiking tomorrow."

He looked back at her, his eyebrows raised in surprise. "Okay."

"By myself."

"All right. Where you going?"

"Acadia." They had planned to go there together someday; that was why she picked it. She thought if she told him she was going alone to a place they were supposed to go to together, he'd get the hint that something was off.

But he didn't.

"You need gear?" he asked. That was when she realized what she really wanted was for him to stop her from going. To say, "No, stay. Hang out with me. Be with me."

She was lonely. Her mother was dead; her sister was a crackpot. Her three best friends were scattered across the country. None of them was married. None of them would understand. Molly judged her for getting married in the first place. Didn't approve. Mae was too nice, too afraid to step on anyone's toes. It was impossible to get a genuine response from her. The one person who could give her honest advice was embroiled in an epically stupid affair. She had no advice to give. She was in the position only to receive.

"Yeah, I need gear," she said. As she followed him down to the basement, she thought maybe it was good to put some space between them. Give him a chance to miss her.

She didn't sleep much that night. She got up before the sun, had some coffee, headed out. She listened to sugary pop music on the drive and sang along loudly, shamelessly botching the lyrics. She was excited to clear her mind, for some alone time, for an adventure. It was the right call. She was feeling good. She was feeling free.

"Free," she says, "is my favorite feeling."

It was a perfect day. The sky was a pure, vivid blue. The air was fresh and delicious. She locked her car, double-checked her pack, threw it over her shoulders and took off running.

She ran! She couldn't walk! She couldn't wait another second to leave the rest of the world behind.

From there, her memories get foggy. They cut in and out. She knows she set off on a particular trail, but she can't remember which one. She can't remember when her excitement faded, when the initial wonder of nature gave way to boredom and unease. Moss. She remembers moss. Moss-covered rocks along the trail. She remembers thinking of moss as "forest mold" and being angry at herself for having thoughts like that. Ruining the experience.

Being in the woods, she realized she had let her husband brainwash her into thinking she was outdoorsy. He was the one who liked to hike and camp, to rub sticks together and eat freeze-dried food. He was the one who could identify poison ivy and true north. Not her. She liked air-conditioning and lattes and clean bathrooms. Being outside made her itchy. She hated being itchy. She hated bugs, and outside is where all the bugs live.

The woods gave her bad vibes. The trees stood around like sullen overlords, dense and dark and ancient. The other plants, fern-looking things, she didn't find particularly impressive. She distrusted them. She suspected they were harboring bugs.

After walking for a while, she decided she deserved a rest. She came across a fallen tree overlooking a shallow stream. She sat on the tree and bit into one of the protein bars her husband had packed for her. It tasted like rubber. She took out her phone, pulled up Maps.

It was around this time she became aware that someone was watching her.

She got a sensation like pins and needles from her shoulder up the side of her neck. She didn't want to give any indication, acknowledge its presence with the eruption of sudden movement. She slowly turned to face the trees behind her. There was a rustling of branches, but no person. No animal. No eyes emerging from the shade.

A squirrel. That was the narrative she decided on. It was a squirrel.

She returned to her phone. Something wasn't right. According to Maps, she was a blue dot in a sea of white nothing. She hadn't brought a paper map. Hadn't thought she would need one.

She put her phone down, took another bite of her protein bar. The brief lapse of mental stimulation made her vulnerable. It allowed doubt to creep in.

There was no way that was a squirrel. She saw the branches move. She heard them murmur. There was too much movement, too much noise to come from a squirrel. Cuter rats, as she called them.

It could have been a fellow hiker, which should have brought her comfort, because she realized she hadn't seen any other hikers in a long time. An hour at least. It was a weekday, so maybe the park wasn't crowded. She tried not to overthink the situation. She tried to ignore the image she had in her head of some man leering at her from behind a tree.

She could go home. She could walk back the way she had come, get in her car, drive. Stop at some random diner, drink buckets of coffee and get the solo time she'd been craving. Or go straight home, rest safe in her husband's arms.

Maybe this was the answer she was after. She missed the sense of security she felt when she was with him. The feeling of home. She missed being in their beautiful dream house, being able to crack the windows and hear nature but not have to be *in* it, slapping off mosquitoes and managing squirrel paranoia.

Maybe she needed to try harder to make her life work.

She tucked her protein bar wrapper in her back pocket, drank a few swigs of water. Took a moment to appreciate the shimmer of sunlight on the stream.

She was ready to turn around, head back, but she found something about the path that unspooled behind her less appealing than the way ahead. The leaves weren't as green.

She reconsidered leaving. She had come for a reason. She didn't want to bail. That was her habit, wasn't it? When things got hard, she left. When they weren't hard, she got bored and she left. She didn't want to be that way. Always leaving.

She chose to forget about whatever was watching her from the woods. It wasn't watching her then. At least, she didn't feel like it was. She didn't know it was.

She followed the stream, carefully selecting which stone to step on next, like an elaborate game of hopscotch. She avoided checking the time, knowing if it was earlier than she expected, she would get impatient, and if it was later, she would feel rushed.

Only she realized she'd wandered off the path, and she wasn't sure how far she had gone or how long she had been on this detour. She didn't want to give in to negativity, but the truth was, she was fighting a losing battle against escalating dread.

She reasoned with herself. She'd been in worse binds than this. She'd been stuck in Amsterdam with no money, her passport lost, her phone smashed, and still she had made it home. She'd figure it out, find her way back. She always did.

She ignored her distress. She set her pack down, hydrated, peed behind a tree, got herself together.

She went along, concentrating on the satisfying crunch of ground beneath her feet. Then she heard the first twig snap.

She spun around before her fear could stop her. In the woods behind her, obscured partly by the slope of the land, was a person. Not really a person. A figure.

What scared her most wasn't that it was there, that she shared the woods with someone or something else. It was that whatever it was, it was dressed in head-to-toe black. It cocked its head to one side, looking at her with curiosity, but it didn't have eyes. None that she could see.

Her body reacted strangely, adrenaline pushing her forward instead of pulling her back. When she took a step toward the figure, it dropped on all fours and scuttled into the brush.

She stood there for a minute.

The way it had moved, there was no way it was human. But she'd never seen any animal stand upright on its hind legs like that. Even bears hunch. And its arms. It had long, skinny arms. She couldn't quantify its size because of the distance. It could have been under three feet tall. Could have been over seven.

There was no question of going back now. To go back would be to walk toward it. Her only option was to hurry forward and hope it didn't catch up. Or to find other hikers and make fast friends.

It'd become too difficult to run in her bulky hiking boots, strapped into a heavy backpack. She power walked, took long strides, tested her legs. Her shins ached, her quads, her shoulders. Her feet were blistered. She looked straight ahead. She didn't let her eyes stray. She didn't want to see. Didn't want to know.

She thought about calling a park ranger, but she had zero reception. They say to bring a walkie-talkie or some shit, but she hadn't.

She tried Maps again. Nothing. Not even a blue dot.

The hike became more challenging, the sun less generous, the trees taller.

The wind picked up. That was her first clue about the turn in the weather. The forecast was all cute yellow sun, but the smell in the air was unmistakable. It was the smell of the earth ripening for a storm.

The reality sank in.

People disappear. It happens all the time. They leave to pick up bread or soap or cigarettes or AA batteries, and they never come back. Their families are left to wonder. They can't eat toast or wash their hands or smoke or use the remote control without it coming back to haunt them. Kids wander off at the playground or in grocery store parking lots or waiting for the bus, and they're never seen again. Their parents plead on the news, put up posters. They're dead, she used to think. *Do they know, or are they delusional with hope?*

When she was a kid she pictured her own face on one of those posters. It didn't scare her. She always coveted attention. She imagined her classmates crying, hugging one another. People searching with German shepherds and flashlights. Calling out her name over and over again.

Now the idea made her woozy.

Because the figure was behind her again. Not exactly behind her. It walked beside her. But in the woods, concealing itself. It was so dark, so tall and gangling; it was like a walking shadow. She was able to pacify herself a few times by telling herself it *was* a shadow. But then she'd see the trees move, hear its footsteps.

Her phone wasn't working, but she pretended.

"Hey . . . Yeah, I'll be there soon. . . . You're there? Yeah, I'm, like, right by you. I'll be there soon. Are Chris and John with you? . . . Cool . . . Cool. Yeah, see you soon. . . . You, too. Bye."

When she fake hung up, she thought she heard laughing. A low, evil laugh, unlike anything she'd ever heard before.

She tried to move faster, but her legs refused. Her adrenaline wasn't working the same. It wasn't sustaining her.

Her realization was punctuated by the first flash of lightning, followed by a booming clap of thunder.

She couldn't stop to take out her poncho. She didn't have time. She was being hunted. She knew, by the severity of her panic, by the tenseness of her body, that she was prey.

By the time the rain came, she was running. She wasn't fast enough. It clipped her ankle and dragged her down. She fell face-first into the mud and hit her head on a rock. The impact knocked out her vision. She clawed around in the dark. She couldn't scream because of all the mud she'd swallowed. She couldn't say anything.

In the darkness, she tried to calm herself down, to sense whether she was in any pain. Her ankle burned, but the pain wasn't terrible. She tried to rotate her foot and realized whatever had caught her was still holding on. Its hand was wrapped around her ankle. Its hand or a rope or its mouth. She couldn't tell.

She kicked.

The laughing came again. It was a sound she says she can't describe, but even if she could, she wouldn't want to.

She says she prayed. She prayed to a god she didn't believe in until that moment. She thought about her husband at home, and the candy wrappers in the sink she no longer gave a flying fuck about.

She kicked with her free leg. Her foot connected with something. Her vision came back, blurry, her eyelashes encased in mud. She saw she was free and that whatever was attacking her was far enough away that if she ran, if she ran hard and fast and for her life, she could get away.

So that was what she did.

She couldn't breathe. Her chest was on the verge of exploding; her legs were on fire, but she was creating distance. She was escaping.

She didn't know then. There was no escape. She didn't understand until it caught her the fourth time. Both her ankles were shredded to the point that she could see the skin hanging off like party streamers. She didn't know until she felt the size of the gash on her neck, until she pulled her hand away and saw how red it was. It had let her go. When it wanted, it let her go. It was a game. It was sport.

She hid anyway, knowing it would find her again. Knowing there was nothing she could do but buy herself more time. She hid in the hollowed trunk of a dead tree, marveling at the magnitude of her fear.

And when it took her, took her the last time, she was able to see what it really looked like.

She said, "Please."

She thought she was asking for mercy. Maybe that was what she got.

It pinned her to the ground, each of its long, spindly branches, not limbs—that was not what they were, not exactly—digging into her, cutting off her circulation. Its head hovered over her head. Its mouth—not a human mouth or an animal mouth, but a fissure, a nest, a leak, a void—clamped down.

She didn't want to be afraid anymore. She was about to die, and she resigned herself to it. In her final moments, she decided she wanted to think of her happiest memory. She found it easy.

"The last thing I saw," she says, smiling, "was your face."

Next thing she knew, she was buried in the dirt. Not deep. Through it, she could see sunlight. She could breathe. Instinct would have her break out, but something stronger stopped her. She stayed.

Not because of it. She knew the creature that put her there wasn't a threat to her anymore.

Her thoughts were familiar. They were her thoughts. Julie's thoughts. Only it was like she was reading them off a cue card, or they were being fed to her through an earpiece. There was a disconnect in how she thought, what she thought and what she felt. A detachment.

The truth was, she didn't feel much of anything.

She'd always been someone with strong emotions. Sensitive. She walked around feeling like a raw nerve. She couldn't watch the news, because it would make her hysterical, send her into an existential crisis. She couldn't have a weird dream without it ruling her day. A rude barista at Starbucks could keep her up at night. All of that was muffled now. Some monster had stalked her in the woods, attacked her, buried her, and she was feeling fine. Not great. Not bad. Fine.

She doesn't know how long she stayed buried there. Eventually, she got hungry.

Getting out required more digging than she expected. That didn't matter. Her nails were long now. Sharp. She thought about how human nails keep growing after death. That was a thing, wasn't it?

When she saw it again, however long later, she felt an immediate kinship. It watched her emerge from the dirt. It wasn't so ugly to her now. It turned away from her, revealing its exposed spine, its bones. Its skin, maybe bark, was tight and stretched thin. It looked like ash. Like it was something else once, burned beyond recognition.

She was following it now. But that was what it wanted. That was what they did. They followed.

They lived together, in shadow. They and the others. They traveled together, from place to place. They preferred the woods, the camouflage of the trees, but it didn't really matter. What mattered was that, wherever they were, they could feed.

She didn't know what they were, not exactly, but she knew she was one of them. She knew she had been chosen, but she didn't know why.

"Really, I think I chose for myself," she says. "My whole life, I wanted to be something else. Wanted something more. To escape my body, my life as it was. It could sense that in me. My hunger, my longing. My fight. My strength."

She seems confident in this. I'm sure it's easier for her to accept if she tells herself it was her choice, that it wasn't decided for her. That it wasn't something that happened *to* her. I can't blame her for this. I won't take it from her, even though I don't believe it. I believe she was taken because she was there. A pretty blonde. Alone in the woods. Lost.

There are many reasons why bad things happen to young women, and at the same time, no reason at all.

Julie knew that she died and wasn't dead.

She knew that she was hungry, so she ate.

There was a faint voice that sang in her ears sometimes as she fell asleep. Her memories. Of her husband, of her house, of what it was like to drive a car, of how good it felt to have a stiff drink on a Friday night. Of her friends.

Of everything and everyone she had left behind, I was what she remembered the most. She worried the most about me.

The worry distracted her. The distraction made her weak. The others took notice. When she asked if she could go, they nodded. The nod was consent. They couldn't speak. Or they could, but she didn't yet understand the language.

When she left for her former home, they didn't watch. They didn't follow.

Her memories came back in droves. The closer she got, the more she felt like herself again. She even *looked* like her old self. She was really, truly coming back to life. By the time she arrived on her front porch, she was 100 percent certain.

VIII

She looks at me, her eyelids drooping to her earlobes, lashes splayed like spider legs. I can no longer read her expression. She might be nervous.

I take a strained breath. "Remember that time we saw that stupid horror movie in the theater, the one with the machete guy? And you asked us all if we were in a horror movie, who would die first, and we said you, and you got so mad?"

"Fuck you," she says, laughing. "I actually thought about that as I was running."

"You've been kept alive all this time on spite."

"What was the order again?"

"You, Mae, Molly, me."

"Interesting," she says, tucking a leg beneath her. Her joints screech. "So, you don't believe me?"

"No," I tell her. Looking at her now, how could I not? "I believe you."

"Are you afraid of me?" she asks, smiling to reveal that she's lost every last one of her human teeth.

"No," I lie. Then I tell the truth. "I love you."

Because it's still her, isn't it? In some form? And Julie, in any form, is better than no Julie at all.

She lets out a sigh of relief that breaks my heart.

It sways me to tell her something else.

"I've seen it."

"Seen what?"

"What took you. What you described. I've seen it. Here in the hotel. I've had . . ." I hesitate. She's inching too close. Her breath is poison. "I've had dreams. Visions."

She reaches for my hand. Hers is cold. It's ice. Her nails are yellow, overgrown, pointed. For how long they are, they don't look weak.

"Come with me."

"What?"

"Let me take you."

"Take me?"

"Back with me."

"Back where? Back to Acadia?"

She shakes her head, shedding hair in the process. "It's hard to explain."

I don't understand. Panic rises; my blood whirs in my ears. "Why would we go there?"

"Because," she says like I'm an idiot, "you're lost, Lise. Like I was. You're hurting. I was, too, but I'm not anymore. I can give that to you. And we can be together. Together every day, like we used to be."

"Jules," I say. I'm afraid to break eye contact, but I do it anyway. I scan behind her. The hallway, the staircase.

It smashes into my head like a sledgehammer.

"Where's Patsy?"

She turns away, leaning back casually. "What do you mean?"

"Patsy was here. She went upstairs to get my bag."

"Haven't seen her."

"We should check on her," I say, standing.

"We're in the middle of a conversation," she says. It's a voice I know well. She's in her pouting phase. It's the prelude to Julie anger.

"I'm nervous she hurt herself or something." I cross behind her on the couch. She grabs my arm to stop me.

"Wait," she says.

I pull out of her grip.

"Elise."

"I'll be right back," I say, breaking into a power walk/jog. Not a run. It can't look like I'm running away.

I expect to walk down the hall, to open the door to my room and find Patsy there, huffing, packing up the rest of my stuff. I expect to get my bag and tell her she needs to leave the hotel now. I'll insist.

I expect to walk with her past Julie, who will still be sitting in the lounge. I expect Julie to be upset, but I don't expect her to do anything about it. There would be real-life consequences. Julie doesn't like to be caught. She likes to be free.

I expect Patsy to get into her car, her frown lines deepening as she begins to understand the scope of what has happened over the past few days, accepting this permanent stain on the reputation of her hotel. She'll cry when she sees it in the rearview, because she won't see it as it looks now; she'll see it in its inevitable end state of disarray. Gables crumbling, balconies collapsed, paint disintegrated. That's the hotel's future. She'll think it's her fault.

I expect to start my car with a combination of guilt and relief. I'll plug my phone into my car charger, have a thousand messages from Molly and Mae. I'll meet them somewhere, wherever they are now. We'll put this weekend behind us, find a way to move on. I expect time to heal us. I expect to be healed.

What I don't expect is to find Patsy dead in the hallway.

She's pale, drained of blood. It trails behind her. Her arms are out in front. She dragged herself this far. There are small tears in the carpet. One of her legs is missing. I can see because her pants are ripped, the fabric wet and red. Her head is twisted to the side, neck broken. Her eyes are open, white like hard-boiled eggs. Her tongue spills out of her mouth.

"Lise?" Julie calls.

I step around Patsy. The longer I look at her, the more I want to lean over and shout, "Get up! Stop it! Get up!"

"Elise!"

I stumble to my room. The door is locked. Where is my key?

I don't have it. I don't have my room key.

I try a few other handles along the hall. Locked, locked, locked, locked, locked.

There's nothing in my stomach but acid, and it's clambering up my throat.

Finally, I find an open door. I step inside. I lock it behind me, my hands so shaky and sweaty, it takes me three tries to turn the dead bolt.

The theme of this room is blue. There's awful neon carpet. A set of leather couches. Checkered wallpaper. All blue. A round blue bed covered in blue crushed velvet. There's a set of blue doors on the back wall. They're curved like fun house mirrors. I open the first. A closet. The second, a bathroom. Between the blue vanity and the blue tub, there's another door. It's so small I have to duck to get through it. It leads to a sitting area with blue beanbag chairs and a blue wicker armoire. Beyond them is a set of sliding glass doors leading to the balcony.

Do I run now?

I feel in my pocket for my car keys. I do it again to make sure. I have them. Yes, I have them. Right? I don't trust my senses anymore. Did I really see Patsy dead in the hallway? Is my best friend downstairs, or did I imagine her? Did she really sit across from me, rotting before my eyes?

I take out my keys. My wallet. I have everything I need. If I open the sliding doors, I should go to the right. There should be stairs around the corner. There have to be.

I don't want to leave unless I know where I'm going. I go back into the bedroom to find the fire-escape plan. It's up on the wall by the door.

"Lise?" Distant. She's coming up the stairs. "Lise? Elise?"

She's getting louder. Closer. I back away from the door.

"You didn't let me finish," she says. "If you just let me explain."

I hold my jaw to keep it from trembling. I'm too afraid to breathe, to move, to blink.

"After everything I've been through—after everything *we've* been through—don't abandon me."

What choice do I have? What am I supposed to do?

"Elise!"

She's right outside my door.

"Elise?"

My hand is over my mouth now, holding my face together. If I let go, it'll fall open. I'll scream.

"Please," she says, her voice breaking. "Please."

She's crying. Her sobs soak through the door. I'm reminded of all the times I've heard her cry before. How warm her tears were when I wiped them away with my thumbs. How her sniffles were cute and small. Nose hiccups, I called them.

I can't help it. It's instinctive; it's reactive. "Jules?"

"Elise?"

"Don't cry, Jules."

"Where are you?"

"I'm here."

"Where?"

"Please don't cry."

Two fists. Two fists bang on the door. It cringes.

"Open the door," she says.

"No."

"Why?"

"Patsy is dead. Haven't you noticed? There's a dead body in the hallway, Julie! What the fuck?"

Her wheezing breath lets me know she's still there. She's thinking.

"It doesn't matter," she says finally.

"Doesn't matter?"

"You don't trust me."

"Can you blame me?"

She pounds her fists again. Some dust flies loose. "You didn't let me finish!"

"Patsy's dead!"

"Elise, I swear."

"Swear what? Tell me you didn't kill her." I count five seconds. It's five seconds too long. "Tell me it wasn't you. Tell me it was that thing. That thing I keep seeing. Tell me it came from Acadia and killed the pig in the kitchen and killed Patsy."

Silence.

"What got you in the woods, Jules? What hurt you? That's what got Patsy, too, right? The tall creature? The one with the long arms and legs? The one I told you about, the one I saw here in the hotel?"

Nothing from the other side of the door.

"Julie. Tell me. Tell me it was that thing."

"I can't."

"Why?"

"If you would just let me explain."

"Why, Jules?"

"You know why!"

"Say it. Tell me the truth. It was you, wasn't it? It's been you this whole time. In my room, out on the balcony."

"Open the door."

"What about the glasses? I saw that girl's glasses in your room, the girl from reception. Why did you have her glasses? Oh God. Julie, what did you do?"

I don't know why I ask. I don't want her answer. I don't need it. I already know.

Everything I doubted, everything I tried to write off as my own crazy paranoia. Every creak of the floorboards, every elusive shadow. The noise inside the walls. The substance dripping from the vent that Julie was so quick to dismiss.

I know now.

I can identify the smell.

"Open the door and I'll finish explaining," Julie says. "I'll explain everything. You'll understand. I know you will. We get each other. We always have."

"I need a minute to think."

"What's there to think about? It's me, Lise."

"Please? Just a minute."

I back away from the door, each step carefully calculated, as quiet as possible. I feel like a marionette again, like I'm suspended over this hideous blue carpet. I'm so terrified that my fear is warping everything in my view. The door is bending in toward me, the walls elongating, the furniture expanding, the floor sinking. The bed begins to creep up the wall.

I make it to the bathroom. I crouch through the small door.

"Lise?"

I get to the balcony. The air is frigid, and it smacks me out of the foggy state of shock I've been operating in. I round the corner, looking for the stairs, but they aren't there. It's a dead end.

There's a white lattice fence that's too tall to climb. If I fall, I would fall seven feet onto concrete. Through the gaps in the fence I see a hot tub. The goddamn honeymoon suites.

I run back to the room. I hear destruction inside. She's breaking down the door to get to me.

She won't stop. Julie always gets what she wants.

I try the door to the next room over. Locked. I'm grateful for the stupid shared balcony now. Fuck.

The second one down is open. I sneak inside, lock it, draw the curtains.

There's a mural of a windmill set back in a field of tulips. The opposite wall is fake stone, like in Molly's room. The other two walls are painted glittery green. There are birdhouses hanging from the ceiling. Pink, purple, white, black. They vary in size and intricacy. There are two queen beds, both on top of platforms covered in Astroturf. There are a set of wooden chairs and a mustard-colored couch. This room is significantly smaller than any of the others I've been in and significantly weirder.

It's not the ideal place to hide for my life.

There's a chance I can escape through the hotel. If she's out on the balcony, I can go into the hall, downstairs, out the front door. I can't hide in here forever, and I know I can't wait her out.

I listen. Press my ear to the door. There's a rattling. But it's not coming from out in the hall. It's coming from somewhere behind me. Somewhere inside the room.

I follow the sound. Beyond the vibrating birdhouses, there's a vent. It's coming loose. Through the narrow slants reach ten long, gnarled fingers.

I go. I open the door and run.

I tell myself I'm not going to get caught. I'm going to get out of here. I'm going to make it out to my car. I'm going to call 911.

I'm sure of this until I hear her coming down the stairs behind me.

I veer off, go right instead of left. I'm running away from the front door. I won't reach it in time. I'm running deeper into the hotel. I don't bother with the rooms; they're probably all locked. I make a left down a flight of tiled steps. The smell of chlorine shoots up my nostrils.

The pool is shaped like a giant kidney. The surrounding walls, floor and ceiling are all faux stone. Or real stone. What do I know? Flowering vines hang from the ceiling and weave up the walls. The water is illuminated by green lights. I can see the steam rising in pretty curls. There's a waterfall, a slide. It's a shame I'm not down here to enjoy it.

I run past a sign that reads in bright red letters: NO RUNNING.

There's a sauna. Bathrooms/changing rooms. I'm looking for a door outside or another stairwell. I remember from the website a picture of a patio with retro lawn chairs and umbrellas resembling humongous mushrooms. It would make sense for there to be a way to get there from here.

I'm not going to get caught.

There can't be only one way to get to the pool. I can't be trapped down here.

I'm not going to get caught.

I put my hand over my chest and feel my heart beating against it. I'm gasping, taking in rapid sips of air. I'm struggling to breathe. It's not subtle. It's not quiet.

I need to put myself away somewhere. I run into a changing room and hide. The door locks twice. There's a button on the handle and a bolt up top. I don't like the way it feels to be in here. I'm cornered.

I change my mind.

When I open the door, Julie is there.

Her eyes are bloated. They bulge from mounds of gathered skin. She's covered in sores. There's one that takes up the entirety of her cheek. It's deep pink but bubbling with yellow pus. I see movement, like there's life inside it. I'm proved wrong immediately. It's not life I'm seeing; it's death. The wound is expanding. I watch it chew away more of her face. She doesn't notice, or she doesn't care.

The last strands of her hair fall over to one side. The skin on her scalp has split, and through the gaping lesions, I can see bits of ivory white skull.

She smiles at me with a mouth not her own. Her breath carries a dizzying stink. "Found you," she says.

"Julie."

"Come on," she says. She's holding the door open for me. "I only want to talk."

I can't move because I can't catch my breath. My lungs have forgotten how to breathe.

She puts a bony hand on my shoulder. "Elise, calm down. Breathe. I'm not going to hurt you." She leads me out to the pool. "Sit," she says. "We can put our feet in."

I sit. My hands are shaking with such ferocity, Julie has to take off my shoes and socks. I watch her skinless fingers take my feet and place them in the water. She does it gently, like a patient mother.

"I can't believe I had to chase you around this hotel just to talk to you," she says. "Do you know how that makes me feel?"

I can't answer because I can't speak. My tongue is a coward; it refuses to go out past chattering teeth.

"I'm trying to find the right word. 'Disappointed'?"

"S-s-sorry," I manage. "I'm sorry."

"We've always been on the same page. I don't get it," she says. "I thought you'd want to come with me. Be what I am. You and me together again. Free."

"Together where?"

"Wherever we want to be." One of her eyes slips out of place, and she pushes it back in. "And the best part is, you wouldn't be like everyone else anymore. Not like you're like everyone now. We've always been different. We've always known we were special."

I'm not sure where she's getting this from. Julie and I have a lot in common, but not everything. I've never felt different or special. This has happened before, when she lumps me into one of her beliefs, about the world or about herself, and I'm left to wonder what else she assumes about me. But I never correct her, because I know her well enough to know she does it to feel less alone.

Or maybe I've made some assumptions of my own. Maybe I only ever saw what I projected onto her, what I wanted to see. Maybe I never really knew her at all.

"There's the hunger, but it's really not that bad once you get used to it," she says. "I kind of like it, because what it really is is power. Control. We like to be in control."

Doesn't everyone? I don't think I'm a control freak. I don't think she and I have ever talked about how we like to be in control. Mae likes to be in control. I tell her this. She frowns.

"I'm not talking about Mae. I'm talking about us," she says, her frustration apparent in how she strains on each word.

"Why me? Why not Mae? Why not Molly?"

"They're not like you and me," she says. "We love them, but they're not the same. Besides, we're not as close to them. They're closer to each other."

"I don't think so," I say. I'm not sure why I'm contradicting her. I felt the same way in the past, thought about the four of us in rigid terms. Us and them. But friendships are mercurial. They're shape-shifters. I've learned to allow them to fluctuate and take new forms. I love my friends; that's all that matters. I would take a day wiping up Mae's vomit over any day without her. Anything to be in the same place as her, and Molly, too, even when she's raking me over the coals for my relationship bullshit.

"Our friendship is special," she says.

"I know it is."

"You're my favorite person. You know that, right?"

"I do now."

"You are. I tell you all the time."

"You could have changed your mind."

"Me? Change my mind? Never."

We laugh weakly.

"So, what do you think?" she says.

"I don't know what you're asking me."

She sighs. "I'm asking you to come with me. Follow me down this new path."

"What does that mean, exactly?"

"You just have to trust me."

"Julie," I say slowly. "You're sick."

"I'm not sick."

"You are."

"I'm not sick. I'm changed."

"We can try to find you help." I don't know what else to say.

"I don't need help! You're not listening to me!"

"I am. I'm telling you the truth."

"The truth is, you don't want to come with me."

"I don't get what you're asking me to do! You want me to go with you to Acadia. Then what? I have a job. I have family. Molly, Maebs. I have a life."

"What life? All you talk about is how much you hate your life."

The pool lights cycle from green to purple. The whole room's darker now.

"I'm not happy with where I'm at," I say, softly. Vocal kid gloves. "But I don't hate my life."

"You've told me, verbatim, that you hate it."

"That's venting."

"Didn't sound like venting to me," she says. "I think you like being unhappy. I think you enjoy it, feeling sorry for yourself. It's safe."

"No one likes to be unhappy," I say. If she didn't look the way she looked, if her teeth couldn't rip my arm clean off, I'd shove her into the pool for saying that to me. For being a bitch.

"You do. That's why you're still in Buffalo even though you're done with him. You're afraid of happiness. You're afraid to really live," she says. Her amber eyes are on fire now as she leans in toward me. She's shrouded in the ethereal glow of the pool lights. It gives her some authority. "You're paralyzed by fear."

She's right. I've made some big mistakes, and now I'm so terrified I'll make another one, I'd rather punish myself for the rest of my life than try to be happy and risk fucking it up more.

"You don't have to live in fear anymore," she says. "I can give that to you. A new life, Lise!"

Right now I can't imagine anything but fear, because of the size of her new teeth and how hoarse her voice has become over the past few minutes. It almost sounds like two people speaking at the same time.

"Come with me."

"Jules."

"I can't stay here. That's not an option."

"Why not? Don't you want to?"

"What I want is to go and for you to come with me."

I wish I could escape my body. It's nothing but a casket, an inevitable end. The pool lights turn pink. The color reminds me. "Is this about Tristan?"

"What about Tristan?"

"I said I was sorry. Nothing happened, I swear to you. We were friends. Close friends. We mostly talked about you."

She starts to laugh.

"What?"

"This is your problem. You make everything about men. You think everything is about a man, a man, a man. This isn't about Tristan. This isn't about your professor. It's about *you*. And me. Our happiness, our future."

"You're not mad?"

"No, not really," she says, still laughing. "You just do things, don't you? Then you feel guilty about them but don't think about why. Why you did what you did or why you feel guilty. You're so perceptive, and yet you're the least self-aware person I know. I don't get it."

It's a mean thing to say because it's true. And of course, I, not self-aware, didn't know this about myself until now.

Something changes. I feel like I've been betrayed somehow. Like she withheld information from me about myself on purpose just to watch me screw up. Like she's not really on my side.

She doesn't want what's best for me. I tried to be honest with her, and she's laughing at me.

She's not offering me some wonderful new existence. She's trying to drag me down with her.

"I don't want to go with you," I tell her, ignoring what she looks like in my moment of defiance. Forgetting Patsy dead upstairs.

She sneers with a nonexistent top lip. "What?"

"I'm not going with you," I say. "You do what you have to do. I don't want any part of it."

Her hands are around my wrists before I can blink. Her fingers wrap all the way around almost twice. They dig into my skin, muscle, bone. The bruises don't wait.

"I'm not going to watch you make another bad decision," she says, standing. She releases one of my arms and drags me by the other across the floor. She does it like it's easy, exerting no effort at all. I struggle against her, but her hand doesn't budge. She's not even paying attention. "You'll see. You'll be thanking me. You don't know what's good for you. You never have. I do."

"Julie, let me go!" I scream. I'll dislocate my shoulder if I pull any harder. I swing around, writhe like a fish on a line, gain enough momentum to get my legs out in front of her. I clip her foot, and she falls forward, releasing me so she can break her own fall.

I launch past her, but she's got my foot. I kick back. Harder than I mean to.

"Goddamn!"

She looks surprised. Her nose is broken. I can tell because there's no skin there.

She laughs, spitting fragments of bone from her mouth. Fixated on the state of her face, I do nothing to fight back. She pins me. She presses her shins and forearms against mine. Her face hovers an inch over my face. I gag at the smell of her, at the sores and simmering wounds that threaten to ooze onto me.

She opens her mouth, and I can see all the rows of teeth, her decimated tongue, her wide red throat.

Of all things, of all people, I hear Tristan's voice saying, "It's not Julie."

I see Molly, the tension in her brow and jaw as she asked me, practically begged me, to have the conversation. I see Mae, her sweet, worried expression.

I see them crying at Julie's funeral, their arms linked, passing each other tissues and ChapStick.

Two and a half years, and I've been wrong the whole fucking time. I married myself to this wild, ignorant hope. I allowed myself to think it made me smarter than everyone else. That I knew better.

I can add it to the long list of my mistakes.

Julie died. She died two and half years ago on a solo hiking trip in Acadia National Park. She's dead.

I lost her.

But I couldn't let her go. I've been clinging to the small parts of her that are left, that are some echo of her former self, because I couldn't accept the change. I couldn't accept that she's not the same.

I guess I love her that much. I was willing to take the scraps. Any piece of her was better than nothing. It was better than conceding I didn't recognize this person in front of me. I can't deny it now, as she unbuckles her face, as her mouth expands and closes in.

"Julie, please," I say, and from the sound of my voice, I realize I'm crying. I squirm. "Julie, please. Please, no!"

She's not listening. She's not stopping.

I wriggle an arm free, pound a fist against the side of her head. I find the few strands of remaining hair and pull. They come free easy, her scalp along with it, with a sound like Velcro.

She rips backward. She scurries away from me on her hands and knees. Her spine is arched. The colored lights have changed again. They're red now, and her silhouette shudders in their burn.

I push myself back. My head hits the bottom step. I turn and begin to climb. I'm halfway up when I hear her screaming. Low, guttural moans.

"You abandoned me! You abandoned me! You never loved me."

She's almost getting to me again. Almost getting me to stay.

"You don't care! You don't care about me."

I never abandoned her. I'm not abandoning her now. She's trying to kill me.

I'm lumbering down the hallway. I'm at the lobby. I'm at the front door. I'm going to get away.

"You weren't there for me!"

I push the front doors. They won't open. I pull. They won't open. I heave my whole weight against them.

"You weren't there when I needed you."

She's coming toward me. Slowly. A walking corpse. Her skull is entirely exposed. There's some skin on her face still, if it can be called that. One shoulder wilts. She leads with her left foot; the right drags behind.

"I needed you," she says.

"The doors, Julie. What did you do to the doors?"

"You weren't there."

"You never asked! You never said you needed me. You never asked for my help!" I say, banging my fists against the doors, pulling at the handles. "How was I supposed to know?"

She's closing the distance between us.

"All you want is to get away from me," she says. "You left me. You don't want to be my friend anymore."

"Julie, you're not the same. I don't know what happened," I say. She's getting too close. "Maybe we can figure it out. Find a specialist."

She laughs soberly. "Figure it out."

It's too late to run. All I can do is lie. "You can get better. Get back to yourself."

"I am myself," she says. "Maybe you can't accept that."

"I guess not." My hands are numb from pulling at the handles. "Are you going to kill me?"

"I came back for you," she says. "I thought . . . Well, doesn't matter what I thought now."

"Are you going to kill me?" I ask again for no good reason.

"I don't want to."

"Then let me go."

She reaches out her hand. Her sleeve falls away; her skin peels. I see muscle and vein spun together, soft and delicate as lace. She's falling apart in front of my eyes. She lifts my chin with the bone of her thumb. "I can't."

We look at each other for a moment, as if we might burst out laughing, as if we both wish we could.

The phone rings behind the front desk. She turns. The back of her skull is like a pale moon.

I want to break it.

I shove her to the ground. I expect resistance, but I must have caught her by surprise, because she falls face-first.

I bring my foot down on the back of her neck, where her spine splinters out of the skin. Her limbs spasm. It's like crushing a bug. It's exactly like crushing a bug.

I stomp down again. Something spatters. What should be but isn't blood.

Again.

I observe this out of body. Study this violent stranger.

Finally, she's still.

It takes too long for me to get to the phone. By the time I pick it up, no one's on the line. For some reason, I go on asking the dial tone for help.

I notice a small red button. There's a grimy piece of masking tape underneath it with the word *DOOR* written in smudged Sharpie.

My fingers don't do what I tell them. They're weak and evasive. *Press the damn button.*

I try to make a fist. I've got two flaccid hands. Fuck this fucking front door. I use my palm, but it's too slick with sweat. I slam my arm against it.

There's a distant click.

It's the most beautiful sound I've ever heard.

It revitalizes me.

I nearly trip over Julie's body on my way out. The doors open, and a sob escapes me. This is the closest I've ever come to believing in God.

The air smells so good. I didn't realize. It smelled like death in there.

It's not raining anymore, but it's still cloudy. I manifest momentum, propel myself across the parking lot. My legs are stiff, tired, weakened with the relief of being out of that damn hotel.

The lot is mostly empty. I count four cars. The one in the far corner is mine.

As I get closer to it, I can tell there's something wrong, but I don't know what. My eyes aren't focusing. Everything is covered in fuzz.

I pull my keys out of my pocket and hit UNLOCK. Nothing happens.

My tires are slashed. All of them. Completely deflated.

It doesn't matter. It's a problem for me in two minutes. Future me.

I pull open the door. My car is already unlocked.

I shove the key in the ignition and turn it. The engine stammers. I assume it won't start, but it does.

I lock the doors and find my car charger. I plug my phone in. I take a second to wipe the not-blood spatter from my eyes, to take a deep breath in an attempt to steady my hands. They're trembling so badly, I can't grip the steering wheel.

My phone chimes. Messages crowd my screen. Voice mail: Maebs. Voice mail: Molls. I don't know how many there are, and I don't wait to count. I dial.

It doesn't even ring. She answers that fast.

"Are you coming?"

"Molly," I say, crying so hard, I don't sound like myself.

"Are you still at the hotel? Are you still with her?"

I hear Mae in the background. "Lise, are you okay? Lise?"

"I'm leaving. Where are you?"

"We're at a clinic. I sent the address. Fuck! I shouldn't have left you. Elise, please come."

"It's okay. I'm coming. See you soon," I say, or maybe I don't. There's shattered glass everywhere. It's in my hair, in my mouth. It's on my lap. There's a rock in my passenger seat. Julie's on my car, climbing through the windshield, pulling away the remaining shards of glass with her bare hands. They don't bleed. I do. I'm bleeding. I can taste it. I spit the glass from my mouth.

She's climbing in headfirst. Her skull is split open, exposing green rot.

"Did you think you could get rid of me that easy?" she asks.

She's almost inside. Her clothes are in tatters. I can see her body, her bones. Something worse.

I ignore the glass going through my hand. I put the car in drive and unleash my foot onto the pedal.

There's a moment of acceleration, the unearthly pitch of my

nonexistent tires against the pavement, the fight of the steering wheel. The tree.

I open my eyes into the white cloud of the airbag. It smells like an attic. Like mothballs.

There's an emptiness in my ears. I'm the last one left at the party.

It's sort of like I'm drunk. I can taste whiskey, only I know it's blood.

My head delights in its throbbing. Welcomes the proof of life.

I still have all my fingers. At least, on my left hand. I count them as I open the car door, collapse out onto wet dirt. It stings my wounds. It's too late. It's in me now.

There's no one in the passenger seat. There's no one underneath the car. Doesn't appear to be anyone between the car and the tree, but they're smashed together pretty good, so who knows? Anything's possible.

Don't I know it.

That's something Lu says whenever I tell her something she agrees with. "Don't I know it."

I miss her. I'd really like to see her again. To have her fuss about my split ends and make me Frito pie.

Would it be better to go along the road, or to cut through the woods?

The woods get me to civilization faster, but I have a better chance of being seen on the road. I don't know if that's good or bad. I'm too dizzy. I'm really very dizzy.

The woods rearrange around me. Every few steps the trees get up, dance around, shuffle back and forth. I wonder if they know all the dances you're supposed to know. The ones that go along with those songs. The ones they play at weddings.

There was a time when I thought I would never get married, because I was in love with a married man. But then I thought, *Maybe.*

It's not the trees that are moving.

What did she say?

She pretended to make a phone call.

What else?

It was like a walking shadow.

She said she was afraid.

"You know," I say. I sound funny because of the cuts in my mouth. "I felt abandoned, too. You went to California. You went to Europe. You went to Maine. But you never came to visit me."

I pause to give her a chance to respond. She doesn't. Maybe she doesn't want to give up her position. Maybe she knows I'm right.

"It wasn't easy for me. I was alone. You had your mom. You had Tristan. I had no one. And it's not like Molly and Mae were supportive. You weren't, either, really. Just more understanding."

I see something. To my left.

"I do love you. I always have. But I was jealous of you. I know it's an ugly thing to admit. I know I'm not supposed to tell you. But it's the truth. And I resented you because your life turned out so much better than mine. I want you to know I'm sorry about that. I'm sorry about Tristan. I'm sorry about all the things I've done to let you down. I guess there's a lot of them. But you should know, you let me down, too."

To my right now. She's circling me.

"I can't do this anymore. If you're going to kill me, just do it. You'll have to live with yourself."

She steps out of the trees.

She's fully transformed. I'm not sure if there's any of her left anymore. Not until she speaks.

"I'm sorry," she says. "I can't help it."

I think she's crying. It's hard to tell because there aren't any tears. I don't think her new eyes make them. "I can't help it. This is what I am now."

She's on her knees. Her hands are on her skull. She rocks back and forth in agony.

"I'm so hungry," she says. "I can't help it."

"Julie."

"Go!" she screams, a darkness harmonizing underneath. "Leave!"

"Julie. I'm so sorry."

"Go! Please! Now!"

"Jules."

"Please."

This will be the last time I ever see Julie. This creature in front of me who once shared my bed and fed me Gummy vitamins, who borrowed my toothbrush and I didn't even care. I can't comprehend it. The world we built. The jokes that only we understand. The weird nicknames. The memories. We're each other's witnesses, sole witnesses to so much that will now be lost. Gone forever.

I will never stop mourning the future we were supposed to have. I will never get over losing my best friend.

"Elise," she says, and I think I'll stay. Wouldn't it be better than being without her?

"Please," she asks, and when I look at her, I'm reminded she's already gone.

So I run.

. . .

I'm thinking about them. I summon their faces before me. Their bodies walking ahead. I see silvery white hair. The sway of hips, uneven steps. I hear their voices. Almost.

The woods remind me of the house I shouldn't have gone into. That wasn't mine. I'm an intruder. Only this time, there's no thrill. All I am is sorry.

I've been wandering here for hours. Maybe days, weeks. Attempting to trace my footprints back to the parking lot, making more footprints. I'm frantic for the influx of light, the retreat of the trees, when I can welcome that monster of a hotel back into my sight.

What I'd give for a cigarette.

I separate my fingers, lift an invisible one up to my lips. Inhale. Hold. Exhale.

Anything to ignore the fear. It's unlike any I've ever experienced. Not like the kind that lurks under the bed or inside dark closets. Not like a slow knock on the door late at night. Not like being next in line for an old, rickety roller coaster. It's free of anticipation and full of acceptance.

I never thought much about death. I figured the lights would go out, and it wouldn't matter, because I wouldn't know the difference. But it does matter.

I can't remember a time when I felt like I belonged in the world, but I'm not ready to leave it. I'm suddenly drowning in affection for everything. For my friends, yes, and for Lu, Rick, but also for me. For my stupid, messy life, all the minutiae. Sipping foam from a cappuccino, putting on socks warm from the dryer. Hitting the snooze button. I would give anything to be back in Buffalo, dead smack in the middle of winter, freezing but alive, alive, alive. And in the summer, it's really something else. Blue sky, walking along Canalside in the shade of the silos, the smell of Cheerios wafting from the General Mills plant. It's perfect.

And my apartment! My shitty studio apartment. It's small, but it's mine, and I would kiss that drafty window. If I could go back, I would bake cookies for my mean landlord and say hi to my neighbors. Be polite.

I would wake up early, eat a proper breakfast. Eggs and fruit and whole grain toast and orange juice with reduced sugar. I would volunteer on the weekends. Wear sunscreen. Floss.

That's not true. I probably wouldn't do any of those things. But I would try harder. I would do better. I wouldn't waste so much time. I've wasted so much time, and now I have none left.

I'm not ready.

My left foot might be broken, and I'm bleeding, but I don't know from where. The pain is searing, but I'm in love with it, because it means I still have my body, I still have my life. There's no future beyond the next slow, labored step except another step. Maybe it would help to picture something more. A future where I have a new job that's fun and fulfilling, where I wear tailored blazers and my hair is always done. A future where I travel to Italy, sun myself on the Amalfi Coast and stand in the ruins of Pompeii.

Honestly, I don't care what the future looks like, however wonderful or mediocre or disastrous. I just want it.

But there's the whispering of leaves in the wind, the snapping of a twig somewhere. What might be there. What might not be ready to let me go after all.

I can't move any faster. I gather my sleeve in my hand and wipe the blood from my face. It's too dark to see. A terrible cold rises from the flats of my feet and finds its way up my calves. It's spreading. I'm losing circulation. I'm going numb.

"No, no, no, no!"

At first, I think it's the echo of my cries, but it isn't. It's a deep growling, fast approaching. Two yellow eyes in the complete, total darkness. They find me, and I feel nothing. Not even fear.

As I wait for the ambulance, cloaked in a Mylar blanket, drinking tepid water that stings like antiseptic, that tastes like rust, I shake my head in utter disbelief.

"I didn't realize it was a car," I tell the officer. "Not until it almost ran me over."

"What'd you think it was?" she asks, concerned for my sanity or genuinely curious.

I shrug, holding the truth under my tongue.

IX

We get back from dinner soaked to the bone. Mae gives us fresh towels, turns up the heat. Another rainy, cold October.

It's been a year. The first anniversary. We don't know what else to do but to be together.

"I'm going to make tea," Mae says. "I have green peach, Earl Grey, matcha . . ."

"Earl Grey," Molly says.

"Me, too, please." We've been drinking a lot of tea lately. Molly says it's because we're getting old. She says it's only a matter of time until we're carrying around coupon books and grapefruit spoons.

"Don't you say anything," Mae warns Molly from the kitchen. "We're not old!"

She's right. We're not. But I welcome the years. I will take as many as I can get. I look forward to them, to the life I have left to live. There's only the one thing.

"Lise," Molly says, twisting her wet bangs into a single spiral. "What is it? You've got your thinking face on."

"It's just hard," I say. "I want to put it all behind me, but it's bittersweet because the more time that goes by, the longer we've been without her."

Before, we would've let the conversation die here. The subject would be changed, a joke would be made. But things are different now. I poke with my tongue at the insides of my cheeks, these back alleys of my mouth, cuts that didn't heal quite right, stitches that were meant to dissolve but instead were absorbed into my skin, a new part of me, sharp and small.

"I get it. I know what you mean," Molly says. Her mouth isn't the same, either. She used to wear a perpetual grin, subtle, almost smug, like she knew something you never would, but if you did, man, you'd be grinning, too. It was part of the DNA of her face, but I didn't really notice until it was gone.

"Yes," Mae says, setting down coasters on the coffee table. "I understand."

Maybe it's good we don't look the same, because we aren't the same. It's good there's physical evidence. In my mouth, Molly's mouth. In Mae's now-imperfect posture, her shoulders hunched from the weight of what we've been through. In the way my neck is fucked because I'm forever looking over my shoulder. There's no forgetting what happened, because we see it in one another.

We don't want to forget. We don't want to bury it under the floorboards.

Mae sits in the armchair across from me, rests her feet on my lap.

"You okay?" she asks me. "You need anything?"

"I'm good, Maebs."

"What about you, Molly? What's on your mind?"

"Well, I was just thinking," she says, and pauses for a deep sigh, leaning forward, "about that peanut butter bread pudding. You remember? We had it the first night at the hotel. Fucking amazing."

Things are different, but not so different. I'm grateful for that.

"Trip wasn't all bad," Molly says.

Mae makes her clicking noise.

"I can almost hear her laugh," I say, and it's true. I can hear Julie's laugh, like she's next to me, like she's got her head on my shoulder. I can smell her shampoo, her scalp. That's what intimacy is, I think. That's love. Knowing the smell of someone else's head. I get whiffs of it sometimes, randomly. What a funny kind of ghost. A phantom scent.

We sit drinking our tea, the city sputtering around us, and beyond the city, a web of suburbs, and more cities, and more suburbs, and rivers and lakes and farms, and sad old bus stations and dive bars where women dressed in new denim are a whiskey away from meeting their soon-to-be exes. There are interstates and back roads and police cars and diners with weak coffee. There are people safe in their beds about to turn out the lights, little girls trading secrets and friendship bracelets from parallel sleeping bags. And beyond and in between all that are stark, wild woods and what I know roams there. I know what waits there. And I wonder if it's alone, if it's sad or angry or remorseful or any part human. I wonder if it remembers me. I wonder if it knows where I am.

Because I still think about her all the time.

She's the footsteps that approach a little too quickly, the odd shape moving in my periphery. She's the inexplicable chill. The hum of an awakening vent. She's every shift in the silence, every creak of the floorboards, every elusive shadow.

She's with me. In my fear, my loss. Wherever I go, I know. She will follow.

Acknowledgments

I would like to thank my agent, Lucy Carson, for believing in this book, and being the most incredible advocate and an all-around superstar. I'm forever grateful to my brilliant editor, Jessica Wade, for her wonderful insights, and to Tawanna Sullivan, Miranda Hill, Alexis Nixon and the truly spectacular team at Berkley. Many thanks to Eve Hall for her good faith and enthusiasm, and to everyone at Hodder & Stoughton—you rock! I'll never get over how many super smart, talented, hardworking people put their time and energy into making this book. From the bottom of my crusty black heart, thank you. Thank you, thank you, thank you.

A big thanks to Emerson College for teaching me about the power of storytelling, and to Catapult for giving me a place to become a better writer.

To Courtney, twinset, for sticking with me. B Vanilla forever. And Abby, my North Star. Heather, for the good vibes. And Maria, the bravest person I know, my scary-movie buddy for life. You four make me better. My love for you is in these pages; this book wouldn't exist without you.

Thanks to Deanna, Heather M., Tina and Christy for being true friends and cheerleaders over the years.

Thank you to my mom for always encouraging my creativity, and my dad for showing me what it is to work hard and for working hard for me. To Joseph, for being a good sport. And Julia for the entertainment; life would be dull without you. Thank you to my extended family for their support, and to my new family, Karen, Mark, Kate & Co.

And to Nic, for everything. You make it all possible. Thank you. And Gatsby, I guess, for the company.